THE CROSSBOW MURDERS

THE CROSSBOW MURDERS

KENNETH BUTCHER

W**O**RLDWIDE

TORONTO • NEW YORK • LONDON
AMSTERDAM • PARIS • SYDNEY • HAMBURG
STOCKHOLM • ATHENS • TOKYO • MILAN
MADRID • WARSAW • BUDAPEST • AUCKLAND

W❂RLDWIDE™

ISBN-13: 978-1-335-42525-6

The Crossbow Murders

First published in 2023 by The Wild Rose Press, Inc.
This edition published in 2024.

Harlequin Enterprises ULC
22 Adelaide St. West, 41st Floor
Toronto, Ontario M5H 4E3, Canada
www.ReaderService.com

Printed in U.S.A.

For Char-Char and Benito

PROLOGUE

THE MACHINE FIT snugly in the bed of the Ford pickup truck and the three boys fit snugly on the bench seat. The uniform of the day for them, the uniform of every day for them, consisted of blue jeans, T-shirts, greasy looking ball caps with shark hooks clipped onto the bills, and work boots. The shark hooks were especially incongruous since the three of them lived in the mountains of North Carolina, nowhere close to the ocean. Two of the T-shirts had pictures of a round snuff can and the name of a well-known brand. The third T-shirt bore the letters "WHM—Be the Pig" along with a profile of a white pig.

The machine, an acquisition from earlier that evening, was covered by a tarp and held down firmly with bungee cords. It was constructed of rough-sawn timbers with metal fasteners, springs, and cogged wheels. It was heavy and it had required all their strength and their limited knowledge of leverage to hoist it into the truck bed and they had no intention of repeating the process if they didn't have to.

It was dark by now which suited their purpose because they weren't sure exactly how to operate the machine and did not want an audience until they figured it out. They pulled the truck into the field behind the high school football stadium, a school in which they were enrolled and where they occasionally attended.

The truck was aligned with the tail gate toward the football field and about twenty-five yards from the bleachers. The boys dismounted and moved to the bed of the truck, released the bungees, and pulled the tarp off. For a moment they regarded the contraption they had borrowed (They did expect to return it at some point). It was a replica of a fifteenth century catapult, the machine of war used to break sieges by hurling stones or other projectiles. The boys had been giving considerable thought as to what else it might hurl. They had not seen it in action yet, thus the test firing tonight. The youngest among them, Garth by name, claimed some authority since he had delivered the timbers from his father's saw mill and heard the designer and the builders discussing some of the details of construction and operation.

Before the heist there had been debate about the first projectile they would place into the basket at the end of the flinging arm. They had settled on a large balloon filled with two gallons of white paint. Their objective was to toss it over the bleachers and land it around the fifty yard line of the football field where they expected it to make a pleasing white splash mark they could admire from their second story remedial math classroom the next day.

Garth climbed into the truck bed and the other guys handed up the bag of paint. As soon as he placed it in the launch basket the reality of the situation hit him. They were really going to do this. It wasn't just talk. He figured the others must feel the same way because they were laughing and saying things like, "Oh, man," under their breath.

"What's next?"

"Next, we crank it down to cock it," Garth said in a coarse whisper. He grasped a handle on a curved metal arm and cranked in a circular motion. The mechanism clicked with the sound of a ratchet wheel. After half a dozen cranks he stopped and inserted a wooden pin in a slot. The wooden pin was attached to a loop of rope which he tossed over the side of the pickup.

"All we got to do is yank this rope to release it," he explained when he jumped down.

"You didn't crank it down enough," said his older friend. "You should give it a few more turns." He was the owner of the truck and therefore claimed a certain authority of his own.

"I don't think we should," Garth said. "The guy that designed it said—"

"I don't give a shit what the guy said. We don't want to come up short on this, then we got nothing."

"I don't know," Garth said.

"Get your ass back up in the truck and crank that monkey down."

Garth complied. He reset the ratchet, removed the pin, and slowly cranked. He could feel more resistance as the mechanism made creaking and groaning noises, building up tension and suspense. He stopped and looked at the owner of the truck.

"One more crank," the truck owner said.

Garth slowly advanced the crank another half a turn and said, "That's it." The other boy nodded and Garth climbed down.

He took the rope in his hand and said, "OK, y'all. Watch this."

The others took a step back, happy for a little distance.

"Count me down," Garth said.

"Three. Two. One. Go!" They chanted, and Garth pulled the rope.

The power of the release caught them off guard.

"Ho-ly-crap," one of them said as they watched the balloon sail high over the bleachers, field, and stadium, and disappear above the glow of the security lights. It must have sailed on past the driveway over the announcement board and at last it reentered the light and smashed against the school building itself, crashing through the office window. Garth was just imaging the explosion of glass shards and white paint that must be happening inside when the alarm went off.

"Oh, shit," they all said at once. They scrambled into the truck, and started off. They stopped in a few feet, one of them jumped out and grabbed the tarp, got back in, and they headed out into the night.

ONE

Westerville Pub

WALTER WAS TALKING to Segal. Walter was a black man with blocky shoulders and perfectly fitted sport coat, a little gray mixing into his dark hair. Segal was a thinner white man more often taken for a college professor than the police detective that he was. A worn gray sport coat hung loosely on his frame. The top of a paperback book could be seen sticking out of the left-hand pocket. Segal was looking down at the table top. More specifically, Segal was looking at a notebook which he had earlier opened on the table after wiping away the moisture left from cleaning. Without looking up at Walter, Segal took a pen from his pocket and began drawing a small figure on the right-hand page. The left-hand page was filled with notes made earlier that morning concerning the robbery case at UNCA. At the top of that page *Mechatronics Department* was printed in neat organic letters. It was a curious theft, but Segal was not overly worried about it.

An observer might have thought Segal was ignoring Walter, but the observer would have been wrong. Segal was listening very intently, calming his hands and his mind with drawings that came from somewhere below the surface of the pool of consciousness. Among other things this habit made for an interesting set of notebooks.

"So then she asked me did I ever hear of the Women of Color Against Violence," Walter said, bouncing his head back to signify astonishment. Walter was talking to Segal about a conversation with his wife, Nancy.

This made Segal look up. "But you are a man of color."

Walter looked at him with some combination of curiosity and disgust. "Yes, Segal, I am aware. Pretty sure the fact did not escape Nancy either."

Segal looked back at the notebook, his gesture for Walter to go on with the story. Walter did, settling back into the cadence of "she said, so I said." It was a story of a wife worried about her husband being a policeman and, at the same time, coming up short of asking him to change jobs. Segal figured that for Nancy, as for most people, the fear of change exceeded the fear of violent death, alienation from community, or anything else. So in this discontented equilibrium they seemed destined to stay. At least that's how Segal read it.

He listened to Walter, but at the same time he understood that Walter was not asking him for help. Walter was venting and all he needed from Segal was to listen with empathy.

His attention to Walter and to the notebook did not mean he was unaware of his other surroundings. The main room of the Westerville Pub in West Asheville was rather long and not so wide. The bar ran down most of the length of one side. The bartender maintained that constant state of motion that the profession demands, and yet somehow maintained a stop and go conversation with two girls near the center of the bar. The owner came and went with purpose, moving kegs and consulting with employees and patrons in quick efficient bursts. In an adjacent room at the front, a pool table was in use. Through the doorway Segal could see the guys moving around the table and hear the collisions of the balls. Servers came and went with trays of food and drinks. It was lunch time: pretty busy.

One guy at the bar caught Segal's eye. Heavy tattoos showed on his arms and neck. Segal read him as a little drunk, or high on something else, or maybe both. One of the tattoos read WHM beside the small outline of a pig. He copied this into his notebook, thinking to maybe look it up later. The guy looked around a lot, a little too quick, nervous. Nothing terrible, just someone Segal's cop sense told him to keep half an eye on.

The back door opened and a young woman came through. She was small with a huge shock of frizzy hair trailing behind. The way she moved made Segal think *athlete*, that and she carried a large gym bag. She nodded to Walter as she passed their table and Walter nodded back. She met Segal's eye, too, for just a second. He had the feeling he should know her, but then a lot of women sought out his eyes, blue in contrast to his brown hair.

All this took only a second or two of glancing around the room. Walter talked on. Segal sketched, those blue eyes popping up now and then. Their waitress approached Segal from behind and reached around to place a plate in front of him. This motion put her mouth close to his ear and she whispered, "Cheeseburger," in the voice of an angel. She delivered Walter's plate with a less personal touch. In fact she may have revealed a slight level of disgust at his choice of an Italian sausage sandwich smothered in gravy.

Segal put the notebook aside to give his full attention to the burger which he considered to be one of the major achievements of modern civilization, at least when it was made properly. And at the Westerville Pub, it was. He picked it up and took his first bite.

Walter stirred the gravy around on his plate, but before he began to eat he looked over Segal's shoulder, furrowed his brow, and said, "Oh, shit. You better check this out."

SEGAL TURNED IN his chair. Across the room near the door a waitress was trying to take the order of four people sitting at a table. Meanwhile, a boy in his late teens was desperately trying to talk to her.

It was Tommy, Segal's second cousin, son of his cousin, Deidra; Tommy was clearly off his medications. It was the expression on Tommy's face that told him so, a kind of brooding grimace. That, and the fact that his hair was wild, even by Tommy standards, and the neck of his T-shirt was stretched and misshapen. Segal figured he had been pulling on it, a nervous habit exaggerated when his mind was in a bad place.

Segal put the cheeseburger down and went over to help. By the time he got there, Tommy's voice was raising a bit. The poor waitress was doing her best to be good natured about the interruption and to minimize the awkwardness of the situation. As Segal got there, Tommy put his hand on the waitress's arm and she jerked it away by reflex.

Segal put a hand on his shoulder and turned him away from the table. Tommy looked surprised at first, but then, when he realized who it was, his face broke out in a wide grin.

"Segal!" he said, still a bit too loudly.

By this time Segal had moved him a couple steps away from the table while nodding back toward the waitress and the people trying to order and mouthing the words, "Sorry."

"Come over and sit with me and Walter," Segal whispered to Tommy. But the owner stepped into their path.

"Don't bother to sit down, Tommy. I told you, you can't come back here," he said.

Tommy pulled back and looked confused, and then turned to Segal. Segal started to plead their case, but the owner raised a hand, stopping him before he could get started.

"Segal, I mean it. I'm sorry, but I have my customers to think of here." He said this with a note of finality that told Segal the conversation was over. He nodded and turned Tommy toward the door.

"Let's go out for a minute, Tom," he said. As he guided Tommy toward the door he looked back at Walter who motioned for him to go ahead. When they got outside Tommy started to talk immediately.

"Segal, she's my girlfriend—" he started, but Segal stopped him.

"Are you talking about that waitress, Beth?"

"I thought she was my girlfriend." Segal didn't know where to start explaining how Beth was twenty-five and Tommy was seventeen and how he couldn't interrupt people in the middle of doing their job.

"Wait a minute, Tommy," he said. "How long is it since you've eaten?"

"I don't know, but Segal, my girlfriend said—"

"Did you eat anything for breakfast or lunch today?" Tommy looked around as if he didn't know exactly where he was or what time it was.

"Let's go over here and get you something," Segal said. He started toward the bakery which was just a couple doors down the street and across a small parking lot. He knew that low blood sugar was one of the factors in Tommy's descent into this state of mind. It wasn't the trigger or the main cause, just one of the steps in the downward spiral which had to be reversed before Tommy could return to anything like normal.

A few minutes later he had Tommy sitting down eating a cinnamon roll and drinking a cup of coffee with lots of milk in it. Tommy had resisted, but as soon as Segal got him to take one bite his appetite kicked in.

"Segal, you got to tell me about girls," Tommy said when he had settled down a little.

"What do you mean, Tom? What do you want to know about girls?"

"You said you would always tell me anything I wanted to know."

This was true. It made Segal think back to years ago when Tommy was eight or nine. Tommy's father left, and he took it pretty hard. He wasn't like he was now. There were no signs then of mental health issues, just a very sad, shaken little guy. It broke Segal's heart. He decided back then to help as best he could: be more of a big brother, not just a remote second cousin. Part of that had indeed been a promise that Tommy could ask him anything he wanted to know, and Segal would give him an honest answer.

Tommy's voice brought him back to the present moment.

"How do you make a girl like you?"

Segal recoiled. Of all the questions he might have asked, it had to be this one.

"That's not so easy. That is *the* question men have been asking themselves since the beginning of time."

Tommy just kept looking at him. Segal realized that he fully expected a concise and actionable set of instructions. Segal looked around as if the answer to the question might come driving down Haywood Avenue. In a way it did. He saw Tommy's mother driving slowly along, obviously look-ing for her son. He waved at her and she pulled into the parking lot beside them. She let out a long sigh of relief looking at Tommy and then she turned toward Segal. The look on her face said everything that needed to be said. Segal just put a palm on each of her cheeks and kissed her forehead and smiled. They both looked over at Tommy who arose from the bench where he was sitting and taking the last bite of his cinnamon roll. He walked obediently to his mom's car and got in, reminding Segal of that eight-year-old boy he used to be. Segal bent down lower so he could see him through the window.

"Be good, Tom. Listen to your mom." And then to both he said, "I'll check in later and see how things are going." Deidra just put a hand on his forearm and squeezed a little.

Tommy leaned toward him to make eye contact. "How about my question, Segal?"

"Hang on," Segal said.

He ran over to his own car, which was parked a couple spaces away, opened the door, and rummaged around in the pile of books on the back seat until he found the thin, well-worn paperback he was looking for.

"See if this helps," he said as he tossed it to Tommy.

Tommy held it up and he and his mother read it out loud in unison, "*The Tragedy of Romeo and Juliet* by William Shakespeare." Tommy seemed well pleased and calm. Segal watched as he opened the book to the first page and the car pulled away. The image of the cheeseburger re-entered Se-gal's mind and he turned back toward the bar.

"YOU GOT TOMMY settled down?" Walter said when Segal sat back down. This was not the first time he had seen Segal administer a little mental health first aid.

"Maybe for the time being," Segal said. He picked up a french fry and dipped it in ketchup as a prelude to the main course. He also took a drink of his cola, wishing it was beer. Just as he felt his attitude beginning to adjust back to pre-Tommy conditions there was a commotion at the bar.

It was the guy Segal had spotted before. He was yelling at the bartender, something about the food. Segal took a quick longing look at the cheeseburger in front of him as he pushed his chair back, ready to stand up and help the bartender and the owner deal with the situation. Walter slid his chair back at the same time but then stopped. He put a hand on Segal's forearm and said, "Hang back a second."

Segal looked back to the bar and saw the short girl with the big hair he had noticed before approach the guy. She leaned on the bar beside him and withdrew an object from a pocket in her shorts and showed it to him. She spoke to him in a voice too low for Segal to hear. The guy started to respond, but she held up a hand and said something that stopped him.

Slowly, he slid off the bar stool. It wasn't until he stood up to his full height that Segal realized how big the guy was, an impression made all the more dramatic by the girl's small stature. The tattooed arms looked thick and powerful.

Segal tensed. If there was going to be some unpleasantness it would come now, but instead of turning to confront her the guy turned toward the back door and began stalking out. The girl escorted him, walking to his right and half a step behind.

They walked quickly until they got to the door where the guy turned, possibly to shout some final insult toward the bar. In the instant the guy shifted his weight to make the turn the girl grabbed his wrist and bent his arm up behind him far enough to make Segal wince at the pain it must have caused. In the same motion she shoved him through the door, and they were out.

Segal realized that the noisy room had gone silent. When the door closed everyone exhaled and the noise resumed as before.

Segal and Walter looked at each other both raising their eyebrows.

"Who the hell was that?" Segal said.

"That's our new girl," Walter said. "Just started last week. Came over from the Charlotte force. Officer Rude-something. Rudisill."

"Damn," said Segal.

They watched the door to see if she would come back in when Walter's phone sounded. He answered, frowned, and then hung up.

"You better pack up that burger to go, Segal. Somebody got themselves murdered in the River Arts District."

TWO

The Artist's Studio

THE RIVER ARTS DISTRICT was only a short drive away, down Haywood Avenue then winding through a sharp left turn and descending into the river valley and across the bridge to the flats on the east side of the French Broad. At the bridge they stopped to let a girl walking an Afghan Hound cross in front of them. The hair flowing from the dog's back was strikingly similar to the girl's hair, both in color and texture. The girl wore a gown and an unusual cloth cap which tied by a strap under her chin.

They both watched the procession and then Walter addressed the unspoken question. "Probably something to do with the music festival coming up. Remember, the theme this year is Renaissance Fair."

Segal nodded. "I thought every day was Renaissance Fair in West Asheville."

Segal took a couple of bites of the cheeseburger, but it was cold and the events had taken away his appetite. He tossed the bag in the back seat next to the pile of books. It was an eccentric jumble ranging from Carl Hiaasen to Hillerman to Hemingway to Shakespeare, but there was more Elmore Leonard than anything else.

"So, dispatch said murder? They actually used that

word?" Segal asked. It was unusual for dispatch to identify a fatality as a murder before detectives had even visited.

"That's what the lady said." Walter scratched the back of his head as he did when pondering the curious or unexpected.

"Cause of death must be pretty obvious," Segal said.

Walter grunted in agreement.

They turned onto Lyman Street and followed it along the river until they came to a large brick industrial building sprawling the length of a city block or more. Originally it had been a factory of some kind, but Segal knew that it had been converted into a hive of artist studios. Though he had never been there in an official capacity he had been to parties and openings a few times and knew something of its complexity; not a welcome feature in a murder investigation.

Segal saw a couple of police cruisers at one of the entrance doors near the center of the building. A uniformed officer stood by the door talking to a small group of people. Segal drove slowly along the length of the building, taking his time, studying the scene. When they parked the officer nodded to them and motioned to the nearest entrance.

"In here and up the stairs," he said.

They entered a vestibule and saw a directory listing the room numbers occupied by various artists and groups. The faded look of it made Segal question if it was up to date. The area was bright and freshly painted, a little better cared for than he recalled.

"Of course, it's up the stairs," Walter said. He was looking at the long metal stairway that led off to the right. "Why can't anybody get killed on the first floor for a change?"

They trudged up the stairs, longer than a normal flight owing to the high ceilings of the building. Upstairs the halls were darker and narrower. Down the hall to the right they could see another officer standing by an open door with a length of yellow crime scene tape draped across.

Segal nodded to the cop and ducked under the tape like a boxer entering the ring. Walter followed and they stood together taking in the room. It was large and bright, the light coming from a set of frosted windows facing north and set high in a skylight. A counter ran almost the whole length of the wall with the door through which they had entered. Every square inch of the counter was covered by containers, brushes, and pieces of equipment, most of which Segal did not recognize. Below the counter were shelves and drawers likewise filled to capacity. A set of larger shelves occupied the left-hand wall and to the right was an old couch and arm chair. Behind them a section of the room had been divided off with a curtain.

Near the center of the room stood a large easel facing a platform on the opposite wall. In front of the easel and a little to one side the body of a man lay crumpled on the brown wooden floor. His knees were pulled up part way, almost a fetal position. His head lay limply to one side. The pose was entirely awkward and unnatural and lifeless. There was considerable blood.

Segal's eyes went to the canvas on the easel. In contrast to the artist on the floor, the scene painted on the canvas was alive and beautiful. Depicted there, the figure of a young woman was standing proud and turned three quarters toward the viewer. She wore a hooded sweatshirt and shorts. Over this she wore a shining armor breastplate. Her thighs were bare and well curved below a fringe of chain mail, but her shins and knees were protected with armor as well. Her left hand curled around a helmet which rested on her hip. She was standing with her weight on her left leg which cocked the hip supporting the helmet. In her other hand she held a sword. On her feet were pink running shoes somewhat worse for the wear. She had short brown hair shiny enough to catch a glint of light and partly wet from sweat. There was an expectant look in her large brown eyes which conveyed the idea that she was waiting for the viewer to do something. *Joan of Arc Postmodern,* Segal thought.

He returned her gaze for a moment feeling a tinge of guilt that he was paying more attention to the painting than to the body of the man who had painted it. *Maybe he would have wanted it that way*, Segal thought. Presently he began circling the body, making a wide arc to his right. He moved in an unhurried way; He took out pen and notebook and began jotting down the occasional word or phrase as impressions of the scene entered his mind.

He circled until he was looking at the front of the body. There he saw a wooden shaft with feathers. It was stuck into the chest with the body curled around it. The thumb of one hand touched it as if the artist were about to pull it out.

As Segal knelt for a better view he said, "Walter, there's an arrow here."

Walter, who was examining the floor in front of the easel, turned toward him.

A voice from the back of the room said, "Bolt."

Segal and Walter both turned. It was Crawford, the medical examiner. *How could anything of such a size enter the room so quietly?* Segal thought. Crawford was already dressed in his paper Tyvek suit, and he was pulling on a pair of surgical gloves.

"The projectile shot from a crossbow is called a bolt. It is much like an arrow but it's shorter and often a little thicker."

Segal looked back at the body. It was true. If it had been a regular arrow the point would have been sticking out of the victim's back, but such was not the case. He glanced at the painting of the girl in armor again. He remembered a factoid he had read about crossbows. They could penetrate body armor. He jotted a note to himself in his small note-book though he understood it almost surely had nothing to do with the case.

"Looks like the assailant must have been standing over there to the right, probably a little further away than you are now," Crawford said, "but we'll know better when we can measure the angle."

Segal stood up. He had in his mind the image of a figure with a crossbow held up to his shoulder and as he scanned the room, he tried to imagine the man standing in various places. His gaze lifted to the high ceiling where the vertical panes of glass in the skylight admitted abundant white light.

"Hey Doc, one of those skylight windows is ajar."

Crawford leaned back and squinted, then turned toward the body.

"Right. We should be able to tell from the angle of the bolt whether it originated from there or from ground level.

Crawford approached the body and Segal backed away to give him room. The doctor took out a small digital recorder from the kit he carried and began to mumble observations into it. This routine reminded Segal of a priest muttering the rote words of a standard prayer under his breath as he went through the motions of a blessing.

Crawford interrupted his ritual long enough to reach toward the body and remove the man's wallet. He made a perfect underhand toss to Segal without looking up. Segal snatched it from the air.

When Crawford withdrew a thermometer from his kit Segal took that as a sign that he would not be needed there for a while. He motioned to Walter, and they left, giving the room one last scan.

Outside in the hallway two crime scene technicians pulled on their own paper suits and gloves while a uniformed officer acted as gate keeper. Segal nodded for the techs to go on in.

"Who discovered the body?" Segal asked the officer.

"Girl from one of the potteries came looking for someone here," the cop said. He handed Segal a slip of paper with the girl's information.

"You have the name of the deceased?"

"Julius Hargrove," the cop said.

Segal raised his eyebrows in recognition of the name. This was an artist well known even outside of Asheville. He handed the wallet to Walter.

"You want to go through this? I'm going up on the roof to check things out."

Given Walter's fear of heights Segal knew he would get no argument. And besides, he could use a little air and a few minutes alone to process the information he had already taken in.

HE EMERGED INTO daylight up on the roof, a very agreeable place. His eye was drawn first to the French Broad River flowing smoothly a short distance away. Opposite, after a few blocks of flat land, a steep hillside led up to what he knew to be downtown Asheville, though he could see nothing of it from this vantage. In between the river and the hill was the River Arts District, mostly old industrial and warehouse buildings like the one he stood on. Some were still empty, but many were repurposed as studios, shops, bars, breweries, and restaurants.

He directed his attention to the building itself. The roof

was nearly flat for the most part and covered with tar and fine gravel. He could see a number of skylight structures similar to the one he had noted from below in the victim's studio. These were right triangles, with panes of glass in the vertical face. The roof was also populated with various chimneys and pipes and vents. He walked carefully in the direction of the Hargrove studio and when he passed a wide chimney, he found a circle of folding lawn chairs.

He approached the little seating area. Apparently, he was not the first to enjoy the view from the rooftop. In addition to the chairs there were several ceramic bowls which were clearly used as ashtrays. They contained cigarette butts; commercial ones as well as hand rolled, probably tobacco and other substances as well. Also, cigar butts and loose black ash. Possibly used by pipe smokers too. To Segal it conveyed a pleasant convivial air. He could well imagine artists and friends getting together there for a break or perhaps after a day's work. He made a notation in his notebook. They would have to find out who frequented the roof. Possible witnesses.

He moved further on the roof until he thought he found the skylight structure above the crime scene studio. A quick look through the opened sash confirmed that he was right. The techs were moving carefully around the room and Crawford was putting something back into his traveling kit. *He's probably ready to move the body*, he thought. He scanned the area but saw nothing of interest around. *What had he been expecting? A discarded crossbow? Interesting thought, though. How do you come and go inconspicuously with such an unwieldy object?*

He took one more glance around and made a note to have the techs come up and dust for prints, especially on the window and frame. And on the door at the top of the stairs, he added as he started to head back down.

He skipped lightly down the flight of stairs, turned quickly into the hall, and stopped short as he literally ran into a young woman coming the other way.

He drew in a breath as the girl jumped back, clearly as startled as he was. He began to apologize, but when he saw her face, he stopped.

Standing there before him was a girl, maybe eighteen or nineteen. Dark brown hair. She was wearing a violet tank top and black shorts and thin-soled shoes that looked similar to ballet slippers. It was the girl in the painting. Joan of Arc Postmodern.

THREE

Jody Mare and the Marks Brothers

AFTER A COUPLE of beats Segal found his voice and said, "I'm sorry, Miss. We have to talk." He said this as much to himself as to the girl.

The girl took a step back and Segal realized that he had not identified himself. He withdrew his badge and held it up to her. "My name is Ira Segal. I'm with the Asheville police department and we are investigating an incident that took place here earlier this morning or perhaps last night."

The expression on the girl's face did not change much. Her eyes were still wide and her mouth open a little.

"I take it you work with Julius Hargrove," Segal said.

This seemed to snap her out of it. "That's where I'm going now," she said. "In fact, I'm late, and he does not like people being late." She took a step toward the studio before Segal stopped her, putting a hand gently on her arm.

"Hold on, Miss, I need to ask you a few questions before you go anywhere." Segal looked up the hall toward the studio that was the crime scene. There was no good place to talk.

"First of all, could I have your name?" he asked.

"Jody Mare," she said.

Segal nodded and wrote the name in his notebook.

"Listen, Miss Mare, let's go downstairs for a minute

and talk. Could we do that?" He nodded at the stairs and she turned toward them. She took a step but then turned back to him.

"We could talk in the studio, I should let Jules know I'm here," she said.

"Let's not worry about that for a while, let's just go downstairs for a minute." On the way he phoned to check in with Walter.

"It's going OK. Crawford is almost done and his guys are here. Techs are getting through the scene." Segal told him he was going down to interview Miss Mare. Walter didn't ask who Miss Mare was.

"What happened up there?" Jody asked when they walked outside.

"That's what we are trying to piece together," Segal said. He had settled them on a bench where they turned slightly toward each other, their knees nearly touching.

"How long have you been working with Mr. Hargrove?" he asked.

She lifted her chin and looked slightly up at the sky. Her lips parted a little. It brought her head and face into a pose very much like the one in the picture. There was an innocence about her, but at the same time, an intense geometry. It was an uncomplicated face, very compelling. Segal thought that the artist, Julius Hargrove, had made an inspired choice using her as a model for Joan of Arc. Or was it the other way around? Did Jody Mare inspire him to paint Joan of Arc?

"I took a class from him about a year ago," she said. "Then about four months ago he asked me to model for this project. It was good money, plus he is easy to work with. And I'm learning a ton just listening to him and watching him work."

Segal watched the animation in her face as she talked. He wished he could carry on in this vein for a while, but he realized he could not. It was not ethical to go on referring to the artist in the present tense. He had to tell her what had happened.

Before he could speak he was interrupted by an agonized scream. They both jumped from the bench. Segal took quick steps toward the parking lot while Jody brought her palms to her cheeks.

In the parking lot a uniformed officer grasped a middle-aged woman by her shoulders in a stance that combined restraint and support. She was looking toward the building and sobbing and saying, "No, no, no," over and over again.

Segal glanced toward the building and understood immediately. The middle-aged lady, undoubtedly the wife of the artist, had arrived at the worst possible moment. The coroner's team was wheeling her husband out in a body bag to the waiting van.

IN SEGAL'S EXPERIENCE, when things unraveled they unraveled fast. He found himself looking back and forth between two hysterical women feeling very much overwhelmed which made it an outstandingly good piece of timing when a female officer pulled up in a cruiser. It took Segal a moment to realize it was the young women from the bar; the one who had escorted the troublemaker out. This time she was in uniform. *What did Walter tell me her name was?*

She got out and walked quickly toward him, looking from side to side as she approached.

"Are you Lieutenant Segal?" she asked.

Segal nodded and extended his hand.

"Dinah Rudisill," she said. "Dispatch said you might

need some extra help. What can I do?" She was looking back and forth between the model and the wife as she said this.

Segal nodded toward the model. "That's Jody Mare. She worked for the victim. See if you can stick with her and keep her calm while I talk to this other lady."

Dinah nodded and proceeded toward Jody with no further instructions.

SEGAL APPROACHED THE other woman and the officer. Her back was to him, and the officer gave Segal a look over the woman's shoulder. Segal nodded and came around where the woman could see him.

Her eyes widened when she saw him and presumably recognized him as a person with authority.

"I want to see him," she said.

Segal looked down, finding it hard to meet her eye. He pulled out his badge and identified himself.

"I want to see my husband, Lieutenant," she said, becoming a little calmer and more business-like. Segal regarded her for a moment—dark curly hair, maybe a perm, not brushed. She was dressed in jeans and a gray sweatshirt with a university name on it. White tennis shoes. She was a little below average height, and her figure was on the full and curvaceous side. She might soon be called a woman of a certain age, but she still retained a definite allure.

"And you are?" Segal asked.

"Margery Hargrove. One of the pottery girls called me and told me what happened. You people didn't even have the decency to notify me."

"I'm sorry, Mrs. Hargrove, we've been here only a short time ourselves—" Segal began to explain.

She shook it off. "I want to see my husband before they take him away, Lieutenant."

The men wheeling the gurney had arrived at the back of the van by now and they paused and looked at Segal. In many cases the appearance of the deceased would have made viewing by a relative a very bad idea, but such was not the case here. If anything, Segal thought, the man had looked quite tranquil. He nodded to the men and guided Mrs. Hargrove to the side of the gurney.

When she was in place one of the men unzipped the covering enough to show the face. Margery Hargrove stood perfectly still. Large tears formed in her eyes and the first of them ran down her cheeks. Segal watched her closely. After a moment she took a deep breath and let it out and the tears flowed freely now.

Segal said softly, "You can confirm that this is your husband, Julius Hargrove?"

She nodded. "Yes, that's Jules."

Segal nodded to the technician and after the wife turned aside he zipped the bag closed again. Margery closed her eyes, and for a long moment she stood there stunned. Segal did not intrude on her thoughts. He motioned to the technicians and they loaded the body in the van.

After a moment she opened her eyes. Segal asked, "Would you like to sit down? Can we get you some water?"

"I think I'd like to go home now," she said. "Could I do that?"

"Certainly. This officer will make sure you get home OK, and he will get your contact information." Segal looked up at the officer when he said this, letting him know he was issuing instructions as well as calming the victim's wife. "I'll need to talk to you in detail soon, but for now can you just tell me when you last saw your husband alive?"

She seemed to think for a moment then said, "Days. Three days ago, I think. Wednesday. So May twentieth."

Segal watched her walk away. She moved slowly but seemed steady enough on her feet. The officer walked close by her side. After a couple of steps she paused and looked over toward the bench where Jody Mare sat crying. He thought she might speak, but instead she moved on and got into her car. She sat there for a moment with her hands on the steering wheel, not moving. It seemed for an instant that the flow of time froze and he felt a direct connection to this woman and all the pain and confusion she was feeling. Her world had just changed and there was no going back. Ever.

Segal realized his life had changed too, and it would not be back to normal until he and Walter found resolution to this murder. Walter had frequently warned him not to let his natural empathy get in the way of clear thinking, but he couldn't prevent a certain resonance at moments such as these.

He turned back toward the building where he had left Jody Mare with the new cop, Rudisill. Jody was sitting on the bench hunched over with her hands on her knees and her head down. Officer Rudisill was standing beside her and leaning down so she could speak to Jody in a low voice. Segal approved of how she was handling the situation.

Three young men had also joined the scene. They were bunched together a few feet away. One looked around, apparently trying to take in the whole scene, one watched Jody, and the other looked at the ground, head down, hand on his chin. Segal's read of the body language suggested that these guys knew each other well and that each, in his own way, was upset.

Officer Rudisill looked up when Segal approached. "Miss Mare was feeling a little faint so we're just sitting down and taking it easy for a while," she explained. Then, looking over at the other three, she said, "These gentlemen are students of Mr. Hargrove." The three seemed to take this as their cue to come closer.

After Segal showed them his ID and introduced himself, he said, "You three are students?"

"Apprentices," the tallest of them said.

"I think I should take Jody home," the one who had been watching her broke in. "She shouldn't have to be here now. It's upsetting her."

Segal considered. "I think we'll ask Officer Rudisill to take Miss Mare home."

Dinah looked up at Segal. She took Jody by the shoulders and guided her to a standing position, then turned her to walk toward the cruiser.

Before Dinah walked away Segal put a hand on her shoulder and whispered in her ear, "Get a statement from her if you can. I want to know about the last time she saw her boss alive and what she was doing yesterday, last night, and this morning."

Dinah nodded and they moved off.

SEGAL TURNED HIS attention to the three apprentices who had come closer.

The tallest and thinnest of the three was standing a little behind and to the left of the bench. He was dressed in what looked like a worn-out white dress shirt. Some decorations in black ink had been added; either that or ink had been inadvertently spilled here and there. The shirt was not tucked into his worn blue jeans. On his feet were a pair of black high-top sneakers. One of his shoes was on the bench and the other on the ground and he leaned on the raised leg. Segal thought the pose looked stiff and self-conscious, like a model in an apparel catalog. The man had sandy hair and was clean shaven: quite handsome.

Occupying the center of the bench was a man of medium build, red hair and beard a little on the woolly side. He sat erect with one arm resting on the back of the bench. He smoked a cigarette and brushed some ash off his worn green T-shirt labeled with the logo of a local brewery.

The third man sat on the right side of the bench, bent forward as if he might be dealing with stomach problems. His build was huskier than the other two. His hair was jet black and straight. He raised his head when Segal approached and the look on his face spoke of dejection and misery. Segal also noticed that the royal blue T-shirt he was wearing had a depiction of a robot on the chest and the letters UNCA. *University of North Carolina Asheville*, Segal thought.

The tallest man on the end took his foot off the bench and stood up straight. The red-haired man in the center stood as well and looked attentive. The one on the right cringed and looked away, seeming to withdraw more into himself.

"What can you tell us about what happened, Lieutenant?" the tall man asked.

"First let me get your names," Segal said. He took out a small moleskin notebook.

"Henry Marks," said the tall one. "And this is Mark Morrison."

The one in the center with red hair nodded.

"And down on the end, Mark Engel."

The dark-haired man finally sat up and made a gesture with his hand, but still did not meet Segal's eye.

"What happened, Lieutenant?" This time it was the red-haired man, Mark Morrison who asked the question. "We heard that Jules was killed. We heard all kinds of things."

Segal held up his hand. "I'll tell you everything, or at

least as much as I can, but first I have to ask you some questions." This time even Mark Engel actually looked at him.

"Tell me your whereabouts on Friday night and this morning."

Morrison spoke up. "Henry and I were at a party Friday night."

"A party where?" Segal asked.

"Jules's house," Morrison said. "His wife, Margery, was throwing him a birthday party, only Jules never showed up."

"Never showed up?" Segal asked, "Wasn't anybody worried about that?"

"Lieutenant, Jules did what Jules wanted to do. He never liked all the birthday stuff, so no one was surprised he stayed away." This time it was Henry Marks who answered.

"What about his wife, she wasn't worried?" Segal asked.

"I think she was pissed, but she didn't let on. She was used to Jules disappearing for a few days at a time. Besides, she wanted everyone to have a good time," Henry said.

"And did you?" Segal asked, "Have a good time?"

Henry and Morrison looked at each other and grinned. "Yeah, I guess we had a pretty good time," Morrison answered.

"And what time did you leave there Friday night?"

"Uh, we didn't," Morrison said. "I mean we fell asleep there. We didn't leave till this morning, a little after eight."

"And what about you?" Segal said, addressing Mark Engel. "You weren't at the party?"

Mark Engel looked down again and hesitated before he spoke. "Not for long. I had an early dinner with some people, then I did a little work here, I stopped by the party for a while, then I went home."

"And can anyone vouch for that?" Segal asked.

"Dinner, yes, but after that, no."

"And what time did you leave the studio?" Segal asked.

"I'm not sure. Maybe around nine, nine-thirty."

"Did you see Julius Hargrove or anyone else while you were here?"

Mark Engel looked down again and shook his head. "But I wasn't in the main studio where Jules worked. I was in the little one next door."

"He means our studio," Henry Marks explained.

"But you do have a key to the main studio," Segal suggested, still looking at Mark Engel.

"We all do, Lieutenant," Henry Marks said.

Segal looked up from his notebook, first at Henry Marks, then the younger Mark Engel. *It's like a big brother defending a little brother*, he thought.

"Do any of you know what Hargrove might have been doing up here last night? Would he have been painting?"

Henry Marks and Mark Morrison looked at each other and grinned. It made Segal feel like he had just asked a silly question.

"No, Lieutenant. We only work in natural light," Morrison explained. "That's how it was for the old masters."

Segal nodded his understanding. He wrote down a quick note, then said, "OK, let's go upstairs and have a look around." He motioned for them to go ahead of him.

When they got to the studio the three waited for Segal in spite of the fact that the door was open. The evidence techs were just packing up their kits, getting ready to head out. Walter sat at an antique desk writing notes. He looked up and nodded to Segal and watched the three young men with a practiced gaze.

"The first thing I'm going to ask you to do is look carefully around the room without touching anything. I am primarily interested to know if there's anything missing or anything you see that looks odd or out of place," Segal said.

The men began to browse slowly around the room, reminding Segal of the way people floated slowly around a museum, silently evaluating all that they saw. Segal thought it must be an odd experience for them, treating a familiar room like that.

While they did their silent inspection Walter summoned Segal with a nod of his head. Segal came behind the desk where Walter sat writing. Walter scooted the chair out a little and revealed a bundle underneath the desk, something wrapped in a brown blanket. He moved aside one corner of the blanket to reveal a crossbow.

"Found it in the studio next door," Walter whispered. "The building superintendent told us it was used by Hargrove and his apprentices. He let us in."

Segal nodded.

Presently all three of the Marks Brothers gathered in the center in front of the painting. Though a preliminary attempt had been made to clean up, remnants of a blood stain could still be seen on the wood floor where the body of their mentor had lain. But it was the painting, not the blood stain that held their attention.

"This might be the best of his paintings," Henry Marks said to no one in particular.

"It really works," Mark Morrison said.

Mark Engel said nothing, just continued to gaze at the painting. He started to tear up and he drew his forearm across his eyes.

"Anything missing?" Segal asked, putting them back on task.

Henry Marks approached the second easel, the one with

the reference sketches attached. He lifted a couple to see a few more underneath.

"I'm not one hundred percent sure," he said, "but I thought there were more of these." He looked at Morrison for confirmation, but Morrison only shrugged.

"Would they have been sketches of the background?" Segal asked.

"Maybe," Henry said. "I asked him about the background, but he seemed kind of touchy on the subject. The way he was doing this was not usual. It's typical to leave details in the background for later, but by now something should at least be sketched in, at least some fine locator marks."

"What do you make of that?" Segal asked.

"I don't know. It's like he was reluctant to commit to it for some reason, or maybe he hadn't made up his mind."

"I was hoping he'd ask us to do part of the background," Morrison said.

Segal made a notation in his book: *Who finishes the painting now?*

They were quiet for a moment, all looking at Joan of Arc Postmodern. After a pause Segal broke the silence.

"You said your studio is next door."

The three of them nodded.

"Let's go look around there, too."

This room was smaller than the main studio, less than half its size, but the light was just as abundant. The space was divided into four areas, one for each of the apprentices and one common area with shelving for storage.

Segal and Walter followed them in as each apprentice gravitated to his own area. Walter caught Segal's eye and nodded toward the area where the youngest man, Mark Engel, stood. Engel seemed to be searching for something.

He moved canvases, looked under his work bench, and picked up some clothes that were piled on a wooden desk chair. The search grew more frantic as he repeated all these motions again.

Segal walked closer. "Missing something?" he asked.

The other two apprentices who were calmly inspecting their own work areas looked up, and Walter watched closely too.

"I am going to be in so much trouble," Mark Engel muttered.

Segal took another step toward him and raised a hand as a sign to calm down. "What are you missing, Mark?"

Mark Engel looked from Segal to Walter and said, "A crossbow."

In the silence that followed Segal noticed dust mites in the shaft of sunlight which illuminated the young man.

The silence persisted a few more seconds before Walter turned to the other apprentices and said, "Could you two gentlemen maybe wait for us in the main studio a few minutes, please."

The two moved reluctantly to the door. After a pause and a look back, Henry Marks said to the younger kid, "You don't have to tell them anything, Mark. Tell them you want a lawyer."

Walter frowned at Henry and guided them on out of the room and shut the door behind them.

"Why don't you sit down here a minute," Segal said. He took the pile of clothes off the chair and plopped them onto the workbench. Mark Engel lowered himself into it and took a deep breath, clearly trying to calm himself.

"Tell us about this crossbow you're missing," Segal said

The kid took another deep breath and said, "I borrowed it from the Biltmore Estate. Jules needed to draw one in the Joan painting and I told him I remembered seeing one at the Biltmore estate. I talked the guy there into loaning it to us and he's going to be really pissed when I have to tell him it's gone."

"What's the man's name?" Segal asked.

Engel told them. Segal nodded toward Walter who jotted the name down and left the room, pulling his cell phone from his pocket.

Segal decided to shift away from the weapon for a minute until Walter got back. He wanted to calm the kid down so they might get him to talk more freely.

"I see you have a UNCA shirt on. Are you studying there as well as working here?"

"I'm just taking a few random classes: a few that sound interesting."

"Such as?"

"Right now, I'm taking a history class and an engineering class." Engel said. He seemed to relax a little.

"Engineering? Isn't that a long way from art like you're studying here?"

"Not really. Look at da Vinci. He was an artist, designer, engineer, everything."

Segal looked around the room at the drawings in pencil, ink, and chalk, at the plaster busts and easels and brushes. *Yes*, he thought. *Leonardo da Vinci would have felt pretty much at home here.*

"Why did you decide to apprentice with Julius Hargrove?"

The kid, Engel, looked at Segal like he was crazy. "Didn't you see the painting next door? Have you seen any of his other work?" Engel shook his head as if that were all the explanation anyone should need. "If I could learn to be anywhere close to that good…" His voice trailed off. His face changed from animated to sad as if he was only just processing the reality of his mentor's death and how that was going to change his own life.

Walter leaned back into the doorway and summoned Segal with a sideways nod of his head.

In the hallway he gave Segal the news. The guy at the Biltmore estate confirmed the story that Mark Engel had told them about the antique crossbow. The guy also said it couldn't possibly be the murder weapon.

"YOU THINK HE really didn't know a crossbow was used in the murder?" Walter asked. After releasing the three apprentices for the time being, they had repaired to the Hole Doughnut Shop across the river.

"If he did he's a lot better actor than I'm giving him credit for," Segal said. He took a bite of the cardamom-glazed pastry, savoring its restorative power.

"The curator at the Biltmore, you said he was pretty sure about the crossbow not being the weapon?"

Walter nodded. "He said that thing is over four hundred years old. You put much tension on it and he wasn't sure what would break first, the string or the bow, or the release mechanism. That wood was very brittle. There's virtually no flex left in it. Not functional."

"Well I'm not going to be the one to crank that thing back and break it just to prove the point," Segal said.

"I know a guy we can check with," Walter said.

For a moment they fell silent and concentrated on the doughnuts.

"What did you think about the whole story of the birthday party that lasted all night even though the guest of honor was not there? Seemed a little curious to me," Segal said.

"If by curious you mean odd as hell, makes no frigging

sense, and they're not telling us the whole story, then yes, I find it mildly curious." Walter said.

MOUNTED TO THE door of the Hole Doughnut Shop was a little bell which alerted the staff when a customer entered or left. Segal and Walter both looked up when they heard it sound.

Dinah Rudisill entered, looking around in the way that told Segal this was her first time in Hole. She spotted them and came over to their table.

"I got Miss Mare home, and I stayed a while until one of her roommates came home. The captain said I should come back and see if I could help out more with the investigation."

This took Segal and Walter a little by surprise and they looked at each other.

"Did he say anything else?" Segal asked.

"He said do whatever you asked me to do and to pay attention because I might learn something," Dinah said.

Segal looked back at Walter who nodded wisely. *So what Walter had heard was true. They were grooming her for bigger things.*

Dinah was looking around the shop again.

"Well, Officer Rudisill, the first thing you can learn is to have them give you one of the doughnuts. I recommend cardamom honey."

FOUR

Silence in the Studio

SEGAL AND DINAH knocked at the door of the pottery studio even though it stood half-way open. A girl looked up from a pottery wheel when they entered, but did not take her hands off the clay form that spun in front of her. Her straw-colored hair was pulled back into a ponytail and the top of her head was covered by a sky blue bandana. Segal guessed she was in her early twenties. Below each eye was a patch of clay smeared on like war paint, but there were also some streaks through the clay. Segal concluded that she had been crying and trying to wipe her eyes with clay covered hands.

"Mary Jane?" Segal asked. He often addressed people by their first names in situations like this to put them at ease.

The girl nodded. She lifted her feet off the kick wheel and took her hands off the clay cylinder, letting it coast. This was the person who had found the body and called it in. She did not seem surprised to see them.

Segal had dropped Walter off at the station. Walter would write and file the initial report and other paperwork which Segal hated to do. Meanwhile, Segal met Dinah back at the studio building to interview other occupants. He wanted to work together with her, at least on the first couple, to make sure Dinah knew how he expected her to proceed.

Mary Jane's eyes filled with tears. She leaned forward to rest her head on her arms. Dinah found a paper towel and handed it to her, putting a hand on her shoulder, but saying nothing.

After a moment Mary Jane recovered enough to speak.

"I'm sorry," she said.

"No need to apologize," Segal said. He went on to introduce Dinah and himself.

"Could you tell us briefly what happened this morning," Segal said.

Mary Jane took a deep breath and pushed out her brief account.

"It was around eleven. I came over to see one of the guys that works with Jules."

"Mark Morrison?" It was a pure guess on Segal's part, but as it turned out, a correct one because Mary Jane nodded yes.

"I knocked on the door, but no one answered. I pulled on it and it opened so I guess it wasn't locked. I went on in." She hesitated and Segal had the good sense to say nothing. He noticed Dinah said nothing either. A *good sign*, he thought. So many interviewers felt the need to push at all the wrong times.

After the pause Mary Jane continued.

"The first thing I noticed was how still it was in there. There was always so much going on in that room any other time I've been there. Right away it didn't feel right. I saw the painting Jules was working on, the Joan of Arc. I took a couple of steps toward it and that's when I saw the body on the floor and all the blood."

"Did you go over to see if there was a pulse, to see if he was alive?" Segal asked.

Mary Jane looked at him. "Oh, he was dead. There was no doubt. I ran out in the hall and called 911."

"And you didn't go back in?" Segal asked.

She shook her head no.

This story was consistent with what he heard from the first police officers on the scene.

"Could you tell what killed him?"

She again shook her head no. "I never got that close."

Good, Segal thought. *Maybe we can keep that factoid under wraps.* At this point he nodded to Dinah, indicating that she should ask the next questions.

"When was the last time you saw Julius Hargrove alive?" she asked.

Mary Jane thought for a moment. "I guess it was last week sometime."

"You didn't see him last night?" Dinah asked.

"No, I went to his birthday party, but he never showed up."

"Have you noticed anything out of the ordinary recently? Anything going on? Any people here you haven't seen before or who seemed out of place?"

"Now that you mention it I did see a guy in a suit come out of the studio. Like a business man or something. That's kind of unusual for this place. This was a few days ago."

"Did he seem threatening in any way?" Dinah asked.

"He seemed pissed is what he seemed. He was walking fast and swinging his arms, and he seemed to be talking to himself."

Dinah went on to get a description of the man which wasn't very specific. After asking a few more questions it was clear they had learned about all they were going to learn from Mary Jane. Segal thanked her and left a card, letting her get back to her pottery wheel meditation.

Once they were out of the pottery studio Segal said, "You did well in there. For the rest of the people working here I think we'd better divide and conquer." He had seen enough of Dinah in action to believe she could do these initial interviews on her own. They went to the entrance of the building where the list of studios was displayed and divided up the territory.

This was the shoe leather part of detective work, knocking on doors, asking questions, knowing that helpful information might be sparse if it was there at all. After spending the rest of the afternoon on the interviews Segal returned to the studio. He wanted to be alone there for a little while. He wanted to think and to process and to let the room speak to him. As he entered he looked at the painting on the easel. *Joan of Arc Postmodern.*

He stepped up for a closer look, first at the painting, then at sketches on the easel nearby. He pulled himself away and wandered around the room, picking up objects and putting them back. Looking at documents and sketches, all of which seemed unrelated to the violence that had taken place. After a few minutes of that he gave up on the rest of the room and settled down into a canvas director's chair in front of the painting.

His phone buzzed with a message. He checked it out and saw it was only his This Day in History app. On May 23, 1616 William Shakespeare died, the message read. Segal snorted. *And here it is four hundred years later and he's still the best I could come up with for Tommy.*

There was a soft knock at the door though it stood open. He glanced back over his shoulder. It was Dinah, leaning in.

"Lieutenant, I finished the interviews, at least at the studios where anyone was working." She was talking in a low voice as if she had picked up on Segal's contemplative mood. He appreciated that as well as the extra effort she was showing.

"Come on in, Officer Rudisill."

She took a step into the room, looked around and then advanced slowly, eyes wide.

"Ever been in an artist's studio before?" Segal asked.

"Not like this one." Her voice was still scarcely above a whisper. "This must be what Leonardo da Vinci's studio looked like." She was looking at a couple of plaster busts on one of the back shelves.

"You're probably closer to the truth than you realize," Segal said, turning toward her. "Talking to people this afternoon, I learned a lot about what kind of art they work on here. This guy was very literally old school. He learned from a master and he went through the same kind of training that students have been going through since the renaissance. His master was trained by a master, and on and on back in time. These guys can literally trace their art heritage back to the fifteenth or sixteenth century. One of the steps a student must go through in learning to draw and paint is drawing those busts. It's the same set of busts that Leonardo and Rafael and all those guys would have drawn as part of their training, mostly plaster casts of statues from ancient Greece."

"Jody told me a little about Hargrove's three apprentices. Everybody calls them the Marks Brothers because they're all named Mark," Dinah said.

Segal grinned and nodded. He had a hunch people might open up to Dinah. It looked like his hunch was paying off.

"Walter and I talked with them a little today, but we hadn't heard the Marks Brothers thing. That's pretty good."

Dinah approached closer to the painting at the center or the room.

"That's her all right," she said. "He was making her look like a saint or something."

"What did you think of her?" Segal asked. "I mean when you were sitting with her and taking her home. What impression did you form of her?"

Segal noticed that Dinah did not answer right away. It was another thing that impressed him. She seemed to be giving his question some thought and consideration which was more than he could say for a lot of people.

"I formed the impression that she's young, nineteen, trying to figure out what the world is all about, trying to figure out what her place is going to be in it. She seemed scared about what happened here, truly shocked."

"Did she say anything about her background?" Segal asked.

"Her mom owns a bookstore a little south of here. She worked there when she was in high school. She came up here to Asheville and started at UNCA; thinking about majoring in art, but she wasn't sure. Then she met a guy who introduced her to Julius Hargrove and she enrolled in one of his drawing classes. Now she's thinking she could learn more here than at the University. At least that's what she was thinking before this happened. So that's another thing she's upset about. Murder is bad enough, but in this case it also totally derailed what she was going to do with her life. She's more confused than anything."

"What about her living arrangements?" Segal asked.

"She's living with some other girls in a house off of Montford Avenue."

"Good," Segal said.

Dinah gave him a curious look.

"I mean I'm glad she's not alone," he explained.

She nodded and looked back at the painting.

"It looks like he was nearly done painting her and he was moving on to the background."

"So it seems," Segal said. "Although, if you look at the sketches here it's not too clear what the background was going to be."

Segal was pointing at several small sketches on paper taped to another easel to the right of the painting. Some were details of hands and one was a close up of her face. Two or three others seemed to be rough layouts of the entire painting, only, as Segal had said, the background was different in all three.

Dinah felt one of the sketches by rubbing it between her thumb and middle finger.

"This paper feels different than regular paper," she said.

Segal did the same. It was a little stiffer and thicker than most common paper, also just slightly off white. You might call it ivory. The surface had an interesting texture. It seemed familiar to him, like he had held something like that recently.

"Why are the sketches done in that reddish color?" Dinah asked.

"That's called conté," Segal said. "The old school guys liked it as a drawing medium especially for figure drawing. In the old days they used sanguine chalk. It came from a certain quarry in Italy."

"No wonder," Dinah said, "It's exactly the color of dried blood."

They both fell silent for a moment after she said this. For Segal the mention of blood brought him back to the fact that a few hours earlier a man's body had lain a couple of feet from where he now stood, and it was his job to figure out what happened.

"Where do you even start on a case like this, Lieutenant?" It was almost as if Dinah had read his mind.

"Certain basic questions," Segal said. "Time of death. Cause of death. Who was the last person to see him alive? Who had access to this place? Who had motive to kill him? The kind of stuff we did this afternoon."

He looked at Dinah and smiled. He felt like he had been giving a lecture, but the look on her face told him she was interested, not just making conversation.

"Anyway, if you can get some answers to those basic questions a picture starts to emerge. That and people talk." He stopped and grinned. "People always talk."

Segal felt himself hit the wall of fatigue and realized there was nothing more for him to do there that night.

"Let's get out of here," he said and Dinah preceded him into the hallway outside. He turned and locked the door and they walked down the hallway and began to descend the stairs. When they reached the first landing Segal said, "Damn."

"Forget something?" Dinah asked.

"There was an address book I was going to take with me." He turned and retraced his steps up the stairs. Dinah paused on the landing, evidently unsure if she should follow him back, proceed down the stairs, or remain where she was and wait for him to return.

Segal turned off the stairway and walked into the gloom of the hallway. He fumbled in his pocket for the key, but before he could fish it out the door exploded open, swinging to the side and knocking him to the floor. A large figure stumbled out, a man dressed in black with a hood covering his face. The way his body was turned to the side Segal could tell he must have hit the door from the inside with his shoulder like an NFL lineman.

"Police! Stay where you are," Segal shouted, although it must have seemed less impressive from his crumpled position on the ground. He struggled to his feet, but the instant he was up the hooded man swung at him and caught him with a vicious blow to the side of the head. It knocked Segal back into the wall where he slumped to the ground. In the moments it took his head to clear and for him to get to his feet the man was gone. In his groggy state he registered the sound of running footfalls in the hallway followed by the clanging foot falls on the metal stairs leading to the roof.

Then he heard light footsteps clanging up the stairs leading from the ground floor. It was Dinah, bounding up, clearing the top landing like a deer.

"Are you all right?" she asked Segal.

He nodded.

"Which way?" she asked. Segal noticed she had her side arm drawn.

"Up those stairs to the roof," he said, nodding his head in that direction. She took off and he followed, though he was no match for her speed. She was up the stairs in a few leaps but when she pushed on the door it did not open. She pushed again and it gave slightly.

Segal arrived beside her and they both gave it their best try. It slowly yielded and at last they were out in the night air.

They both listened for a second but when they heard nothing Segal pointed to Dinah and then off to the right. She moved off carefully in that direction; Segal went the other way.

After a moment his eye caught movement to the left and he gave chase. He could just make out the guy high stepping over some obstacle half-way across the roof. As he gave chase he found the footing treacherous with the small loose gravel and the various pipes and vents and windows appearing at the last second out of the darkness. He lost sight of the guy, but his general direction led to the back of the building. Segal moved around the pipes and the vents and then seemed to be in a clearer section and put on a burst of speed.

Before he realized it he was coming up on the edge of the building and he put on the brakes, but the pieces of gravel were like ball bearings under his shoes. His foot hit a piece of conduit running across the surface and he pitched forward. At the last second he felt a hand grab his jacket from behind and he felt his center of gravity pull back from the ledge.

He turned to see Dinah. He looked at her for a second then bent over and breathed hard, trying to regain his composure after his near death experience.

As soon as she saw that Segal was OK she moved to the edge of the roof, looking down, then to the left. "Fire escape," she said.

Segal recovered enough to join her there, looking down, trying to spot any sign of movement, but they saw none.

"Long gone," said Segal.

"Like a turkey in the corn," said Dinah.

They waited a couple more beats then began retracing their steps back toward the entrance to the stairwell.

"Did you get a look at the guy?" Dinah asked.

"Not really, he had a mask," Segal said. "He was big, though, I can tell you that. He knew his way around, too. Knew about the fire escape, knew about this stairwell."

"Even knew about this," Dinah said. She knelt by the partially open door to pick up a small wooden wedge.

She handed it to him. He looked at the wedge and then at her. "Good eye for detail." Another thing about Dinah that impressed him.

"Let me ask you something. Earlier today at the pub, what did you say to that big guy at the bar that settled him down and persuaded him to leave?"

"Oh, that," she said and gave a little laugh. "The guy was all upset because they had left the slice of onion off his burger. The cook brought a slice out to correct his mistake, but the guy wouldn't stop yelling, said it was too late. I showed him my badge and told him it was time to pop smoke."

"Pop smoke?"

"Yeah, its military slang for leaving. I could tell from one of his tattoos he had been overseas. When you're being extracted from a war zone by helicopter you set off some smoke grenades so the pilots can see your location and which way the wind is blowing. Time to pop smoke means time to leave."

Segal nodded.

"Anyway, the cook was standing there with the chef's knife still in hand. I said if the knife was sharp enough to slice an onion, think what it could do to you. Only difference between you and the onion is no one would cry if you got cut."

THEY RETURNED TO the studio where the door stood open and the light bled out into the hallway.

They moved around and inspected the room carefully to see if anything was missing or if there was any other clue about what the man had been doing there.

"Thank God this is OK," Dinah said. She was standing in front of the Joan of Arc painting again.

Segal realized that he felt a sense of relief as well. He also realized they had both already formed an attachment to the painting. *Is that how you know it's a good work of art*, Segal wondered.

He glanced at the other easel to his right and took in a breath.

"At least we know why he came here," he said.

Dinah came up beside him.

"Remember those conté sketches you asked about?" Segal said. "Some of them are gone."

FIVE

Police Station

WALTER GOT TO the squad room early the next day, as was his custom. Well before Segal. Gina, the squad's secretary/ administrative assistant, watched him trundle through the room toward his desk. It was a toss-up each day as to which one of them would get there first. This morning Dinah Rudisill came in early, too, looking a little lost.

"Can I help you with anything?" Gina asked.

"Just waiting for Lieutenant Segal," she replied. "The chief asked me to work with him for a while."

Gina smiled. She had heard rumors that this girl was on a fast track for detective even though she had only recently arrived from the Charlotte police force.

"Segal and Walter can use all the help they can get right now," Gina said, and poured Dinah a cup of coffee.

"Segal's not in yet," she said. "Maybe we should confer with Walter."

She showed Dinah over to the nook where Walter and Segal had their desks. It was almost as good as having their own office.

Walter looked up and smiled when he saw them.

"Looks like you and Segal have some extra help for a while," Gina said, by way of introduction.

"That's what I heard," he said. He glanced back at the computer screen.

Dinah stood there a minute looking at him, perhaps waiting to see if he had any instructions for her.

"I've got a laptop with me, I guess I could start on my reports from yesterday," she said.

"What are you working on, Walter?" Gina asked.

"I'm hoping I can get this report done, the call we were on just before this homicide came up. Kind of clear the boards, you know?" Gina knew Walter was like that. As meticulous about his paperwork as he was about his appearance.

"A homicide, especially one like the one in the River Arts District, tends to push other cases aside," Gina explained.

She turned to Walter. "That other case, was that the professor at UNCA that had something stolen?"

Walter nodded.

"What was stolen?" Dinah asked.

Walter turned away from the computer screen, apparently giving up on the idea of concentrating on the report.

"That was one of the strange things," he said. "The professor called it in and he didn't want to tell us over the phone what was missing."

Gina asked, "What department was it?"

"It turned out to be," Walter dragged out the last word while he spun in his desk chair to retrieve a brochure, "Mechatronics."

"Mechatronics?" Dinah asked. She wrinkled her forehead.

Walter took a sip of coffee. He was the kind of storyteller who was in no particular hurry to get to the juicy parts of a tale.

"According to this brochure, it's a combination of mechanics, electronics, and computer programing."

"Like everything they could think of that's hard," Gina said.

"Yeah, that's what I thought, but Segal said it sounded great. I thought he was going to enroll himself on the spot."

Gina nodded and grinned. Walter grinned too. She enjoyed trading Segal stories with Walter and she knew he enjoyed it too.

"So we drove over there and we found this professor, the one who called it in. He was really nervous and shaky. A lot of people are like that after something is stolen or they've had some other kind of problem. But this guy was off the charts. Before he would even tell us anything about what happened he said we all had to go and meet with the president of the University."

Walter paused to take another drink of coffee. Gina and Dinah leaned forward with an expectant looks on their faces.

"So we all trudge over to the president's office and they take us to a meeting room and it's us, the president, the professor, and a couple of lawyers, and they all seem nervous as hell, just like the professor was in the first place."

At that point Walter pulled a sheet of paper out of the folder on his desk. It was large enough that it had to be folded three times to fit in a normal folder. The paper itself was off-white and the intricate drawing was done in brown ink.

"It reminds me of one of those da Vinci drawings, like the ones in his notebooks," Dinah said.

"Me, too," Walter said. "Can you tell what it is from the drawing?"

"Is it a...catapult?" Dinah asked.

They all studied the drawing. It showed a machine made

mostly of heavy wooden beams and planks. The fixtures looked like parts taken from heavy farm equipment. There was a long adjustable arm with a metal basket on the end. Walter explained it was the main throwing arm. There were some big metal springs and a cranking mechanism.

"Is that what he told you had been stolen?" Gina asked.

Walter just nodded his head and grinned.

"What were they doing with a catapult anyway?" Dinah asked.

"Engineering competition," Walter said. "Apparently, among the groups that stage Renaissance Fairs, there's a competition on catapult building. It started as a challenge to throw a hundred-pound rock a hundred yards, and grew from there. Originally catapults were used to throw rocks to break up the walls of fortifications. Sometimes they threw balls of rags soaked in oil and lit on fire. They would hurl those over the castle walls to start fires. They called them comets."

"Did it work? I mean, this catapult. Did it actually throw things?" Dinah asked.

"According to the professor it worked better than anyone expected. I mean this year's model did. Before this year it was just a few history majors messing around with it. They got tired of losing so they recruited some of the engineering students and between them they made something that looks authentic and works, too. It was the idea of one of the students who happened to be taking an engineering and a history class at the same time."

"So why were the president and the lawyer in on the meeting?" Gina asked.

"Liability," Walter said. "They're scared to death what someone's going to do with this thing, especially what the University might be liable for."

Gina nodded. "So then what did you do?"

"We all went traipsing out of the conference room and around back of the engineering building where they had been working on it. We could see some tire tracks. Segal thought it looked like a heavy pickup maybe. There was some soot deposits nearby so Segal said it was probably a diesel.

"Then he noticed this brown stain or splash of something, partly on the sidewalk, partly on the grass. He pulled up a few blades of grass and sniffed them. Then he held it out to me and told me to smell it. You ever notice when someone tells you to smell something, it's always bad?

"I almost puked. Segal just said, 'Someone's been dipping snuff and they spit it out here.'"

"Did that make the president and the lawyer feel any better?" Dinah asked.

"Segal made them feel better. He told them he would be surprised if their machine wasn't back to them by the end of the week. That made them feel a lot better. They said they were supposed to do a demonstration with it at the music festival at Lake Eden next week. The theme is Renaissance Fair and they're supposed to fling one of those flaming balls."

"So what are we going to do to find it?" Dinah asked.

"I asked Segal the same question. I said what are we going to do about this, and he said, 'Nothing.' He didn't think we needed to do a dang thing. He predicted that they would make themselves known soon enough."

"He said that?" Dinah asked.

"What I said was stupidity of that caliber cannot be hidden under a bushel. It must be allowed to shine out in the world. They will make themselves known soon enough without us looking for them. We just need to keep our eyes and ears open," Segal said, entering the room and setting his briefcase on his desk.

SEGAL STOOD BY his desk and regarded the little group. He was wearing his usual gray sport coat. Also, as usual, the top of an old paperback book could be seen sticking out of the right pocket, one of Elmore Leonard's set in Miami. One time Walter had pointed out that this arrangement meant that it would be much quicker for him to pull out the book than to draw his gun in case of emergency.

"That's the way it should be," Segal had told him.

"Is that supposed to make me feel better?" Walter had asked.

"Stories are much more powerful than guns," Segal said, not for the first time.

This morning Walter said, "I was just telling these two about our catapult case at the university."

"Ah yes, the catapult case," Segal said. "Are you up for taking the lead on this one, Dinah?"

Dinah looked a little surprised, but quickly replied, "Yes, sir," revealing a little of her military background. Segal spent a couple of minutes outlining how she might get with dispatch and route certain types of calls through her for the next few days.

Gina handed Segal a number of pink message slips. As he took them from her she said, "The chief wants to see you and Walter at your earliest convenience."

Segal nodded and glanced briefly through the slips. Walter stopped typing on the computer. He looked at Segal and raised his eyebrows. "You ready to talk to the chief?"

Segal nodded and got up. They both knew what the chief meant by "At your earliest convenience."

The chief's office was classic old school, fronted by half-length windows with Venetian blinds kept at a perpetual closure of about eighty percent. With very few alterations it would have fit in perfectly in the nineteen twenties. Segal and Walter waited for a moment outside the open door. They could see the chief sitting behind his old wooden desk in shirt sleeves and suspenders and wide tie. The picture would have been perfect if the phone he held to his ear had been made of heavy black plastic with a looped cord.

The chief hung up and motioned them in and without preamble said, "Tell me about the homicide."

Segal and Walter took turns briefing him on the facts they knew so far.

"And what are you doing next?" their boss asked.

"Well, Crawford should get us a time of death this morning, official autopsy report in a couple of days maybe, but, of course, cause of death was pretty obvious when we got there," Walter said.

Their boss looked at the paper in front of him. "Is this right? Crossbow?"

"That's what Crawford says," Segal said. He explained about the length of the arrow.

"Bolt," Walter corrected.

The chief shook his head and looked back at the report for a second. "Look," he said, "I've already got a call on this from Raleigh this morning."

"Since when does anyone in Raleigh care about anyone west of Charlotte?" Segal asked.

"Since this guy who got crossbowed to death is the governor's brother-in-law," the chief said.

"Brother-in-law?" Walter said.

"His wife's brother," the chief said. "Needless to say she's pretty distraught which makes the governor pretty distraught himself. He wants to send in the SBI."

Segal and Walter both started to object at the same time, but the chief held up his hand.

"Don't worry, we're not going to have the lot of them

swarming the station here, at least not yet, not if we move on this with some dispatch." He looked up at the two detectives to make sure they understood. They nodded in unison.

"Meanwhile," he continued, "give the SBI something to do. That's the best way to keep them and the governor off our backs. Send them something for chemical analysis, something to put in their electron microscope, anything."

"OK," Segal said, "we can do that."

"Let's send them the arrow," Walter said.

"Bolt," Segal said, "Perfect."

"Also, the wife is at the Western Residence. Apparently, she came over from Raleigh as soon as she heard. I need you to go up and meet with her and make her feel better. Let her know we're on this."

"Right, boss," Segal said.

"What about the other thing?" the chief asked.

"Other thing?" Segal said.

"The robbery?" Walter asked.

"Yeah," the chief said. "You were called to the University on something."

"Department of Mechatronics," Walter said.

"Mechatronics?"

"And History," Segal added, as if that would clear anything up.

"Is it anything we have to worry about right now? Do we need to put someone else on it?"

"I gave it to Dinah," Segal said. "I'm pretty sure the culprits will make themselves known soon if we just keep our eyes and ears open."

He and Segal stood up and turned to go, but the chief said, "Segal, stick around for a minute." Walter shot Segal a look as he brushed past, and Segal turned back to the chief.

The chief leaned forward and spoke in a softer voice.

"I'm assigning Dinah Rudisill to you for a while for three reasons."

He held up his hand and started counting with fingers.

"One, you can use some extra help to clear this murder quickly. Two, from her resume and from what I'm hearing, she has some real potential." He handed Segal a folder with her name on it.

"What's the third reason?" Segal asked.

"I want you to watch her and give me your opinion," the chief said.

Segal nodded and began to get up, but the chief held him by raising a palm.

"One more thing, Segal, unrelated. I heard there was another incident with Tommy yesterday."

Segal recoiled. The chief was famous for hearing about everything that happened in Asheville, but damn. Bad news traveled fast.

"He didn't really do anything this time. I just had to get him settled down and get him something to eat and he was OK. He's with his mom now."

"Good thing you were in the right place at the right time is what I heard," the chief said.

Segal nodded. "Yeah, maybe."

"Trouble is, you won't always be."

"Nobody seems to know what to do with him," Segal said.

The chief just let it sit there a moment. Then he said, "Let me know if there's anything we can do." He lowered his eyes down to the papers on his desk as a signal the conversation was over. Segal left. He knew the chief and probably everyone else at the station thought Tommy should be in an institution. None of them said it out loud, at least not to Segal. He had to give them credit for that.

SEGAL RETURNED TO his desk next to Walter's and pushed the wad of pink message slips aside.

"Why do you kill someone with a crossbow?" he asked Walter.

"You could break the question down," Walter said. "First, why do you want to kill this guy at all, and then secondly, why do you choose an archaic weapon like a crossbow?"

Segal followed this stream of thought. "OK, the first part is no different than any other murder we've ever worked. You kill someone for money, for revenge, in self-defense, in a fit of jealous rage, to keep them from doing you some kind of harm, to silence them, all the usual stuff.

"The second part, why do you use a crossbow as opposed to some other weapon, I would say, you could break down further. You could break it down into practical reasons and symbolic reasons, symbolic as in you're trying to make some kind of statement."

This was one of the things that Segal liked about working with Walter. They could have conversations like this, brainstorming and bouncing ideas around like a shared stream of consciousness. Thinking out loud.

Walter picked up the thread. "So for practical reasons, you could say the crossbow is quiet, at least compared to a gun."

Segal nodded.

"Also, you can kill at some distance from the victim. It's not up close and personal like a knife or some other bladed weapon. Also, it doesn't take as much physical strength, cause a knife is probably going to result in some hand-to-hand combat action," Walter continued.

"To say nothing of the messy nature of a knife fight. Getting blood all over yourself and so forth," Segal said.

"Lots of evidence involved: bloody clothes you have to get rid of, fingerprints, shoe marks."

They thought for a moment.

"Why not a regular bow, like a target bow or hunting bow? There are plenty of those around." Walter asked.

"Shooting a crossbow takes less skill and practice than a regular bow. At least that's what I've read. That was one of the reasons they became popular for a period of time. That and the fact they were powerful enough to pierce armor," Segal said. "In this case, though, I'm not sure if either of those factors hold up. Any modern hunting bow would have plenty of power. There is no armor involved. And at that short distance inside I don't know how much skill is needed. Seems like you could hardly miss."

"You might be underestimating the human capacity to F things up, but I get your point," Walter said. "What was the other kind of reason you said? Using the crossbow to make a statement."

"Yeah, like it would be symbolic of something." Segal said. "What do you think of when you think of a cross-bow?"

"I know what you're going to say," Walter said. "You're going to say two things. You're going to say William Tell and you're going to say that Ancient Mariner thing, which only you would think of."

"You thought of it. Everyone read the *Rime of the Ancient Mariner* in school," Segal said.

"Yeah, but you actually liked it."

Segal sat back and thought for a moment. Yes, he did like it. *Was that so bad*?

"OK, but since you brought it up, let's talk about the *Rime of the Ancient Mariner*."

"Here we go," Walter muttered underneath his breath.

"In the Rime, the mariner shoots an albatross with his crossbow. The albatross is a symbol of guidance and goodness, and some people would say of nature. Some even say symbolic of a Christian soul flying up to heaven. In any case it was definitely bad luck to harm one. The crossbow was a symbol of strength. It was associated with protectors and fighters and maybe with human technology, so it could be a technology verses nature kind of thing."

"Seems pretty esoteric to me," Walter said. "If the killer was trying to make a statement connected to that stuff it seems like there aren't many people who would understand the statement outside of you and the English department at UNCA."

Segal thought for a moment. "OK, what about something a little more general. The victim was an artist who used materials and techniques from the renaissance, and he gets killed by a weapon from the renaissance. It fits."

"It would fit in one of your books, Segal. But this here," Walter said twirling his hand around, "is what most of us call real life."

"Or in the case of Julius Hargrove, real death," Segal said, sitting back in his chair. "Meanwhile, to more practical matters, which one of us should go up to the Western Residence?"

Walter just raised his eyebrows with a look that said, "Don't ask dumb questions."

SIX

Flying Monkey Syndrome

SEGAL DROVE HIS aged Volvo up the twisting road following the contours of Town Mountain. He pulled off into a driveway which led to a huge iron gate in a stone wall. A state trooper's car was pulled off to the side just past the gate. The trooper, a man of exceptional size, was standing next to it. He approached the gate and stood with arms crossed.

If they wanted someone to intimidate the general public, they picked the right guy, Segal thought. Segal got out and approached the gate from his side. He pulled out his ID and reached through the rungs of the gate to hand it to the trooper who took it from him and examined it with a little more scrutiny than one might have expected. He glared at Segal but the gate swung slowly open powered by some unseen mechanism, and the trooper motioned him in.

As he followed the drive that curved up the hill Segal got his first look at the house known as the Western Residence, home of the governor of North Carolina, on the rare occasions he or his family visited this part of the state. The house was a little smaller than he had imagined, made of stone and timbers and very wide expanses of glass. In fact, Segal was surprised to find that he could see clear through portions of the house and out the windows on the other side.

It struck Segal as slightly dated, a forerunner of the upscale mountain homes being built today.

As he pulled closer he saw a man standing by the front door, apparently waiting for him.

The man was thin, slightly below medium height, slightly bent. Segal thought he wore his nondescript navy-blue suit like a uniform. Segal could read little in the man's face other than a vaguely worried look as he shook his hand and introduced himself.

"Lieutenant Segal, I'm John Davenport. The governor's wife is expecting you," he said. He opened the door and motioned for Segal to walk in. Segal found himself in an entrance hall facing a rounded stone fireplace. A guest book lay on a wooden stand, and he found that his detective's instincts drew him to it to read the most recent names, even though he knew it would have nothing to do with the case.

John Davenport led Segal further into the house, but then hesitated and turned to him with solemn face.

"Mrs. Price is very upset about her brother's death," he said.

"Understandable."

"Maybe even more upset than you might imagine," Davenport said. The worried look on his face had not changed. "We wanted you to understand before you meet her, just so you will not be surprised if she says anything irrational or makes any unreasonable requests."

"We?" Segal asked.

"The governor and myself," Davenport said.

"Is the governor here?"

"Not as yet. He plans to be here in a day or two, as soon as he can clear his schedule in Raleigh," Davenport said. "In the meantime he wants to be kept up to date on any developments in the case." Saying this Davenport took a business card out of his pocket and handed it to Segal. Segal glanced at it and saw that Davenport's title was Chief of Staff.

"You can contact me and I will see that the governor gets any message you want to send. He also wanted me to offer again any possible assistance from the State Bureau of Investigation."

Segal tucked the card into his shirt pocket and nodded to Davenport. He thought it a little odd that a chief of staff would be here rather than in Raleigh running the office.

Without further words Davenport led him back into the house proper. They passed through the vestibule and into a short hallway. Several works of art hung on two of the walls of smooth wood paneling. The pieces ranged from folk art to modern paintings which Segal assumed were all by North Carolina Artists. There was a fine example of Cherokee basket weaving, a hand stitched quilt and a few portraits, presumably of characters important in North Carolina history. The final painting that he passed was by James Colebrook, a name known to Segal as it was to most people in the area. It was a small painting, less than a foot square, mounted in an elaborate antique frame. Segal paused to examine it more closely. It was done in the manner of Vermeer, showing a dim kitchen room lit by pale winter light coming in through an elevated window above a sink on the left. Tables and shelves bore numerous crocks, bottles and kitchen implements. On the sink a spotted newt wearing a laced bonnet raised its face to the light.

Before he could study it further Segal heard Davenport clear his throat. Segal straightened up and Davenport waved him into the main living room and then disappeared without another word.

It was a large room with bookcases and more artwork on three of the walls. Simple but comfortable-looking furniture was arranged in a couple seating groups. The fourth wall was a large expanse of glass, floor to ceiling, and this was the wall that grabbed Segal's attention. It presented a perfect view over the city of Asheville and across the plateau on which it sat, and behind that, to the west, Mount Pisgah, and the associated ridgeline. Further still other hazy blue ridgelines faded away into the distance.

"You should see the view out that window when the sun is setting." It was a woman's voice from behind him. Segal had not heard her come in.

He turned and saw Alexa Price, the first lady of the state. He recognized her from photos he had seen in the paper. The photos had not done her justice, he thought. She was around five six, with flawlessly cut and styled brown hair. She wore a casual but perfectly tailored light gray dress of some expensive-looking material Segal did not recognize. She wore black hose and no shoes, which would account for her silent entrance. He guessed her age as fairly close to his own, mid to late forties. She was holding a glass of red wine.

For a moment Segal was speechless, but he quickly recovered and introduced himself. By habit he started to pull out his ID, but she said, "Not necessary, Lieutenant. I recognize you from the news."

Segal looked a little surprised at this, then she added, "Besides, you already got through a state trooper and the watch dog my husband sent to keep an eye on me."

Segal only nodded and smiled. He had not been sure what to expect of this interview, and he still wasn't.

"Would you like a glass of wine, Lieutenant?" Mrs. Price said. "I'm having one."

"No, thank you," he said, although the truth was that

the idea of a glass of wine with this lady, under different circumstances, was very appealing indeed.

"My brother liked wine," she said. She moved across the room to stand beside him and look out the window. "Did you know that about him?"

"We did hear that he liked to hang out at a wine bar with some of his friends," he said. This had come from one of his apprentices.

"You mean the one in the Grove Arcade?" she said. "Yes, that is quite a group that hangs out there."

"Yes, that's the place we heard about, but we have not interviewed any of the people he associated with there. Not yet, that is."

"You're in for a treat," she said. She shot him a look and then turned back to the view.

They gazed out in silence for a moment.

"Some people say that it's not worth the trouble to build in a place like this just for the view. They say you get used to it after a while and don't even notice it. But I never get used to it," she said.

"It's different every time you look at it," Segal said. "Just like the ocean."

She turned toward him with genuine surprise. She looked Segal up and down as if doing a reappraisal. "That's exactly what I was thinking, Lieutenant. Just like the ocean." She narrowed her eyes at him. "You're not clairvoyant are you?"

"It would make my job a lot easier if I was," he said. He gave her a smile.

She smiled too, but then a cloud passed over her face. "What can you tell me about my brother's death? Is it true that he was killed by an arrow?"

"We're keeping certain details under wraps as we generally do in a case like this. If we hear something from a witness we want to be sure it is a true observation, and not something that they read in the paper or saw on TV."

He also made a mental note. They had not disclosed anything about the arrow, or more accurately, bolt. Did this mean that the governor's office had access to their internal reports, either through the SBI or otherwise?

Alexa Price continued to look at him and she slumped, tears forming in her eyes. Segal took the glass of wine from her hand as he was afraid she was about to drop it. He steadied her by grasping her other elbow and led her to one of the low cushioned chairs nearby.

"I'm sorry, Mrs. Price. I didn't say it before, but I am very sorry for your loss," he said. Segal looked around, found a box of tissues on a coffee table nearby and handed her one. She took a moment to compose herself.

"I'm sorry, Lieutenant. I was close to my brother. Our parents passed away a few years ago, and he was all I had left of our family."

"And you made the trip here from Raleigh as soon as you heard the news yesterday?"

"I was actually here on some other business. I came up on Wednesday afternoon to help with the preparations for a reception we're hosting."

This piece of information took Segal by surprise.

"And did you see your brother?"

"I stopped by the studio Thursday for a few minutes. He seemed fine then. I had no idea that would be the last time," she said, and tears formed again.

"Did you come here to the residence alone?"

"That's what I had planned but no, shortly after I got here Davenport showed up too."

Segal took out his notebook and made a quick entry.

"What else can you tell me about your brother?" Segal asked.

"Like what?" she asked, looking up at him now.

"Well, to start with, did he have any enemies that you know of? Anyone upset with him for any reason?"

"I guess any time you try to do something there will be people lining up against you to criticize. I mean actually do something instead of just talking about it," she said.

"Like painting?" Segal asked.

"Yes, like painting. Like doing a lot of paintings. If everyone who called him or herself an artist really worked at their craft there wouldn't be enough walls to hold the paintings. My brother worked at his craft. He actually produced. And people in the so-called art world lined up to yap about what he did like a pack of little dogs."

"What did they complain about?" Segal asked.

"Everything. Anything. If he painted something conventional, they said it was unoriginal. If he stepped outside the box, he was turning his back on his roots."

"And how did your brother feel about those comments?" Segal asked.

"My brother didn't care, or if he cared he blamed himself. I told him one time they would criticize anything, but he said no. He had to believe there was a possibility that you could do something so good that no one could fail to see it for what it was."

Segal let that soak in a minute. "Your brother must have been an exceptional man," he said. "I'm sorry he's gone."

To his surprise Alexa took Segal's hand in hers. "Lieutenant, I would like to see his studio."

Segal started to shake his head, but before he could speak Alexa jumped in again. She squeezed his hand. "Please, Lieutenant. I was warned that it is a crime scene and I could not have access, but I need to be there, to see it and to feel it and smell it. I need to feel my brother's presence there."

Segal hesitated. On the one hand it could be very awkward. On the other hand, they might learn something by watching her there and asking her questions about the work.

"Let me talk to some people and see what I can do," he said.

"Thank you," she said.

"Of course, one of us would have to be there with you," he said.

She smiled. "I wouldn't have it any other way." She let go of Segal's hand and sat back in the chair.

"OK, then," Segal said. "I will call as soon as I can get it arranged." He nodded and turned to leave. When he neared the door she called him back.

"Lieutenant Segal," she said, and then in a voice little more than a whisper, "we don't need to let the governor or Davenport know about this."

DINAH'S PHONE SOUNDED as she and Walter and Segal waited outside the studio building. It was Gina on the phone.

"You said you wanted to hear about any strange calls like unusual objects falling out of the sky or flying overhead?"

"Right," Dinah said. She had left these instructions at Segal's suggestion. Gina had written them down without batting an eye.

"We just got a call," Gina said, "A woman says a watermelon fell out of the sky on I26 Eastbound. Smashed on the hood of her car." She gave the specifics about the location.

"So not near an overpass?" Dinah asked.

"Nowhere close."

"Who did dispatch send?" Segal asked. He could overhear the conversation. Dinah held the phone so they all could hear more clearly.

"No one yet. They're thinking it's a crank call."

"It's not a crank call. Tell them to send someone. They can meet Dinah there," Segal said.

"Got it," Gina said, and she ended the call.

Segal turned to Dinah. "Remember, you're looking for a pickup truck with something big in the back. Check the side streets near the location."

"And an observation point," Walter said, raising a finger.

"That's right," Segal said. They would have posted an observer to see what happened, maybe to video it.

Dinah nodded and took off.

"THIS MUST BE HER," Walter said. He was watching a spotless white Land Rover pull up in the parking lot.

Segal straightened his tie as he stood up. They both watched as Alexa emerged from the large vehicle and headed toward them. She was dressed much the same as when Segal first met her except that she now wore high heels. Walter took in her appearance and the way she moved. He looked at Segal and discreetly rolled his eyes.

Walter had been against the idea of her coming to the studio as soon as Segal pitched the idea. Segal argued that they had the potential of learning some useful information from her visit. It might also keep the governor's office off their backs. That's what sold their boss on the idea.

Segal had failed to mention how attractive the woman in question was nor that she was exactly the type that he, Segal, tended to fall for. Thus the look from Walter and the rolling of the eyes. Walter knew him too well.

Segal nodded and smiled as she approached. Walter kept his thoughts to himself. Alexa Price smiled at Segal and touched his arm in greeting.

"Mrs. Price, this is my partner, Walter Knox."

Alexa Price smiled and nodded at Walter and shook his hand in a light and formal way. Walter nodded and said nothing, inscrutable behind his sun glasses.

After a moment Segal said, "Should we go on up to the studio?"

It was what she had specifically asked for, but now that they were close she seemed to have a problem taking those few last steps. After a moment she nodded.

Segal motioned with his hand for her to lead. Ladies first and all that, but more importantly Segal wanted to see if she knew the way. She did. He followed her into the building and up the stairs. Walter fell in behind. Only when they reached the doorway with the crime scene tape did Alexa show any lack of self-assurance. She hesitated and looked back at Segal. He pulled a key out of his pocket, unlocked the door, and preceded her inside, sensing somehow that this was the way she wanted it. He walked to the center of the room and stood bathed in the glow of natural light from the windows overhead. They had placed a canvas drop cloth over the blood stain that remained on the floor.

Alexa followed him into the room with slow steps, looking as if she might turn around and run out. Walter stepped in too, but chose to stay back by the door, giving the two of them some room and observing the scene.

Segal was afraid she would start asking questions about the details of her brother's death, where the body was discovered and that sort of thing, but she did not. Her gaze settled on the unfinished painting.

"So, this is his so-called Joan, Postmodern," she said.

"You didn't see it when you came here Saturday?" Segal asked.

She shook her head. "No, he was keeping it under wraps, like some big surprise."

"Did your brother tell you much about it?" Segal asked.

"Oh, we knew about it," Alexa said. She did not elaborate, and Segal let it go for the time being.

"No background yet," she said after a moment.

"Just some blocking to build up the color base," Segal said, "But you can't really tell where he was going with it; what the detail was going to look like, but roughly, you can tell there were going to be three figures about here." He pointed at the color blocking to the right of the main figure.

She moved to the easel which had held the reference sketches, minus the ones which had disappeared last night.

"I thought there were more sketches here, lieutenant. Did any of your people take them?" she asked.

"No, I don't believe so," he said. "Did you see them when you visited your brother?"

She paused and then said, "I think that's where they were."

"We try not to bother anything we don't need as evidence," Segal assured her. He chose not to tell her about the incident with the intruder from the night before.

"Can you let me know if they turn up?" she asked. "They really should be kept with the painting."

"Certainly," Segal said. He looked over at Walter who raised his eyebrows.

Alexa withdrew a couple of steps to take in the whole painting again. After a moment she sighed and wandered around the room for a while. Segal was afraid she would ask to take something away, but to his relief she did not.

"What will happen to these things?" she asked. She said it in a sort of musing voice, and at first Segal was not sure if she was asking Walter and him the question or if she was just thinking out loud, but then she looked over at him.

"We'll have to determine if anything in here will be used

as evidence, after that, I guess it will be up to the estate settlement," Walter said.

She made a face as if she had just tasted something sour. "Oh, yes, the wife," she said.

She went back and looked at the unfinished painting. "I wonder what happens to this. Do you think the apprentices will finish it?" she asked.

Good question, Segal thought. He did not have the answer, and he made a notation in his book.

"Did he tell you much about this painting; if he was doing it as a commission or if he was doing it on his own?" Segal asked.

"Oh, it was a commission," she said quickly.

"Do you know for whom?" Segal asked.

"Not specifically, no…" she said, but the way she let her voice trail off led him to think she might not be telling the truth, the whole truth, and nothing but the truth. He glanced at Walter and could tell he picked up on it as well.

Alexa shook off her melancholy and put on her game face. She walked back over to the detectives and this time shook hands with both of them. "Thank you very much for indulging me," she said. "I'll let you get back to your investigation." She began to take her leave, but when she got to the door she turned.

"We're still on for later, right, Lieutenant?"

"Sure," Segal said. He smiled and made a small goodbye gesture with his hand as Walter regarded him with a face of stone.

SEGAL AND WALTER walked into the hall and stood outside the studio, watching Alexa Price walk away. When she got to the stairs she turned and gave them a little wave goodbye. Segal waved back.

He turned to Walter who was standing there with his arms crossed.

"So, you're still on for later, are you?" Walter asked.

"That group of artists I mentioned, friends of the deceased, Alexa told me they're meeting at the wine bar this afternoon: kind of a wake. She offered to introduce me to them if I joined them there."

"Hmmm. *Alexa* told you that, did she?" Walter said without uncrossing his arms.

"Mrs. Price," Segal said, looking away.

"I was just reading an article about something they call Flying Monkey Syndrome."

"Flying what syndrome?" Segal asked.

"Flying Monkey Syndrome. It's where men fall under the influence of a powerful and charismatic woman. You know, like the flying monkeys in *The Wizard of Oz* taking orders from the Wicked Witch of the West."

Segal frowned at him. "Well, be sure to let me know if you see any wings sprouting out of my back."

Walter nodded.

SEVEN

Wine Bar to Roller Derby

"COME ON IN, LIEUTENANT," Alexa said, raising a glass of red wine perilously above the head of a man sitting next to her on the couch. "We're having a sort of impromptu wake for my brother."

Segal had just walked into the wine bar which occupied the southwest corner of the Grove Arcade. It was four in the afternoon. He always found the wine bar a comfortable and inviting place although it was not one of his usual haunts. It was actually a combination vintage bookstore and wine bar, and by vintage they meant valuable antique books for the most part. As bookish as Segal was, his tastes leaned more to the paperbacks he carried in his coat pocket rather than expensive first editions of classics. Nevertheless, this place held a lot of appeal for him.

The couch Alexa occupied was part of a seating arrangement grouped around a coffee table with a stamped brass top. Next to Alexa was an end table with a Tiffany lamp which put her face in soft relief with its low intensity light. On the other side of the coffee table was another couch, not a match for the first, and on either end of the table were armchairs. All the seats were occupied except for one of the armchairs. Segal noticed a pair of crossed paint brushes on this one and divined that it was the symbolic place held open for their fallen comrade.

Next to Alexa on the couch was a man whom Segal judged to be in his mid-fifties. He was dressed in a white shirt with a frayed collar, a pair of khaki pants, and white canvas sneakers. At least Segal assumed they had been white at some point in the past; they certainly weren't now.

The man stood up and extended a hand as Segal came around the couch. He introduced himself and the others as well. For each he gave a name and made some comment about his art specialty. One was introduced as a sculptor, one as a portrait painter. They all seemed a couple drinks into the celebration.

That left the man standing before the easy chair at the foot of the table. He was older than the others, perhaps seventies, Segal judged. He had a short gray beard and wore a ball cap with strands of gray hair escaping from the sides. He was of medium height and build. His face was fixed in an ironic grin, as if he found everything around him interesting and mildly amusing. However, it was his deep-set luminous eyes that struck Segal as most remarkable. He thought they conveyed a keen and calm intelligence and they had been following Segal's every move since the moment he walked in. The eyes, at least on this occasion, seemed tragically sad. It was clear to Segal that he was deeply moved by the loss of his friend and had not yet entered the lighter mood of the wake.

"And this is James Colebrook, aka Pipo, in case you don't already know him," the spokesman of the group said, indicating the older man.

"Very good to meet you," Segal said. He had, in fact heard of James Colebrook as had most residents of Asheville. This was partly due to his reputation as an artist, but also for a famous court case involving him and the rest of the Colebrook family a few years earlier. Segal felt a little star struck to meet him in person. He remembered one of the pieces of folk lore he had heard about him; that Pipo had taken a vow of silence some years ago.

Pipo settled back in his chair and picked up a small notebook and began to sketch. No doubt it was a coping mechanism, one which Segal could certainly understand.

The man acting as spokesman stepped to the end of the couch and said, "Please sit down and join us, Lieutenant." He gestured with his hand indicating the center of the couch between Alexa and himself.

Alexa patted the cushion beside her and said, "Yes, by all means, sit with us."

Segal had little choice but to do as they suggested. Alexa, by this time had kicked off her shoes and tucked her feet up under herself. She was close enough to Segal for him to smell her perfume; close enough for it to be a challenge to his concentration.

There was a short awkward moment of silence. Segal cleared his throat and said, "First of all let me offer my condolences. I understand all of you were good friends with Mr. Hargrove."

"More than friends, Lieutenant, we supported each other in this crazy life we all chose," the spokesman said.

"That's a little dramatic, even for you," the sculptor said. Segal detected just a hint of an eastern European accent. He also noticed some anger mixed with his sadness, but then, as Segal knew well, that was sometimes how grief showed up.

"He means dramatic even for a Pre-Raphaelite style painter," the portrait painter added. He seemed to Segal to be smoothing things out for the sake of their guests.

Pipo just gave a wry smile and continued to sketch in the small notebook he held. Segal knew well that this was not a sign of inattention.

He suddenly felt that this was a bad idea, meeting with the group together. He felt out of place and disrespectful, turning their grieving into a police interrogation. Perhaps it would be better to get them talking about something, anything, and sit back and watch the group dynamics.

"Let me ask you something I was wondering about painting," he said, addressing the group at large. "Do artists ever work secret messages into their paintings, for instance into the background?"

Alexa sat up a little straighter and took a sip of wine.

The question got the rest of them going. They assured him that yes, it was done all the time. Probably not so much like *The Da Vinci Code* stuff, more like subtle inside jokes. They cited examples like God's cape in Michelangelo's Sistine Chapel painting taking the form of a human brain. There were many more examples from the renaissance and later periods, especially the Dutch masters. They talked about little details and people slipped into the backgrounds. Throughout this part of the conversation Alexa was quiet, and Segal thought, a little tense. Eventually the conversation diffused in different directions, and Segal let it go.

They would, from time to time begin on a subject unrelated to their friend's death, but the conversation would invariably drift back to Julius Hargrove.

At one point Segal asked if they knew of anyone who had any special ill will against the victim. Apart from the sculptor, who felt the CIA had been monitoring all of them plus half the population of Asheville for years, no one had any ideas along those lines.

"Although", the portrait artist said, "the last time I talked with him he seemed upset with whoever commissioned that Joan of Arc painting he was working on." Segal pressed him for details, but he had no more.

Segal asked if they had gone to the birthday party Hargrove's wife threw for him. He felt that was more subtle than the classic, where were you Friday night. They were all at a dinner thrown by the owner of a gallery, so Segal knew he could at least cross them off the direct suspect list. He asked them to each write their contact information in his notebook which he turned to a clean page.

The men did as he asked, each one standing and getting ready to go after he wrote in the book. Pipo was last. When he handed the notebook back to Segal he also reached out and squeezed his shoulder. It was a gesture of encouragement and sympathy. At least that was how Segal interpreted it. Perhaps it showed empathy for Segal for the difficulty of his task. Whatever the intention, it gave Segal a sense of special connection with the man. Pipo turned away with a tear in his eye.

Alexa was still sitting on the couch as the others walked away. Her wine glass was half full. She swirled it and gazed into the red vortex. Segal checked in his notebook to make sure he had the information he needed from the men. They had all listed their phone numbers with the exception of Pipo who had listed his address along with a note that said, "Come see me any time."

Segal also found that a loose piece of paper had been inserted. It was the page torn from Pipo's notebook; the sketch he had been working on while the others talked. It was Alexa lounging there on the couch, leaning on the arm rest, feet folded up under her, one side of her face bathed in the lamp light, the other in shadow. It was a beautiful woman in a beautiful pose captured, so it seemed, in a few masterful strokes of sanguine chalk. *This,* Segal thought, *is what makes Pipo, Pipo.* In the lower right-hand corner of the page, apart from Alexa, was a winding road disappearing into the distance, and beside the road was a diamond shaped sign with the word caution printed in the center.

"They're ditching us, you know," she said, coming out of her trance. "They'll end up at some other bar or one of the breweries."

"I don't blame them," Segal said. "I probably shouldn't have come."

"I'm glad you did." Alexa gave him a smile now. She swirled the wine in the glass again and handed it to Segal. "I know you're not drinking on duty, Lieutenant, but you have to taste this."

Segal didn't feel he could refuse. He took the glass, noticed the lipstick mark, and tipped a small taste into his mouth. It was smooth and fruity.

Segal sat down again, in the center of the couch next to Alexa so he could speak to her in a low voice. "You asked me earlier to keep you up to date directly rather than communicating through your husband's office. Is there a particular reason for that? Anything I should know?"

She paused for a moment as if considering how to answer that question. Segal handed the glass back to her. Just as their fingertips touched, they were interrupted.

"Mrs. Price," said a voice from behind. They both turned to see John Davenport standing there with the oversized highway patrol officer beside him.

Davenport regarded him for a moment as Segal stood up.

He thought of trying to say some words of explanation but realized there was nothing he could say that was more powerful than the image of him and Alexa Price sitting together sharing a glass of wine.

Davenport slowly shifted his gaze to Alexa and said, "The governor will be arriving soon. We thought you might like a ride back to the residence." His gaze shifted back to Segal and he frowned, indicating that this information was meant for his ears too.

Alexa slipped her shoes on and stood up, a little unsteady on the high heels. This was clearly not her first glass of wine for the afternoon. Segal reached out quickly to steady her. She leaned on his arm for a moment, then turned and walked out slowly, accompanied by the highway patrolman.

Davenport kept looking at him a moment longer. "I'm sure the governor will want you to update him tomorrow. We'll be in touch." He left and Segal was alone thinking about what Walter said about the flying monkeys.

WALTER TOOK ANOTHER drink of his beer. He held up his arm to admire the sleeve of the new jacket he was wearing. He had been doing this at frequent intervals since he had met Segal at the brewery around six.

"You think this new jacket is fashionable, Segal?"

"If by fashionable you mean geriatric then yes, I think it looks extremely fashionable," Segal said without so much as a glance.

Segal was sitting at the table across from him at the Wicked Weed Brewery checking his phone messages of which there were several. He had filled Walter in on his wine bar meeting, such as it was, including the awkward conclusion.

Walter shook his head and said, "Uh huh… That woman is trouble, Segal, and not in a crossbowing kind of way."

"You're the second old man to tell me that within the last hour," Segal said, and he showed Walter the sketch Pipo had made.

"Wise man," Walter said.

Segal frowned. "Nothing's going to happen with that."

Walter looked unconvinced, but not unsympathetic. "Why don't you come to dinner with me and Nancy tonight? You could lighten the mood. She's been dealing with the insurance company all day."

"I don't think so. I'm meeting some people tonight at the roller derby bout," Segal said. He finished reading the text message then put the phone on the table and picked up his beer.

"Roller derby?" Walter said. "You into roller derby now?"

"Not really. That's what my friends wanted to do," Segal said. "You go ahead and take your wife to a nice romantic dinner. I would be a third wheel, and besides that, she doesn't like me, so there's that."

"Nancy doesn't hate you or anything," Walter said.

"I didn't say she hated me. I said she doesn't like me. She doesn't like it that you're a cop. I'm your partner, so I'm part of you being a cop, so why should she like me?" He drained his glass.

SEGAL WALKED UP Biltmore Avenue toward Pack Square. When he got there the square was busy as he expected it to be on a warm spring night in May. A couple of street musicians played near the corner; a guy on Dobro and a girl weaving between vocals and fiddle. Segal stopped a minute to listen. He liked them, and a small crowd had formed. They would do well. Segal knew most of the street musicians in Asheville, but these two were new to him. People who spent a lot of time on the streets could be valuable sources of information to a detective, and besides, he liked authentic music better than a lot of the over-engineered, over-produced stuff coming out of the studios and big concerts.

He tossed a couple of bucks in the instrument case on the sidewalk. The girl nodded to him and smiled. He would make a point of introducing himself the next time he saw them, when they weren't so busy.

He moved on: left onto Patton Avenue. A couple blocks later he turned and passed Prichard Park. Someone called his name and he looked over to see one of the players at the chess boards wave. He waved back. The guy was a fixture there. Beyond the chess boards was the park proper, a favorite place for people to hang out, to form drum circles and pursue various other activities some of which he did not care to examine too closely. On the sidewalk of College Street, people lined up at a vending cart.

Two more blocks and he was in front of the Civic Center where the evening's competition would take place.

"Hey, Segal!" a voice called to him from behind.

He spun around. It was Shirley Dawn, reporter for the Asheville Citizen Times, a thin young whip of a woman in her late twenties or maybe early thirties.

"You on the clock, or just here to see the roller derby?" Shirley asked.

"I was about to ask you the same question," Segal said. He was grinning. He got a kick out of Shirley Dawn, at least most of the time. A lot of people underestimated her, with her diminutive size and her youth, but Segal did not make that mistake. She was smart and focused, especially when it came to her job. Not only that, she knew when to share information and when to hold back.

"I'm not going to bug you about the murder you're working on if that's what you mean. Not tonight anyway. I'm here to check out the new jammer for the Blue Ridge Roller

Girls, see if there's a story there. I heard she's a phenom," Shirley said. "Have you heard anything about her?"

Segal shrugged. "I don't really follow the sport that closely. I'm just meeting some friends here."

"I thought maybe since you're on the police force?" Shirley said, making a question of it with the inflection of her voice.

Segal was about to ask what she meant when a hand clamped down on his shoulder from behind. He turned to see the friends he was meeting, two couples he had known forever plus one of their "friends" they "happened" to bring along. Her name was Tina something, Segal didn't catch the last name. That the friend was a single woman about Segal's age was pure coincidence, of course.

As soon as greetings and introductions had been made Segal turned to introduce Shirley Dawn as well, but she had already slipped away.

INSIDE SEGAL ALLOWED himself to be seated beside the woman his friends had brought. No surprise or subtlety there. The more he resisted their attempts at match-making the more determined they seemed to be. He knew they meant well but he mostly felt sorry for the poor women they hauled into the enterprise. For some reason it just never worked out. He looked over at her and smiled. She seemed a little uncomfortable with the crowd and the noise and he was about to say something reassuring and apologetic when a huge cheer rose from the fans. The local team streamed onto the oval track to warm up.

Most of the women on the team were big and powerful looking. The smaller ones looked fit and athletic. They all wore helmets. They all wore knee and elbow pads. They all wore numbered jerseys with short sleeves, but that is where the uniformity ended. On their legs some wore tights, some colored hose, some fishnet stockings. Colors varied. Some wore only the team jersey on top, others wore a variety of shirts under the jersey so they had covered and colorful arms and for others the arms were bare. Hair styles were all over the map, but braids seemed to be popular. Tattoos were abundant. Overall, Segal thought, it was an interesting combination of uniformity and self-expression. It was a team, but it was a team of individuals. Perhaps, he thought, it said something about the kind of woman who was drawn to the sport. Or maybe it was just Asheville.

Segal glanced at the woman beside him, Tina. She seemed to be settling in and enthralled with the action. She was a brunette with shoulder length hair, dressed in jeans and a simple bright blouse. She had an intelligent and healthy energy about her, quite appealing in her own way, but nothing like Alexa Price. He could hear Walter's voice in his head just as clearly as if he had been sitting there. *"Too busy thinking about the woman who's no good for you than paying attention to the one you're with. Fly young monkey fly."* Trouble was, Walter was often right about that sort of thing.

On the oval the Blue Ridge team grouped up in a tight formation and began moving their skates in a slow rhythm, all together, with their bodies swaying slightly side to side. They made their way around the oval track like this twice. The crowd quieted as this slow rhythmic cadence built up suspense. In the third lap a drum roll was followed by a loud rim shot, and a much smaller skater burst out from the middle of the pack as if shot out of a cannon.

Segal watched closely, but the skater was moving so fast it was hard to follow her. She was small and looked even smaller because she was skating in a crouch. Her hair was a mass of brown curls sticking out from under the helmet, pulled back in a bunch behind her head.

On the next lap the rest of the team had expanded into a looser formation and the smaller skater zigzagged in and out around and through them with an effortless grace. Segal saw this time that her battered helmet had a white star on it indicating that she was the jammer, the skater who could score points by passing members of the opposing team. He recalled what Shirley Dawn said about the team having a new phenom. She had also said something about the police force.

The realization came to him in a flash.

The crowd started chanting: Din-o-saur, Din-o-saur.

"Of course," he said, "that's Dinah Rudisill. Dinosaur Rudisill."

"No kidding, Segal. Everyone knows who Dinosaur Rudisill is. You work with her on the police force don't you?" one of Segal's friends said, leaning forward in his seat.

"Yes, I do," Segal said, with a new found pride. "I do work with her." He thought about the personnel file the chief had handed him, but he had not found the time to read it.

The warmups were done. Five members of each team lined up in their places, the referee blew the whistle to start the action. Dinah and the jammer from the opposite team were lined up well behind the other players who formed a pack. As soon as the last of the pack passed the pivot line on the track the jammers took off.

The other jammer seemed to get the jump on Dinah but it soon became apparent that this was part of Dinah's strategy. The other jammer hit a solid wall of skaters attempting to squirm through a small opening between the Asheville girls, but that opening quickly closed. As the pack began to writhe with blocking and maneuvering the solid wall lost its shape and definition and it took only a few seconds for Dinah to spot a way through. When she did, she hit the gap at speed, twisted sideways, giving one girl a hip check and ducking by another. She was through before the other team knew what happened. By the time the crowd realized she was through and began cheering, she was halfway around the track setting herself up to begin scoring points every time she passed a player from the other team.

And so it went. The Asheville team was good. Dinah was great. Segal cheered along with everyone else. His friends clapped him on the back as if he were somehow responsible for the star player because they both worked for the Asheville police.

It was getting close to half-time and Segal started to think about beer and popcorn. He leaned over to Tina and invited her to come up to the concession stand with him. It was the least he could do, he figured. When they got out of the main arena where they could talk Segal turned to her.

Before he could ask her if she was having a good time she said, "Oh my God! I can't believe how exciting this is."

"It is exciting, isn't it?" Segal said. He realized he was grinning ear to ear and feeling like a little kid. He hadn't felt like that in a long time, and it made him wonder. Part of it was the atmosphere of the place, part of it could be the speed and physicality of the sport, but that was not all. He realized Dinah was a large part of it too. Anytime someone rose to that level of excellence, Segal thought, it inspired people profoundly; inspired them on a deep level. Segal was a fan of excellence and genius in any form.

Tina took his arm as they headed toward the concession stand. It felt good, her hand on his arm like that. Maybe this time it would be different. Plus she was pretty cute. Maybe this time it would work out the way his friends wanted it to. He bought them a couple drinks and a bag of popcorn.

"Want to step outside for some fresh air?" Segal asked her.

She smiled at him and took his arm again and they began walking in that direction. As they approached the exit, the door to the street swung open and they stopped mid-stride.

It was Walter. His face was all business. They looked at each other for a moment and Segal knew that he would not be drinking that beer, eating that popcorn, or spending any more time with Tina that evening, or probably ever.

EIGHT

A Fortress

"THEY FOUND A body up on Town Mountain Road," Walter said on the way to the car.

"Murder?" Segal asked.

"Oh yeah."

Walter's car was pulled up in a no parking zone just outside. When Segal got in he noticed Walter's wife in the back seat with two takeout bags. Apparently she had moved back there so the two men could talk business. She glared at him when he got in, probably hotter than the food from their interrupted dinner.

"Hi, Nancy," he said lamely.

"Hello, Segal," she said, her voice flat.

"Sorry your dinner got interrupted," he added.

Nancy just looked out the window, away from him. He didn't know why he apologized. He wasn't the one who murdered someone and spoiled their date.

They said nothing else until they dropped Nancy off at her car. Walter tried to give her a kiss goodnight but she had already turned away. Walter drove on toward the east side of town. After a few minutes he asked, "So how was the roller derby?"

Segal smiled. "The roller derby was actually good. Did you know Dinah Rudisill was on the team?"

Walter nodded. "I believe I heard something to that effect."

"Well, she's great. A real star."

Walter nodded and smiled. "And how about the girl your friends set you up with?"

"Who said my friends set me up with anyone?"

Walter just gave him that canny look of his and said, "Segal, please. These are the same friends you usually hang with, right?"

They pulled into the driveway of a modern house near the top of Town Mountain. It was part of a new upscale development of similar homes spaced widely apart. Segal estimated the lot sizes must be in the two-to-five-acre range. This one seemed to be even larger. Much of the forest had been left intact judging from the size of the white pines, oaks, and tulip poplars and the tangle of rhododendron and laurel forming an under story beneath their high canopy.

There were two police cruisers in the driveway along with the van from the medical examiner's office. A uniformed officer was stringing yellow crime scene tape between some of the oaks in the yard. He stood back from the drive and nodded to them when they drove up.

Segal and Walter opened their doors and got out in a synchronized motion. Segal did a slow scan before taking another step. The house had heavy brown timbers and rough field stone and a lot of glass. The front door was massive, made of lightly stained oak.

"Check those out," Walter said. He was pointing to two security cameras mounted above the door of the three-car garage.

Segal saw them and continued scanning. "Yeah, and there and there and there." He pointed out more cameras and the sign of a well-known security company.

"Looks like a fortress," Walter said.

"The action is down the hill on the other side of the house," the uniformed officer said. He indicated around the garage end of the house. "There's a path down there following the right of way for the power lines. A jogger spotted the body."

When they rounded the house they stopped, getting their first long range view that showed them exactly why the house was situated as it was. They could see the closer mountains and beyond to the hazy ridgelines, one behind another. The sun was casting long shadows meaning they didn't have much light left.

"Damn," Walter said under his breath, drinking in the view.

"Almost as good as the view from the Western Residence," Segal said.

A narrow two-track cut diagonally down the hill just below them and led to a ravine where they could see more crime scene tape and some figures moving around. They started to make their way down. The two-track seemed old; Segal thought it must have been part of an old logging or fire control road. It made one switchback before they arrived at a saddle point. Off to the left he saw Crawford, the medical examiner, and two assistants as well as a couple of technicians from the Crime lab.

Crawford looked up and watched them as they approached.

"You guys are staying busy these days," he said.

"You, too," Segal said.

"You're not going to believe this one," Crawford said. He turned around and stooped to pull away a tarp that covered a form on the ground.

"I was afraid it would start raining so we covered everything up," Crawford added.

As experienced as the two detectives were they were not prepared for this sight. It was the body of a man lying on his back, limbs spread as if he had been in the process of doing jumping jacks. There was little left of the man's face and a deep and wide streak of red ran the length of his torso. A couple of feet to one side of the body a multitude of brass shell casings were scattered and piled. A couple more feet away was a rifle.

"AR-15," Walter said. "Military version. Fully automatic and quite illegal. Looks like the standard clip, so I'm guessing when we get around to counting we're going to find around thirty shells." Unlike Segal, Walter had been in the military earlier in his career, so he would know this from personal experience.

Segal didn't doubt that Walter was right, but thirty shell casings in a small area looked like a lot of shiny brass, and the damage thirty high velocity rounds did to a human body was ghastly.

"Adrien Koll," Crawford said. "At least I assume so from the wallet in his pocket." He handed the wallet to Segal.

Segal took out the driver's license. "Adrien Davis Koll. He would be, let's see, sixty-one. Picture ID doesn't do us a lot of good." In another pocket were a few business cards. "Continental Drift Financial Planning—*We Take the Long View*," he said, reading one.

"So nothing here to connect this to the other murder, right? The one in the River Arts District," Segal asked.

Crawford and Walter both stopped and looked at him. Dealing with two independent murders was bad enough. To think they might be connected was orders of magnitude worse. If connected, it could mean a serial killer or worse.

"Right," he said. "Let's hope not."

"You got a time of death yet?" Walter asked.

"Right now I'm putting it between six pm and midnight Friday." Crawford said. He knew he didn't have to give them the usual caveats.

Segal scanned the wider area. The two-track path they had followed led to the right-of-way the officer had mentioned. He could see how the body would be visible but not obvious from there. On the other side of the two-track path the ground fell steeply down. The other way, a narrow ravine cut into the hillside. Deep into the ravine he could see some hay bales and targets.

"So what is this, a shooting range?" he asked.

Walter and Crawford turned to follow his gaze.

"Looks like one," Walter said. "The way the hill is shaped, it would be a good place. You could fire down that ravine with virtually no chance of a stray bullet going toward the road or any other houses around. It would probably even absorb a lot of the noise."

"So how do you see it?" Segal asked. But the question was really rhetorical as he proceeded to think out loud. "He's down here with someone, taking a little target practice, and there's some kind of dispute, in which case we're looking for someone he knew."

"That or someone drops him from some distance with a shot or two then comes in to finish him off from short range," Walter said. "In which case he might not have known the shooter."

"Either way you're looking at someone standing here practically on top of the body spraying it with a whole magazine," Segal said. "Does that seem a little excessive?"

"If by excessive you mean deeply deranged and sadistic, then yes, it was a little excessive," Walter mused.

"This is more than a homicide. This is someone making a statement," Crawford said. Segal and Walter looked at each other.

"Seems like a lot of statements being made lately," Segal muttered.

They turned their attention back to the body itself. Fatigue jacket and dark khaki pants tucked into military boots. The jacket was printed with camouflage pattern known as ACUPAT.

"There's a patch on the sleeve," Segal said. Crawford pulled it around so they could see more clearly. "White Hog Militia" Segal read. The patch also had a pair of crossed assault rifles done in black stitching over a light green background and the stitched outline of a pig done in white thread.

"I've heard of them," Walter said. "Big gun group. They're the ones you join if the NRA is too progressive for you."

"I'm curious about the gun," Segal said. "Does it belong to the deceased, or was this a kind of bring your own gun party?"

"We'll know that soon enough," Crawford said. "As soon as the techs dust it for fingerprints they can get the serial number and run a trace."

Segal was less confident about tracing the gun. His attention fell on a section of cinder block wall built into the side of one of the banks of the ravine. There was a heavy steel door and higher up, a couple of vent pipes emerged.

"What the hell do you suppose that is?" He approached the door, slipping on a pair of gloves.

"My guess is it's a survival bunker," Crawford said. "The guy was probably a prepper. It fits with the White Hog Militia stuff."

"You mean a survivalist?" Walter asked.

"Yeah, someone who is preparing for survival in a post-apocalyptic world. After nuclear war, revolution, general collapse of the culture and the economy. That sort of thing. They stockpile guns, food: anything they think they might need. They also study up on survival skills of all kinds, especially self-defense. I guess marauding bands of bandits are assumed to be a big part of the post-apocalyptic landscape," Crawford explained.

"I heard about people like that but I never actually met any," Walter said.

"I wouldn't be so sure, Walter. I bet you do know some only you don't know they're preppers," Segal said.

By this time Segal was at the door, but when he pulled, he found it locked. Just as he was turning to ask, Crawford came up behind him with a set of keys.

"These were in his pocket," Crawford said.

After a couple of tries Segal found the right one and opened the door.

He saw immediately that Crawford had been right. It was a survival bunker. He could see that even from the small amount of light passing in from the doorway. He soon found a switch and when the lights came on Walter said, "Damn."

The room was much more spacious than Segal had imagined, at least twenty by twenty. The ceiling was high, around ten feet, he judged. These dimensions, and the ample lighting kept the place from feeling too claustrophobic. With the exception of exposed steel I-beams in the ceiling, the interior surfaces were covered with some smooth material which Segal guessed must provide insulation and a barrier against moisture from the soil that surrounded them.

To the left was a king-sized bed and a couple of easy chairs. To the right was a desk and some electronic equipment. Toward the back there were several sets of shelves holding canned and freeze-dried food, tools, and various other essentials. There was also a small kitchen area and near the desk, a short-wave radio.

The most prominent feature of all in the front part of the room was the large gun rack, or more precisely, weapons rack. Each weapon was surrounded by an outline on the wall much like the tools in a well-organized workshop. The outlines left no doubt about what went where.

They saw two more versions of the assault rifle they had seen outside plus an empty outline of one. There was also a longer rifle with a scope, a couple of shot guns, and several pistols. There were a number of knives and a toma-hawk and a compound bow.

All three men stood looking at it for a moment.

"To me it looks like a combination of storage rack and display case," Segal said.

"Yeah, this was a man who liked him some guns."

They looked for a moment more. "You know," Segal said, "it looks like there's an empty space here." He indicated a space on the rack beside the compound bow with another outline and a couple of brackets.

Walter said, "Looks like we're missing a weapon."

Segal and Walter looked at each other. Segal was thinking crossbow and there was no doubt in his mind that Walter was thinking crossbow too. Neither wanted to say it out loud, but Segal knew their hope that the two cases were not related just dissolved.

"Segal," Walter whispered, "we're not in Kansas any-more."

NINE

In the Neighborhood

THE NEXT MORNING Segal pulled into a parking place near the Old Europe coffee shop, a few blocks from the station. After their initial visit the night before they had decided to put off further investigation of the murder scene and the house until the light of day.

He settled back and pulled a paperback book out of his coat pocket. *Bandits* by Elmore Leonard. He found the bookmark which he had made by cutting a strip of cardboard from the side of a Cheerios box, and opened the book with a sigh.

A few pages later he heard a sound and turned toward the passenger door. It was Walter with a bag and three cups of coffee. He reached over and pushed the door open enough for Walter to work a knee in and maneuver his considerable bulk into the car without spilling a drop.

"Who do you love?" Walter asked, handing him one of the cups. Walter was a morning person; Segal was better at late nights. It was one of the things that made them a good team.

Segal accepted the cup and skimmed off the first sip. It was perfect. The right temperature, the right strength, and exactly the right amount of cream.

"I love you, Walter," he said with his eyes closed.

"That makes one of you," Walter said.

"Nancy's pissed you got called away from dinner last night?" Segal asked.

"She understands and she doesn't understand," Walter said.

They both savored a sip of coffee.

"It felt like she blamed me for it," Segal said.

"She does blame you."

"How does she figure that?"

"People don't feel compelled to follow a logical path on this kind of thing," Walter said. He reached into the bag and brought out a cinnamon roll and handed it to Segal.

"My God, Walter. Now I really love you." He started the car and drove toward Town Mountain.

Walter found a cup holder for the third coffee and set the bag on the center console.

"Dinah's meeting us at the scene," he said.

"You're really going to corrupt that girl."

"I'll do my best," Walter replied.

When they arrived Dinah was kneeling near the place where the body had lain while a couple of crime scene techs explored closer to the bunker. She wore surgical gloves as she retrieved and counted the shell casings.

"I found twenty-eight," she said, holding up the evidence bag.

"Looks like you were right, Walter. Just about emptied a magazine."

"Be nice to know if he was first shot at a distance," Walter said.

"Let's have someone with a metal detector search a fifty-yard radius," Segal told the techs. He fished in his pocket and brought out the set of keys which had been retrieved last night. "I assume one of these will get us into the house."

Walter handed Dinah the coffee and cinnamon roll from Old Europe.

"I think I'm going to like it here," she said after taking a sip and looking into the bag.

Walter and Dinah joined Segal in the climb up to the main house. When they came around to the front they were surprised to see their boss pulling into the drive.

"Thought I'd come up and see this one for myself," he said when he got out.

Walter started to do a quick rundown on what they had found so far but the chief stopped him with a raised hand.

"Before we get into this, bring me up to speed on the other case, the artist."

"Julius Hargrove," Segal began.

"Brother-in-law of the governor of North Carolina," their boss added. Segal and Walter both nodded, indicating that they had not forgotten. Dinah stayed in the background.

"Crawford confirms time of death as late Friday night or early Saturday morning." Segal continued. "Cause of death, projectile to the heart."

"From a crossbow?" their boss asked.

"Yes, it still looks that way, but we're keeping that on the down low," Walter said.

"Who was the last to see him alive?" the chief asked.

"So far it looks like his model, Jody Mare. They had a session earlier Friday evening."

"Anything suspicious about her?"

"Not her directly. But she may have been a point of contention among Hargrove's apprentices. Maybe the wife too. The girl's pretty cute, even as models go. I'm thinking the wife may have been jealous. Apparently she threw Hargrove a big birthday party on Friday night, only he didn't show up and Jody Mare was not invited," Segal explained.

"Skipped his own birthday party? Where was he?"

"That's one of the things we're trying to find out," Walter said.

"I also met with the governor's wife like you asked me to," Segal said.

"Yes, I got an email message this morning about that." The chief squinted and pulled a printout from his pocket. "From an agent Kelly, SBI, on special assignment to the governor's office: *Awaiting update on Hargrove case. Suggest Lieutenant Segal spend less time drinking wine with the governor's wife and more time in pursuit of perp.*"

Segal winced. "That was not what it looked like," he said. He explained about meeting her at the wine bar along with some of Hargrove's friends, but even as he said it, it sounded lame.

"So I established all of those guys had alibis. We'll have to run down confirmation but I don't doubt what they told me."

He handed the chief a paper with some notes he had typed up. The chief skimmed down the page then gave a little chuckle.

"James Colebrook," he said.

"Is he someone we should concentrate on?" Walter asked.

"He's someone you should pay attention to: a very interesting guy, but as far as being a suspect, no."

Then the chief asked, "So what do I tell Agent Kelly of the SBI?"

"Good question," Segal said. He went on to tell him how both Alexa Price and Davenport, the governor's aide, had asked him to report information directly to them while keeping the other out of the loop.

"That's all we need," the chief said, "to be in the middle of a family feud. So I guess for the time being I tell them as little as possible."

"Or less," Walter said. For reasons he had never shared, Segal knew Walter was even more skeptical of the State Bureau of Investigation than most of the other local cops.

"OK, what about this mess? I got the preliminary report. They couldn't even recognize the remains?"

"Twenty-eight rounds from an AR fifteen," Walter said.

The detectives all nodded and looked down. They had all seen a lot of things, but the level of brutality here was hard even for them.

"Dinah and I can start on the house if you want to take the chief down and show him the bunker," Walter said. Segal tossed him the keys, minus the one to the bunker, and set off down the hill with his boss.

Once in the bunker, Segal gave him a few minutes to look around before pointing out the weapons rack.

"Here's another thing we're keeping under our hats. It looks like there's a crossbow missing," Segal said.

"So you're saying the two cases are related," the chief said. "Shit."

"Other than the crossbow, we don't see any connection between the two men, at least not yet. That's one thing we'll be looking for."

"So you're thinking the same person killed Hargrove and Koll?" the chief asked.

"You could see it at least a couple different ways," Segal explained. "The killer comes up here, does Adrien Koll, steals the crossbow, and uses it to kill Hargrove."

The chief frowned. "I don't like it. He kills Koll, takes the keys out of his pocket, opens the bunker, takes the cross-bow, and only the crossbow, leaves all the other weapons and cool expensive stuff, locks the door, and puts the keys back in the dead man's pocket."

"Unless the killer had his own key," Segal said, thinking it sounded weak even as he said it. He continued, "The other way you could see it is Koll kills Hargrove with his crossbow, disposes of the crossbow because it's a murder weapon, then someone figures it out and comes up here and kills Koll for revenge."

"Or they could be unrelated," the chief said.

Now it was Segal's turn to frown.

"But if the cases are unrelated you have to ask yourself what are the chances that a crossbow shows up in two consecutive murder cases," the chief continued.

"Yeah, that doesn't happen, not even in Asheville," Segal said.

WHEN THEY LEFT the bunker and came outside the air seemed especially fresh and new, and the sun was sending beams through the openings in the forest canopy. Segal showed his boss the four-wheeler sitting on the remnant of the old logging road. The key was in it which gave Segal the idea of offering him a ride up to the house, save the old man from walking. His boss seemed to enjoy it. When they got up to the house the chief got into his car and started to back up, but then paused and lowered the window.

"Segal," he called, and Segal came over to the car. "I forgot to ask, anything on that robbery?"

"It's unfolding about as we expected." He explained about the watermelon on the highway. "Dinah checked it out. She didn't find the culprits, but two of the neighbors saw a Ford pickup with something large in the back. Something covered with a tarp. We put that description out on an APB, so I expect we'll hear something soon."

The chief nodded and shoved the car into gear. He looked toward the road and Segal followed his gaze.

A woman wearing running shorts and a tank top came jogging into view on the road at the end of the driveway. She stopped short when she saw Segal. After a moment of surprise she put her hands on her hips and walked toward him breathing deeply. She smiled as if she were seeing an old friend after years of separation.

When she got up to Segal she said, "Well, Lieutenant, you do get around don't you."

Segal looked at her nervously and then glanced at the car. The woman bent down to acknowledge his boss sitting in the driver's seat.

"Chief Baker, this is Mrs. Alexa Price," he said. It was not until he saw her there out for her morning run that he thought about how close they were to the Western Residence.

"So what brings you up here, Segal?" Alexa asked as soon as the chief had pulled away.

"Official business, I'm afraid," he said.

Before she could ask any more questions a black SUV passed slowly, then stopped and backed up so the driver's window was centered in the driveway. The windows were tinted so he couldn't see who was driving, but he had no doubt it was part of the governor's security team.

Alexa's shoulders slumped and the smile vanished from her face.

"I'd better finish my run," she said. She turned and took a couple strides, then stopped and turned to him and said, "Good luck with whatever you're doing here and let me know about my brother." The smile had returned to her face and she was gone.

Segal found Walter and Dinah in a study at the back of the house.

He scanned the room. Very comfortable. Expensive furniture. American flag on the wall. Photos of the man, Adrien Koll, with various prominent politicians, all members of the far right. There were also some photos of Koll surrounded by other men, all dressed in camo, sitting around a campfire. The room was in the back of the house, giving Koll a nice view down the hill and into the woods.

"You look quite comfortable there," he said when he saw Walter.

Walter looked up. He was kicked back behind the man's desk. In his hand was a controller which he pointed toward a TV and DVD player.

"Check this out," Walter said. He clicked the controller and an image sprang to the screen. It was Koll in front of a group of people. He was giving a speech and the people were apparently of a like mind because they interrupted him frequently with cheers and raised fists.

"That's why we've got to be vigilant," he was saying. "That's why they want to take your guns." At this point he was interrupted by the cheering of the crowd. "We are the thin line, the only line, the only force keeping the enemy at bay. Keeping them from completely taking over this country." More cheering. "They think they've got you beaten down. They think they do, but they don't know how strong you are." More cheering. "They think they can take over here in North Carolina the way they've taken over other states. Well they're going to find out this isn't New York. They're going to find out this isn't California!" Wild cheering.

Walter hit the pause button. "Label on the disc said White Hog Militia Meeting, and it had a date about six months ago. He's got several more here. I haven't watched them all yet."

"What about the rest of the house?" Segal asked.

Dinah spoke up. "As far as Koll was concerned it looks like this was the house. This office room, one bedroom, and the kitchen and one bathroom was all he was using. The rest of the rooms have furniture, but you could tell they weren't being used. I haven't checked the basement yet."

"He wasn't married?" Segal asked.

"Divorced," Walter said, gesturing to another thick folder on the desk.

Segal wandered out of the study and into the kitchen. He opened and closed drawers and cupboards, finding nothing he would not expect to find in a bachelor's kitchen.

"What about the security cameras?" Segal called to the others.

"Looks like the computer is gone," Dinah called back.

"Interesting."

"You can see where the cables came in here to a console, but the monitor and computer are gone."

"And no sign of a cell phone?"

"No, cell. Just like Julius Hargrove," Walter said.

They had discussed this already. If these were crimes of passion, the killer was not so passionate as to forget details in covering his tracks. That part felt more like planning.

He studied the office more closely and mentioned that Alexa Price ran by on her morning jog.

Walter stopped going through papers on the desk. "What the hell does that mean?"

"Just coincidence. She was just out for her morning run," Segal said.

"She lives that close?" Walter asked.

"Yeah, you go up to the left and take that little connector and you're right at the Western Residence. Can't be more than a half mile." Though left unsaid, Segal knew that neither one of them believed in coincidence.

"And you said she got to Asheville Wednesday, so she would have been in the neighborhood Friday night."

"Yes, I suppose she was," Segal said. "And so was that smarmy little dick weed, Davenport."

Segal left the office to look around the house some more. It was, as Dinah said, practically empty. He decided to check the basement and found the stairs. When he reached the bottom and turned on a light he said, "Holy shit." Then louder he called, "Walter, Dinah, you've got to see this."

They came down the stairs a moment later. Dinah had a small black leather book in her hand.

The first impression was a Nazi classroom. There were several rows of chairs facing a lectern, and behind that a big screen TV. On the walls were several versions of the American flag, a Confederate Stars and Bars, and a banner with a rattle snake and lettering which read, "Don't tread on me." There was also a poster-sized version of the emblem of the militia; the same as the insignia on the patches they sewed to their jackets, white pig, crossed AR-15s and all.

"A little something for everyone," Walter said as he walked slowly around the room. "Hey, check this out, Segal."

Walter had come upon a cheap reproduction of a painting of Joan of Arc. Below it someone had taped a sign that read, "Fighting in the name of God."

Segal looked at it and shook his head. "It's amazing how these guys see themselves. Patriots, minute men, rebels, even like Joan, fighting for a holy cause. Only I'm pretty sure their holy cause has nothing to do with kicking the English out of France. People can tell themselves all kinds of stories."

"That could explain one thing," Dinah said. "I just found the guy's address book upstairs."

It was a classic little black book with a worn leather cover. "Lucky for us the man was old school. No one keeps these anymore with all the phones and computers."

Segal nodded.

"Guess who the first entry is under H," she said. "Julius Hargrove."

Before he could respond Segal's phone sounded. He answered and then listened for a moment. Finally he said, "Yes, we could do that," and hung up.

"That was the Western Residence calling. They heard we were in the neighborhood and the governor would like us to come see him."

TEN

Shirley Freaking Dawn

"THINK WE SHOULD check with the chief before we go up there?" Walter asked. They were headed to Segal's car.

"You know what he'd say. He'd say, 'go up there, be polite, and say as little as possible,'" Segal said.

"Or less," Walter added. He glanced back at the house and saw Dinah standing at the door. He tapped Segal on the shoulder and nodded in her direction.

Segal looked back, hesitated a moment, and then gave her the signal to join them. "Might as well let her get the whole experience," he whispered to Walter.

Dinah plowed some paperback books out of the way and scooted into the back seat. She picked one up, looked at the author's name, and asked. "Who was Ambrose Bierce?"

Walter turned his head a little and said, "Please don't get him started on Ambrose Bierce."

They drove in silence. On both sides of the road walls of rhododendron and mountain laurel rose in a dense tangle, except for occasional breaks opening onto spectacular views of the mountains.

It took only a few moments to reach the driveway of the Western Residence. "You weren't kidding when you said it was in the neighborhood," Walter said.

The iron gates across the entrance were closed and there was no one to be seen. They got out of the car. To the left of the gate there was a box with some buttons and a speaker. As soon as Segal started to reach for it the gates clanged, the mechanism emitted a loud hum and the gates swung open. They got back in and Segal eased the car forward. As they followed the driveway up hill and to the right, the house came into view.

The big state trooper waved them on and Segal pulled the Volvo up to the entrance. As on Segal's first visit, Davenport was waiting for them at the entrance. *I wonder if he just hangs out there all day*, Segal thought. To Walter and Dinah he said, "That's the governor's chief of staff I was telling you about."

"Looks like Dracula's servant," Walter muttered under his breath. It was all Dinah could do to suppress her laugh.

Davenport approached the car.

"The governor is on a phone call right now," Davenport told them. "He'll be with you in a few moments." He showed them through to the living room and left them there to wait. They immediately gravitated to the window with the view just as all visitors did when they entered the room.

"Lieutenant Segal, I didn't know you were coming." It was Alexa. She had clearly just showered after her run and changed into a pair of shorts and a blue blouse which fit her perfectly. She looked fresh, clean, and relaxed. "Did you come to see me?"

Segal hesitated just a moment before he said, "Actually, we got a call that the governor wanted to see us."

She continued to smile at him just the same. She nodded to Walter and Segal introduced Dinah.

She seemed about to say something to Dinah, but she glanced over their shoulders and her face changed. Her mouth froze in its smile position but there was a great letdown in her eyes. When Segal turned to see what had changed her mood so suddenly he saw the governor himself walking toward them, coming into the living room from what Segal gathered was probably his private office.

He looked to Segal to be in his mid-fifties. He was a couple of inches taller than Segal's five ten, dressed in a dark blue suit, white shirt, and tie, pretty much the uniform of every politician, business executive and lawyer in the country. He had a cell phone to his ear and was motioning for them to come into his office. Segal could tell he was trying to end the call, saying things like, "OK," then pausing, then saying, "Thanks for the call." He turned and walked back into the office.

Segal and Walter looked at each other as if unsure whether they should follow or not. Segal made an after-you gesture. Dinah and Walter started in. He looked at Alexa who was already retreating. She gave him a little goodbye wave and mouthed the words, "call me", and then she was gone. He followed the others into the office where they found Davenport already there.

The governor had made it to the chair behind his desk and was finally able to end the call with a sugar sweet, "talk to you soon," and tossed the phone onto the desk.

"Which one of you is Segal," he asked with no preamble. The sugary tone was gone.

"I'm Segal."

"What can you tell me about the death of Julius Hargrove?" he said. "My wife is very upset."

Segal gave him a brief summary of the facts, as brief as he could possibly make it.

"Any suspects yet?" the governor asked.

"Nothing firm as yet," Walter said.

"Davenport here, my chief of staff, tells me you are reluctant to share details of the case with him," Governor Price said.

Segal shot a glance at Davenport sitting to the side with a smug smile on his face. He had a clipboard on his lap ready to take notes.

"In many cases there are details that we want to keep under wraps so that if we hear them from a witness we know they're not just telling us something they read in the paper or saw on TV."

"Like in this case the murder weapon?" the governor asked.

Segal nodded and said, "It was a very unusual choice of weapon."

"Then why am I reading about it in the morning paper?" he asked. He reached into a drawer and withdrew a folded copy of the paper and tossed it onto the desk top in front of Segal.

Even before he picked it up he glanced at the headline on the left column of the first page under the fold: Local Artist Murdered by Crossbow.

He picked up the paper without looking at it in more detail and handed it to Walter.

"We haven't had time to read the paper this morning, sir, we've been called to the scene of another fatality, that's why we were up here, fairly close to your house as it happens. In any case, I can assure you the paper didn't get that from us," Segal said. He said this in an even tone, looking Governor Price in the eye. He knew that he was getting the full alpha male treatment and, as usual, he did not respond well to it.

Meanwhile Walter read the article.

"I believe Mr. Davenport here has been in contact with

your boss and offered the assistance of the State Bureau of Investigation," the governor said.

"We did send them some materials for analysis," Walter said. He spoke up quickly so Segal knew he had his back.

"Including the bolt from the crossbow," Davenport said.

At this point Segal and Walter both looked at him. Segal realizing how the information had probably reached the paper: either directly from the SBI, or from the SBI to Davenport to the paper.

"That's all for now. You can keep Davenport up to date. Work directly with him, not through my wife," the governor said, turning away from them and back toward his desk.

"Actually, there is one other thing you might be able to help us with," Segal said. The governor gave him a peeved look, perhaps irritated that his dismissal had not been the last word.

"We could use any information you or the SBI might have on an organization called the White Hog Militia."

The governor shot a glance toward Davenport then said, "Never heard of them." He looked away.

Davenport looked up from his clipboard and an awkward silence hung in the room for a moment. He was looking at the governor. After a couple of beats he said, "I'll see if the SBI has a file on them."

DAVENPORT ESCORTED THEM out and stood at the entrance portico while they started toward the car.

After they had gone a couple of steps he said, "Oh, by the way, the murder you are investigating up here, was that by crossbow too?"

"We didn't say it was a murder," Walter said.

"I just assumed, otherwise why would you be investigating," Davenport said.

"I'll tell you this much, it was not murder by crossbow this time," Segal said. Davenport continued to stare at him.

"By the way," Dinah piped up for the first time, "Where were you Friday evening and Saturday morning?"

Davenport leaned back a fraction and said, "I was here, at the Western Residence. The state troopers keep a log if you want to confirm that."

"If you don't mind," Dinah said.

Davenport ducked into another room and came back with the big state trooper who had the log book in his hand.

"I'll take that." Dinah stepped up to him with a smile, accepted the book, and flipped to the page in question. She ran her finger along the entries, taking the liberty of going back a few pages, then she handed it back with a smile. The trooper glared at her all the while, but she seemed unintimidated by either the glare or his size.

"Did you hear anything unusual? Gunshots or anything?" Walter asked.

Davenport shook his head. He looked at the trooper who shook his head, too.

They turned and walked away. When they reached the car Walter looked back at Davenport, perched by the entrance, just standing there watching.

"Guy gives me the creeps," Walter said.

Walter picked up the paper and looked at the article again. He hadn't bothered to give it back to the governor. "You see the by-line on that story?" he asked.

Segal kept his eyes on the road as he answered in a low and steady tone, "Shirley Freaking Dawn."

IF YOU WERE going to meet with Shirley Dawn, you had to feed Shirley Dawn. That was the unwritten rule, and Segal knew it well. She had the appetite to body weight ratio of a humming bird. Since it was fast approaching lunch time as he drove down off the mountain, he had a pretty good idea of what Shirley Dawn would say when he called.

Walter punched in the number for him and then handed him the phone.

"What are you doing for lunch?" he asked when she answered.

"Dining with my favorite detective?"

"What are you thinking?"

"I'm thinking Katmandu."

"See you there in twenty," Segal said, and hung up.

KATMANDU WAS A place that served food of Nepal. One time Walter asked him if it was authentic and Segal said, "I assume so, but how the hell would I really know? I just know I like it." It was located on Patton Avenue across the street from Prichard Park. Segal dropped Walter and Dinah at the crime scene at Koll's house, drove down off the mountain, parked his car in the garage on Battery Park, walked a few blocks, and pushed open the door, exactly on the twenty minute mark he had predicted. He moved quickly through the little foyer decorated in red and gold, mostly representations of dragons in brass statues and in paintings. As soon as he entered he breathed in the wholesome spicy aroma of the food. He ate there more frequently in the winter because of the hot food, but he was immediately glad Shirley Dawn had chosen it this day. He realized he was quite hungry.

As he expected, Shirley Dawn was already there, sitting at a table for two. She stood up as soon as she saw him and said, "Let's hit the buffet before we talk, Segal, I'm starving."

Segal looked at the hostess/owner and she smiled and nodded, so he made an after-you gesture with his arm and

Shirley, all ninety-eight pounds of her, bounced up to the buffet and grabbed a plate. She wore a loose-fitting flowered dress that came down to about mid-thigh and her brown hair was pulled back in a ponytail, making her look even younger than she was.

Segal took a plate, too, and helped himself to a little of several of the steaming dishes, the names of which he never really sorted out. He also took some naan, the wonderful flat bread they made. All this he topped off with a little pile of their fried onions coated with chick pea flour.

When he sat down at the table Shirley was already digging into the pile of food on her plate which was a good deal larger than the one on Segal's.

She looked up and smiled and said, between bites, "So, are we going to compare notes on the murder cases?"

"Sure, Shirley. You first," he said.

"You seem upset, Segal. Was there something in this morning's story I got wrong?"

"No, there was something in the story you got a little bit too right." He ripped off a small piece of the naan and dipped it into the sauce of the chicken and vegetables on his plate.

"What?" Shirley asked.

Segal couldn't quite tell if she was acting or she really didn't know. He leaned a little closer and said in a whisper, "The crossbow, Shirley. We weren't telling anyone about the crossbow."

"Why not?"

"For one, it was the kind of unusual detail that a person is unlikely to make up. Secondly, we didn't want to sensationalize the story and get every crackpot in the area calling us up with conspiracy theories and false leads connected to the Knights Templar or Big Foot or something like that. You just muddied the water for us, girl."

"But the crossbow is what makes it such a good story, Segal. What you call sensational is what we at the paper call interesting." She leaned forward and said in a very sincere voice, "We are in the business of publishing interesting stories. You take away the crossbow and it gets pretty mundane, except, of course the guy was a well-known artist who happened to be the brother of the state's first lady."

Segal took a bite of the chicken and followed it with some of the fried onions, thinking about what she said.

"Besides, Segal, how was I supposed to know you wanted to keep that secret?" she continued.

"The question in my mind is how you knew about the crossbow," Segal said.

"You know I can't reveal sources, Segal," she said, and she dug back into her meal.

"OK, will you tell me at least if it was one of my people," Segal asked.

Shirley seemed to be calculating for a moment while she chewed. "If I tell you that, will you be willing to fill me in on where you are with this so far?"

Segal exhaled heavily. It was always a negotiation with Shirley Dawn. However, she always honored her part of the bargain, which was more than you can say for a lot of people.

"I'll do the best I can, but a little farther down the line when we have a better picture. Right now, we're having trouble putting the puzzle pieces together."

Shirley must have figured that was the best she was going to get at that point in time.

"Then I'll tell you it was not one of your guys I got that from." She added, "At least I don't think so. First I heard about it was from an anonymous phone call. Some guy, clearly disguising his voice. Just said, 'Hargrove was hit by a crossbow. I thought you should know.' I asked why and he said something like, 'Sometimes you're the mariner and sometimes you're the albatross.'"

"And you ran the story based only on an anonymous phone call?" Segal asked.

"Of course not, Segal. I have my ways of getting confirmation, and don't even ask what they are."

That being settled, they ate in silence for a couple of minutes, enjoying the food, glancing around the room which was filling up with the usual Asheville mix of locals and tourists, students and business people.

Segal was first to break the silence.

"Have you interviewed the apprentices?" he asked.

Shirley grinned. "You mean the Marks Brothers? Did you know that's what people call them? Yeah, I talked to them a little and to some of the other people in that building."

Segal nodded and said, "What did you make of them? Find out anything interesting?"

Shirley took a drink of iced tea to clear her throat. "Let's see. There's Henry Marks. Word on the street is that he's sleeping with Hargrove's wife, Margery. Don't know if that's true or not but I don't find it hard to believe. You can tell he's the kind of guy that moves on women every chance he gets."

"So did he put the moves on you, Shirley?" Segal said with a grin.

"How could he resist?" she said.

"So with Hargrove's wife, assuming it's true, do you think he would do it from attraction or is there a chance he would do it as an act of spite against Hargrove?"

"Men are dogs, Segal, you know this," she said, "You guys don't need all that much extra motivation to go after women. But to tell you the truth, some of the other people in the building did mention that Hargrove was coming down hard on Henry. They thought it was mostly the usual maestro/apprentice dynamic. You know, when the apprentice gets to be nearly as good as the master, or, God forbid, even better."

"Kind of like a teenage son rebelling against his father," Segal mused. He took another fork full of chicken and a few bits of fried onion and chewed with a thoughtful face. "Still, sleeping with your boss's wife is a little extreme."

Shirley shrugged.

"What about the others?" Segal asked.

"The only thing I heard about Mark Morrison was that he has a temper," she said.

"How bad?" Segal asked.

"Like throwing pottery in a ceramics studio mad. Like getting in a couple of bar fights mad," Shirley said. "Some of the people in the studio next door said they heard him yelling at Hargrove. The pair were in a big row over something but they couldn't hear the words clearly."

"When was this?" Segal asked.

"Not long ago. Late last week." By this time she had destroyed most of the food on her plate and was mopping up the sauce with a piece of naan.

"What about the third one, Mark Engel?" Segal asked.

"People didn't talk so much about him," Shirley said. She seemed to search her memory while she took another bite of naan and a drink of iced tea. "He's the youngest of them, like nineteen or twenty. He's very quiet. Almost spooky quiet one of the women said. One person thought he might be religious because they didn't see him drinking or partying like the rest of them."

"Did anyone say how he got along with Hargrove?" Segal asked.

"They said it was like hero worship. He would do anything Hargrove told him to do. The only time anyone remembers seeing him visibly upset was when a guy from a different studio made fun of one of Hargrove's paintings. They said Engel seemed like he was ready to kill the guy."

Segal looked up when she said this last thing.

Shirley raised her fork and said, "I'm sure it was just a figure of speech."

She held up a finger indicating, "Wait a minute," and Segal watched as she went back to the buffet for seconds. When she sat down she handed him a piece of naan. Apparently she noticed he had none left, but he still had a lot of sauce to mop up.

He continued the questioning. "What about their skill level as artists?"

"I was impressed with all of them, but what do I know. I would say they're better than most of the other art you see around," she said. "The general consensus among the artists from the other studios was that Henry Marks is the most talented technically: possibly as good as the master. But, it remains to be seen if he has any soul, like anything important to say. Mark Morrison, they say, is a good journeyman at the craft. He'll be fine, but probably nothing significant. Mark Engel, there was not so much agreement on. Some said he was second rate, some said there was something special there. Something unusual. I could see what they meant when I saw some of his stuff. It all seemed kind of flawed, but there was something interesting there. Hard to look away from."

"What about that last painting Hargrove was working on?" Segal asked.

"The Joan of Arc Postmodern?"

So she knows about that too, Segal thought.

"It's interesting," she continued. "The people from the other studios said he was very secretive about it, would hardly talk about it at all. The rumor is he was commissioned to do it for a ton of money, but no one really knew, and they didn't know who commissioned it either."

"What did the Marks brothers say about it?" Segal asked. By this time he had finished his plate of food and was sipping iced tea.

"Henry Marks and Mark Morrison both thought it was really good work. Henry thought it might be the maestro's best. But, they said Hargrove was sort of freezing them out of the process. Usually they would be around at least part of the time when he was working and he would sometimes talk about what he was doing and why. By the time he finished a piece they would understand a lot about his process from start to finish; what choices he made and why and how he executed. It was part of their learning process. Not on this one, though. One of them thought maybe Hargrove might want to be alone with Jody Mare."

"He kicked them out of the studio when he was working on it?" Segal asked.

"Not overtly. They said he would find some reason they should work elsewhere when he was working on the Joan, and he just didn't talk about it the way he usually did."

"What about Engel?" Segal asked.

"He totally clammed up on the subject," she said, "I got the impression he knew more than the others, but the others said they didn't think so. They thought Engel had a crush on Jody."

I can believe that, Segal thought.

"Have you talked to her?" he asked.

"Haven't tracked her down yet," Shirley said. "Now I have a question for you, Segal."

"Yes?"

"What happened up on Town Mountain last night?"

"What makes you think something happened on Town Mountain?"

Shirley sat back. "Segal, please. We do monitor the radio, you know. You don't send the medical examiner and the forensic team up there for nothing."

After thinking about it for a moment, he said, "No comment."

She leaned across the table. "Just tell me this. Was anybody crossbowed up there?"

"No comment."

Shirley sat back. "Well, if you're going to clamshell up on me that leaves only one more question."

Segal raised his eyebrows.

"Should we get dessert here or do you want to buy me an ice cream when you walk me to my office?"

WALTER AND DINAH spent another hour or so making an inventory of items of interest and photographing the meeting room in Koll's basement. She dropped Walter off at the station and drove a few blocks to Wasabi on Broadway for some sushi to go.

The place looked cozy and inviting as always, and for a moment she considered staying to eat there instead of taking the sushi and miso soup to go. She stood, in uniform, looking around the restaurant, waiting as the chefs, in clean crisp uniforms of their own prepared her California roll.

She turned toward the window and watched the traffic

slide slowly by. The northbound lane on the opposite side of the street slowed. The traffic light down the block must have changed. A Ford pickup slid to a stop opposite her. A large load covered by a tarp filled the bed.

Dinah slid out the front door. She noticed the driver and passenger in the front seat. They were two young men, sitting very close together. In fact, the passenger was pressed up against the driver. Nothing wrong with that, except there was nothing about the truck or about the appearance of the men that seemed to scream couple to Dinah. They seemed upset and they were both yelling and looking to their right. As she crossed the street and got closer she could hear the guy beside the driver yell, "God damn it, Jimmy, stop that. Sit up."

Dinah smiled as she guessed at what was going on. It was the age-old trick. Three guys in the front seat of a pickup. Guy by the window ducks down leaving the other two sitting, to all outward appearances, lovingly close.

She stepped out into the street for a better look. The driver stopped fooling around and watched her, moving his eyes but not his head, picking her up in the rear-view mirror when she crossed behind the truck. As she suspected, a third boy sat up by the passenger window and looked back at her, grinning.

The light changed and the driver reeved the engine and flipped a switch on the dashboard. As soon as the switch engaged a thick cloud of black smoke and soot poured out of the oversized tail pipe, obscuring it from view and engulfing Dinah and the cars behind. She heard the screech of tires as the driver floored it and she heard one of them yell out, "Rolling coal, Baby."

Dinah stepped aside to get out of the cloud of soot. She waved her free arm fanning away the smoke. She tried her best but she could not quite make out the license plate number.

"That's OK," she said under her breath. "I'll get you next time and then we'll see who's rolling what."

ELEVEN

San Isidro

SEGAL'S PHONE BUZZED just as he returned after lunch with Shirley Dawn. He looked at the screen and saw the name "Izzy."

Izzy's real name was Isidro Marquez, second generation Mexican immigrant, pastor of a nondenominational church in downtown Asheville. Some of the Latino members of his church called him San Isidro because he dedicated so much of his time to serving the homeless and the working poor of the city. His knowledge of the homeless community made him a good source of information for Segal, but that cut both ways. Izzy also knew that he could bring certain issues that might be of a legally sensitive nature to Segal without the information working against the innocent or victimized of his flock.

Segal first thought of the missing catapult. *Oh shit, Izzy's going to tell me someone threw a bowling ball through their stained-glass window,* but that was not what Izzy had in mind at all.

"Hey, Segal, I'm here with your cousin," he said.

"You mean Tommy?" Segal asked. He glanced at Walter when he said this. Walter frowned and spun his chair slightly away.

"Yes, young Thomas," Izzy said. "He's calling me Friar

Laurence and asking if I have an herbal potion that can make it look like someone is dead. We're here at the church. Thought you might want to come down."

"I'll be right there," Segal said.

He slid the phone into his pocket and said to Walter, "I guess I better go deal with this."

"What's he up to this time?" Walter asked.

"*Romeo and Juliet*," was Segal's only reply.

Walter just scratched the back of his head.

Segal drove through town thinking about Tommy and Tommy's mom. Was he really helping when he intervened with Tommy or was he just keeping an unsustainable situation afloat? He thought about the murder cases, and in particular how they could possibly be related. When he got to Izzy's church his mind felt like a cluttered warehouse. It needed to be emptied, rearranged, and put back in order.

He pulled into the parking lot and walked past a few homeless people lounging on the steps of the church. His phone buzzed with a message, but it was only his, This Day in History app. May 25, 1925. John Scopes was indicted for teaching Darwinian Theory. Segal shook his head and put away the phone. *At least we've moved on from there*, he thought. *Or have we?*

Entering the church, he was immediately struck by a mural he had not seen before on one of the walls. It stopped him in his tracks and he stood looking at it.

After a moment he heard Izzy's voice behind him. "What do you think of our new fresco, Segal?"

Segal turned to see him standing there with his wide grin. Spontaneously the two of them embraced. When Izzy withdrew Segal got a good look at him. He was a slight man wearing blue jeans, a brown hooded sweatshirt, and sandals. He did look a little like a Franciscan Friar.

"Where's Tommy?" Segal asked.

Izzy motioned with his hand and led him up to the front of the church. When he got to the second pew he stopped and pointed. Tommy was laying there fast asleep. His clothes and hair were a mess and his limbs were at odd angles laying on the narrow bench. To Segal he looked like a broken bird.

"Let's let him sleep," Izzy whispered. He picked up a crate from beside the altar at the front and motioned for Segal to follow him to the back of the church. The crate contained several small milk boxes, the waxed cardboard kind you get in school cafeterias. Sitting on top of them was a box of graham crackers.

They sat in the back pew and Izzy put the crate between them.

"What's this, a new kind of communion?"

"Not a bad idea," Izzy grinned. He handed Segal a brown cracker and a milk box. "Take this, brother, may it serve you well."

Segal accepted the gifts and nodded.

"For some reason Tommy is obsessed with *Romeo and Juliet*. People have been telling me he seems to have the thing memorized, or at least long parts of it," Izzy said. Segal knew that Tommy and his mom were members of the congregation.

"Yeah, well that one might be on me," Segal said, looking down at his hands. He broke off a piece of the cracker and put it in his mouth as he pulled open the top of the little milk carton. It was no easier now than when he was a kid. *You'd think they would have solved this milk carton problem by now*, he thought. He proceeded to tell Izzy about Tommy's breakdown in West Asheville, how he was in love with a waitress there, and his question about guys and girls and about giving him the book of the Shakespeare play.

Izzy shook his head. "Segal, some scholars think *Romeo and Juliet* is more about obsession than love."

"I guess sometimes they show up looking a lot alike," Segal said.

"Except that stories of obsession don't end well," Izzy said. He bit into a cracker of his own. "You've got to be careful. Stories are powerful things."

"That's exactly what I tell people all the time," Segal said. "How can you know something perfectly and not see it in yourself?" He took another hit on the milk box like a man downing a shot of whiskey at a bar.

"Oh shit, Segal. This might mean you're a human being," Izzy said with fake astonishment.

That got a small grin from Segal.

"Don't be too hard on yourself," Izzy said. "No one has a fool-proof playbook for a person like Tommy, or for any of us really."

They sat quietly for a minute, then Izzy said, "I wouldn't have called you if I had known he was going to go to sleep. As soon as we got him calmed down and got him to eat a couple graham crackers he told me he wanted to take a nap. Then, it took him about thirty seconds to start snoring. He just scared me when he asked about a potion that would make it look like a person was dead. Then I remembered *Romeo and Juliet*."

"No, I'm glad you called me. I'll let his mom know where she can pick him up. Meanwhile, it's kind of nice just sitting here in a quiet space, taking communion."

"You on a big case?" Izzy asked.

"Two of them," Segal said. "Actually three. I mean the third one, I wouldn't exactly call that the crime of the century."

"Oh yeah? What's the third one about, if you don't mind me asking?"

"Some guys at the college built a catapult for the Renaissance Fair and someone stole it."

"I heard something about that," Izzy said. "I mean about the catapult, not the theft. They were supposed to do some kind of demonstration with it at the music festival at Lake Eden. Hope you recover it for them."

"It's only a matter of time," Segal said.

After their momentary pause Izzy stood and picked up the crate. "I need to get this over to the daycare for snack time," he said.

Segal stood, too. "Oh crap," he said. "I hope I didn't just eat some kid's lunch."

Izzy just laughed. "Don't worry, Segal. Ours is a world of abundance."

"Thanks again for taking care of Tommy," Segal said.

"No problem. He'll be fine here until his mom picks him up."

Segal took a step toward the door, but then turned around to ask one more question.

"Hey Izzy, what do you know about Joan of Arc?"

Izzy gave him a quizzical look. "Does this have something to do with the catapult?

"No, one of the other cases," Segal said. "One of the victims had been doing a painting of Joan of Arc."

"I see," Izzy said. "Most people think of it as a story about the love of God and the power of believing in him. On the other hand, it, too, could be seen as a story that starts in love and ends up in obsession. It doesn't end well either, at least not for Joan."

"Remind me," Segal said.

"She was renounced by the church and burned at the stake as a witch."

TWELVE

Missing Person

SEGAL WAS AT his desk the next morning trying to update the case file when his phone buzzed. He picked it up with some small irritation at the interruption. Walter must have seen the peeved look on his face because he raised his eyebrows and made a point of looking back to his own keyboard without meeting Segal's eye. Walter and Segal had discussed this many times. Whenever Segal was cross about a phone interruption Walter would say something like, "You know, Segal, it does have an off button. Believe it or not the world can get along without you for an hour or so from time to time so you can finish a task."

Segal knew Walter had a point, but it never felt right to him anyway.

This time it was Joe Meyers on the phone. Segal knew that the other detective team of Meyers and his partner, Ron Philips, had been called out earlier on a missing person case. Segal and Walter had more than enough on their own plate.

"Thought you'd want to have a look at the scene over here," Meyers said when Segal answered. "Our missing person, John Belincort, had a meeting set up with your second victim, Adrien Koll."

"Holy shit," Segal said. "Where are you guys?"

"Grove Park Inn," Meyers said, and he gave Segal the room number.

IT TOOK SEGAL less than fifteen minutes to drive up the hill on the north side of town. He showed the valet his badge and let him take the car. He and Walter pushed through the main entrance and into the famous lobby. As eager as he was to learn more about the missing man and his possible connection to their case, he couldn't pass by this space without a brief pause to look around.

The lobby was large and well-proportioned, with gigantic stone fireplaces to the left and right and a high ceiling. Opposite the entrance, tall windows looked out to the west over the city, to the mountains beyond. The room itself was filled with mission-style easy chairs and couches and rockers. *A person could spend a lot of time in a room like this*, he thought, *but not today.*

Walter checked at the desk and they pointed him in the right direction. The room was in the old part of the Grove Park Inn, the part finished in 1913. As many times as he had been there, Segal had never been upstairs in this part of the Inn, which had hosted so many presidents, business leaders, artists and celebrities of all kinds. When he entered the hallway on the fourth floor he was a little surprised. It was certainly substantial and well cared for, but somehow not as glamorous as he had imagined. The furniture and color scheme were definitely true to the period in which it was built, making it perhaps a little drab for modern tastes.

Down the hall Segal could see a door standing open and when he got closer, he could hear Meyers talking on a cell phone.

When he entered the room with Walter he saw an unmade bed and an open suitcase. Meyers nodded to them without pausing in his conversation and pointed toward his partner, Ron Philips, who was sitting at a desk searching through the drawers. Philips, who rarely said anything, held up a well-worn leather-bound appointment book. When Segal took it from him the book fell open to last Friday.

Segal held the book up so that he and Walter could read it at the same time. The only entry on that day, written with blue ink in clear and precise letters, was the name Adrien Koll and the address on Town Mountain where the body had been found.

Meyers ended his call and turned toward them. "Interesting, don't you think?"

"Very interesting," Segal said. "Where are you with this guy so far?"

Meyers withdrew a small notebook from a pocket and flipped it open and began to read in that flat mechanical tone used for such recitations. "Name of missing person is John Belincort, CEO of Bell Tower Insurance, Inc. In town for a meeting of something called the Insurance Compliance Commission here at the Grove Park Inn. The meetings of the Commission began on Monday, Belincort apparently came to town Friday to play golf which apparently he did. However, he did not go to dinner Friday night with the rest of the guys, saying there was something he needed to do. Then, Monday morning, he didn't show up for breakfast or the meetings. He wasn't answering his phone either. So when he didn't show up this morning the meeting organizers knocked on his door and then got the management to open it when he didn't answer. That's when they called it in."

Meyers flipped the notebook closed and returned to his normal speaking voice. "Anyway, when Ron started going through his appointment book, that's when we called you guys in. Other than that, we're just getting started."

Segal looked down at the antique carpet, trying to think about what to do next. He still had the appointment book in his hand so he opened it again to study the days before and after the page where they had seen the name of their second murder victim. There were no notations on the previous Thursday. Friday was marked Grove Park and 10:20 T, presumably his Tee time for golf, and of course, the name and address of Adrien Koll. Nothing else.

Monday, Tuesday, and Wednesday were all marked Commission Meeting. However, Saturday had one more notation, an address and a time, and the word breakfast.

"You notice this address on Monday in the book?" Segal asked.

"Yeah, we saw it, but we haven't had a chance to check it out yet," Meyers said.

Walter took a look, too. "Down in the River Arts District," he said.

"I have to head over to the River Arts anyway," Segal said. "I'll check it out for you. Let you know what I find."

He and Walter took off. Walking down the hall, Walter said, "So maybe this guy, Mr. Belincort, goes up to Town Mountain and shoots Mr. Koll while he's got a good excuse to be in town."

"Or maybe Mr. Belincort meets Mr. Koll up there and they both get shot only we haven't found the body yet because we didn't know we should be looking for one," Segal said.

"I'm thinking maybe we should get the dogs up there," Walter said.

Segal grinned and shook his head. Walter loved the police dogs. Everyone loved the police dogs, but Walter really loved them. Every time he saw them he said to Segal, "This is what I should have trained for." They went back to the room to get some of Belincort's clothing to give the dogs a scent.

Segal said, "I'll drop you at the station. You can organize that while I go down to the River Arts."

"You want me to go with you? I could take care of the dogs after."

"No, I'll have Dinah meet me there. Probably nothing there anyway."

THE NORTH PART of the River Arts District included a group of buildings well past the point of possible renovation, at least in the opinion of the building inspectors. Some had been torn down, some in the process, some awaiting the wrecking ball and dump truck. The address on the slip of paper in Segal's pocket matched one of these. It made no sense. Certainly no place for a breakfast meeting. He pulled up onto the gravel drive beside what had been a loading dock. Weeds pushed up in scattered clumps on the inhospitable surface, beginning to reclaim this piece of earth. The same could be said for the building itself, with long branches of sumac reaching out of some of the broken windows looking for the sun.

He parked and got out, still looking around. The building itself was the equivalent of four stories high with brick walls the color of ox blood. To Segal it had the feel of a place used in heavy industry. A foundry for rail car parts maybe? To the right a smoke stack clad with the same bricks looked like it might stand there forever.

Next door a crane sat on the flat cement floor inside broken remnants of a foundation that made Segal think of a monster's teeth broken off at the gum line. A little further on he saw a front-end loader and a dump truck. No one was around. *Possibly lunch break,* Segal thought.

There was a high bay door facing the loading dock that must have conveyed fork lifts in and out when the building was in use. There was a heavy roll-up door that looked like it had not been opened in years. However, to the right of this was a normal man-sized door which stood ajar.

He climbed the stairs beside the loading dock. He scanned the area once more but saw no one, then leaned his head into the open doorway and looked around cautiously. In the mottled light seeping through the broken windows and rusted frames he could make out a large chamber of a room. In the main section he could see clear up to the beams and the sagging sheet metal of the roof. To the left a set of stairs led up to a mezzanine level and what must have been an office at one time. There were the remnants of an overhead crane of heavy caliber. Whatever they had dealt with here, it had involved lifting and moving very heavy loads. Everywhere dust, dirt, cobwebs, and rusted machine parts told the story of disuse and abandonment.

Segal stepped on in and yelled, "Hello," but the sound just echoed.

He tried again. "Hello, police."

This time he heard a faint sound to his left and further back in the building. As he turned in that direction he saw a trail in the dust on the floor; partial footprints and marks where something had been dragged. He had an unsettled feeling about this place. He heard the sound of a diesel engine starting up. *Lunchbreak's over,* he thought.

He approached the brick wall. It was windowless, and he realized this was the wall shared by the building that had stood next door at one time. This part of the building was darker, especially the part under the mezzanine. He pulled out his phone and flicked on the flashlight function. As soon as he did, he saw a silver glint of bright metal that looked entirely out of place in this cavern of rust and ruin. He heard a moan.

"Is someone there?" he called but got no answer. He took another step toward the glint of metal and raised his light higher. Now he could see links of a bright steel chain. There was something dark laying on the ground next to it. He did a quick inhale when he realized the dark thing on the ground was a man's body. He heard another moan and quickened his pace.

When he rounded a large engine lathe the picture came into full view. There was a man of middle age, dressed in a disheveled and filthy business suit in a sitting position on the ground. His back was upright against the brick wall. His arms were elevated and spread flat against the wall and Segal could see more chain there. The man's bald head was listing to one side and it moved a little when Segal's light fell on the eyes.

There was another moan. Segal ran up and checked for injuries but saw none. He stooped down so he could see the man's face better.

"Sir, it's the police. Are you hurt?" he said.

He got no response and reached over and tilted the victim's chin up. The man was clearly breathing but not conscious. Segal pulled out his phone to call for backup. When the 911 operator answered he made it short.

"This is Lieutenant Segal with the Asheville Police. Send backup units and medical response team," and he gave them the address, checked that they had it right, and hung up.

Segal stood up to take a closer look at what was holding the man's hands up in this bizarre, seated crucifixion. He could see that the end of the chain had been looped around the man's left wrist and secured there with a padlock. A few links away from the lock a heavy bolt had been passed through a link of chain and secured into the wall. The chain dropped slightly where it passed over the man's head to where his right wrist was secured in a similar manner.

Segal grabbed the chain on either side of the man's right wrist and pulled. Nothing budged. He tried again, jerking harder this time, but again with no luck. He put a foot against the brick wall and put all his strength and weight into it. The bolt stayed firmly anchored. He stood back and cast about the floor for something he could use as a tool.

He found a piece of steel rod, only a foot or so long, but better than nothing. From outside he heard two sounds: nearby, a diesel engine was revving up, and in the distance, a siren faintly wailed. In Segal's stressed and hyped-up mind it seemed that the two sounds were competing against one another.

With the steel rod as a tool he went at the bolt again. First he wrapped the chain around it and tried to use it as a lever. It moved by a tiny fraction of an inch. He unwrapped the chain and tried to use the end of the rod to hammer sideways against the head of the bolt, thinking to maybe dislodge it a little in the brittle brick wall. The bolt moved, at least slightly, and he tried the prying move again. This time the bolt moved by a quarter of an inch or so. When he hammered the head of the bolt a second time he had better leverage and it loosened more. Several times he alternated back and forth between hammering and prying until at last the long heavy bolt burst free from the wall bringing with it a shower of brick and mortar dust.

Outside he still heard the diesel engine, now revving to a new level and accompanied by some metallic creaking sounds. The siren was getting louder, then it stopped. He stood up and took a couple of breaths and allowed himself a brief moment of self-congratulation.

In that instant there was a tremendous thudding crash and he felt the building give a sickening shake.

Segal jumped back, confused. Outside there was more creaking and diesel noise and after several seconds another tremendous crash. This time he watched in horror as bricks exploded from the wall twenty feet away and he caught a glimpse of a giant wrecking ball completing its arc and then pulling away. He started counting, "One thousand one, one thousand two, one thousand three." At the same time he started to work on the chain holding the man's left hand to the wall. Behind him he heard footsteps, but in the back of his mind he continued to count, "One thousand four, one thousand five." There was another crash. He continued to work frantically and he began the count over again. The ball was swinging like a pendulum on a clock, every six seconds.

"Lieutenant Segal!" came a yell from behind him. He turned and saw Dinah there in her uniform with a large flashlight in her hand.

Segal stood up, gasping for air. He held up a hand with four fingers, then put his thumb out to make five then pointed to the wall a small distance away and a third crash occurred.

Dinah's jaw dropped and Segal said, "Wrecking ball." Dinah jumped back when the steel monster made its brief appearance.

This time the hole got noticeably bigger and a piece of brick came skidding toward them across the floor. The ball was getting closer.

"I'll run out and stop them," Dinah yelled.

"No time," Segal yelled back. "Help me with this chain."

Dinah took in the situation with a glance and saw that he was right. Segal struck the head of the bolt with the steel rod again. This one seemed to be anchored better than the first and he could see no movement. Dinah pulled her best on the chain but to no effect.

"We need something longer for better leverage," Segal shouted.

Dinah looked around behind her and saw nothing useful, but further on toward the hole made by the wrecking ball a shaft of sunlight revealed a heavy bar, hexagonal in cross section and forged to a flat chisel blade on the other end. It was about four feet long; the perfect tool for the job.

Dinah took a step toward it but Segal grabbed her wrist as she started to brush by him. A second later the wrecking ball crashed again. As soon as it began to swing back he released her and she bounded forward and grabbed the end of the bar. When she tried to lift it, it would not move. As the dust cleared she saw that a section of wall had fallen on the other end. She struggled to lever it up to free it but it would not move. She wrapped both hands around it and tried to pull. It began to free up when Segal yelled, "Jump!"

She gave one full strength pull like a weight lifter jerking a barbell. The rod broke loose, she and the rod skidded across the floor, and the wrecking ball hit, all in the same instant. There was no doubt about it. The wrecking ball was moving toward them with each swing. It would very soon be on them, that is, if the whole wall didn't collapse first.

Dinah wasted no time. She tried to work the bar under the head of the bolt, but there was not enough room.

"Put the end here and let me wrap the chain around it," Segal yelled.

She did as he said and when he had wrapped the chain around the rod she pried with all her might. The bolt budged a little and the wrecking ball hit again. This time it was close enough that Segal was hit squarely in the back by a flying brick. It knocked him forward to his knees, but he got back up.

He took one staggering step toward the man but Dinah stopped him.

"We're running out of time," she yelled, "Stand back."

With that she lunged forward with both hands on the rod and struck the bolt from the side just where it protruded out of the wall. The end of the bolt sheared off and the man's arm fell free.

Segal wasted no time. He grabbed the man's lapels and hoisted him to a standing position, then ducked and wrapped his arms around the man's legs and let him collapse over his shoulder. He started toward the door with the man over his shoulder, dragging the chain behind them like Marley's ghost. Dinah followed and picked up the end of the chain, making sure it didn't get caught on anything.

When they neared the door Dinah dropped the chain and jumped ahead to open it. The light shone in through the open door and Segal noticed something he had overlooked on the way in. It was a closed-circuit TV camera with a small red light indicating it was active. Dinah followed his glance up there and saw it too. They looked at each other for an instant, then Segal stepped outside to the wide loading dock.

He lowered the man down and maneuvered him off his shoulder. Dinah came to assist and took the man's head in her hands to lower it gently. With the man lying there on his back they finally stood up and took a deep breath in unison.

Segal stood bent over, panting, his hands on his knees. He barely looked up when the ambulance arrived, followed closely by another police cruiser. The cops and the medics opened their doors and stepped out at the same instant and stood for a second taking in the scene.

At that moment there was a sound like thunder as the wall of the building collapsed, shooting a shaft of dust out of the open door.

"I THINK WE can call Meyers and Philips and tell them we found their missing person," Segal said.

"You sure about that?" Walter asked. He scratched the back of his head. He had pulled up just about the time the EMT's were carting the rescued man off to the hospital.

"Not one hundred percent, but I'd bet money on it," Segal said. "They're supposed to call from the hospital as soon as the guy regains consciousness."

The paramedics had checked vital signs before the ride to the hospital. The man appeared to be sedated and dehydrated but otherwise probably OK. Segal was eager to interview him when he came to. Just to be on the safe side, he sent another police officer along with them to make sure the guy stayed put and that there were no more attempts on his life.

Segal and Walter stood by the loading dock.

Dinah came around the side of the building. "The foreman said he wouldn't advise anyone going in there now. It's too unstable with part of the wall knocked down."

"That's what I thought they'd say," Segal said. They had been debating whether to bring in the forensic technicians, but this answered the question. "I doubt we would have found anything anyway, but I would surely like to know who was on the other end of that video camera."

Walter took a step back from Segal and Dinah. "You two are starting to look alike," he said. They were both covered with the gray dust that coated everything inside the abandoned building. They looked at each other and both started laughing.

"I guess I need to get a shower and a change of clothes," Segal said. It felt good to laugh, to feel the giddy experience of being alive when it could well have been otherwise. "I'll need to get this sport coat dry cleaned as well."

"I hate to tell you, Segal, but that thing needed to be cleaned before you ever went into that building," Walter said.

"Check this out," Dinah said. "I had one of the guys take a picture." She held up a cell phone. The picture on it showed Dinah leaning over a giant battered steel wrecking ball. She held onto a massive chain attached to the top of the ball while giving the camera a wide smile. Her teeth beamed white in contrast to her gray face and uniform.

"Damn," the men said in unison. The picture drove home the reality of just how close it had been.

Walter said the dog search of the second crime scene was in progress and he should get back up the mountain. He had been up there when he heard the dispatch call for assistance and he had recognized the address.

"You OK to drive?" he asked Segal.

Segal nodded.

"How about you?" he asked, turning toward Dinah.

She gave him a quick salute. "Ready for duty, sir."

Walter gave a nod and a little laugh. She did look funny with that gray face and a big grin. He ducked into his car and drove away.

Something held Segal and Dinah on the loading dock a moment longer. He looked around and wondered what he was waiting for.

As if reading his mind, Dinah said, "I guess we should let these guys get back to work and finish their job."

"Yeah, I guess we have a job to finish, too," Segal said.

Dinah walked to the corner of the building where she could see the demolition team. She gave a loud whistle and they all looked over at her. She pointed a finger high in the air and made a circular motion with it, a moment later Segal heard the diesel engines fire up.

Equally comfortable giving and taking orders, Segal thought. *The chief could be right about this one.*

He watched her walk back and when she drew near he said, "Thanks for what you did in there."

Dinah looked down and just shook her head. She started to say something dismissive, but Segal raised his hand to stop her.

"No, I mean it," he said. "Do you know how rare it is to find someone who will have your back in a situation like that? I mean, really have your back?"

Dinah was quiet for a moment. She stopped shaking her head and as she looked up her expression changed from an embarrassed grin to a more sad and serious visage.

She held Segal's eye and said, "Yes, actually I do know a little bit about that." Segal recalled then that he heard she had been in combat in Iraq and Afghanistan.

Segal stuck out his hand and she met it with her own. Then they smiled and turned the handshake into a quick embrace, the joy of being alive returning to them once again.

When they backed away from each other Segal looked down at himself and said, "I really do need to go and get cleaned up."

"Me too," Dinah said. "I was responding to a call, but I think it can probably wait while I take a shower and put on a clean uniform."

"Was it the catapult?" Segal asked.

Dinah nodded. "Frozen turkey on to a fourth-floor balcony. Hit the sliding glass door but only cracked it. Must be the same jackasses that were rolling coal earlier," she said. "I think we'll be able to pick them up pretty soon, and I just hope I'm there to be in on it."

"I hope so too," Segal said, and he meant it.

Dinah turned and headed toward her car.

When he got to his car Segal turned back toward the building. He pulled out his phone and called the station and asked for their assistant, Gina. When she was on the line he read off the address of the building. "I want everything you can get from city records. Current and past owners, permits, valuations, everything."

THIRTEEN

Plate Tectonics

SEGAL WAS STILL in the shower when he heard the phone buzz on the counter by the sink. He decided not to make a mad rush for it and drip water all over the place. Instead, he shut his eyes and continued to let the water stream over his head and face and body. When he did get out a few minutes later he heard the ding of a text message. He dried off and saw that the message was from the hospital, just as he suspected. The man they had rescued was awake.

He dressed quickly and hurried out of the bedroom. As he passed the kitchen area of his apartment he patted the side pocket of the clean sport coat he had found. Finding it empty, he turned to a pile of paperbacks on the counter. He grabbed a well-worn copy of *Cat Chaser* by Elmore Leonard and slipped it into the side pocket. He also grabbed a piece of toasted bagel left over from breakfast and headed out the door.

The hospital was only moments from his apartment. It took more time to find a parking place and walk to the emergency room than it took to get to the hospital campus in the first place.

At the desk he showed his badge and the clerk nodded and told him he was expected.

"The doctor wanted to talk to you first before you see the patient," she said.

Segal entered the inner sanctum through the door she indicated and almost ran into a woman dressed in green scrubs. Segal and the woman both recoiled in surprise. It took him a moment to place her. It was the woman he had met at the roller derby match a few nights ago.

"Tina!" he said, "I didn't recognize you dressed like that." He glanced at her name tag and saw Dr. Christina May. It made him realize that he had not spent enough time with her to even find out what she did for a living.

"They said a detective would be coming over. I wondered if it would be you." She smiled.

Segal wondered if he needed to apologize for not calling her but she seemed to sense that before he said anything.

"I've been reading the paper. I guess you've been busy with the crossbow murders," she said.

Shirley Dawn was right, he thought. The name *Crossbow Murders* was catching on.

Segal was standing there with his mouth open, so Dr. May turned on her official persona and raised the clipboard she held in her hand.

"So, your patient is conscious now. He was heavily sedated and dehydrated when they brought him in, so we've had him on an IV drip for fluids and a little nutrition. He had a few scrapes and bruises, but nothing that appeared too serious. We have pulled some blood samples. The initial results don't look too bad. It will take more time to identify the drug or drugs in his system." She lowered the clip board.

"What's his name?" Segal asked.

"Oh, I assumed you knew." She raised the clip board and read the name off the top line. "Name is John Belincort."

Segal nodded. "That's what we thought."

When they entered the room the man on the bed had his eyes closed. Segal saw the IV and the monitors displaying heart rate, respiration, and blood oxygen level. The sounds in the room changed when the blood pressure cuff began to inflate, and the man blinked his eyes open.

"John Belincort?" Segal said.

The man nodded, then looked around the room, and finally his eyes returned to Segal.

"Mr. Belincort, I'm Lieutenant Ira Segal with the Asheville police department. Are you able to answer some questions?"

The man looked around the room again. This time Segal got the impression that it was less from confusion and more like a man looking for a way out.

"How did I get here?" Belincort asked.

"We'll get around to that a little later," Segal said, "right now I'd like to go over what you do remember."

Belincort did not respond. Segal watched his face closely as it seemed to roll through several emotions one after another, apparently struggling to process the situation.

Segal started with the most immediate question. "Who chained you up in that building?"

Now Belincort's face showed authentic confusion. He just shook his head.

Segal knew from experience that trauma could sometimes make the most recent events the hardest to remember. So could some drugs. He backed off a little.

"All right, let's start here. Can you remember when you got to Asheville?"

Belincort had to think a moment. "I got to the hotel a little before noon on Friday. I had a tee time with some guys. We were going to have lunch first but they moved the tee time up so we just took some sandwiches with us on the carts."

"Who were you playing with?" Segal asked.

Belincort told him two of the names. "The other guy, I forget his name. He was a friend of one of the others."

"And what time did you finish your round?" Segal asked.

Belincort still appeared to be a little confused and thinking hard. "It must have been around 5:30, maybe six."

"And after the round?" Segal asked.

"I remember we had a drink in the clubhouse, then we headed up to the hotel."

"And did you have dinner with the other guys?" Segal asked.

"No. I mean, they were having dinner together, but I didn't join them," he said.

"And what did you do?" Segal asked. *This is like pulling teeth*, he thought.

"Uh, I had an appointment to see another individual on a business matter," he said.

"You're an insurance salesman, right?" Segal asked.

Belincort looked irritated. "I am the CEO of Bell Tower Insurance," he said. "Not an insurance salesman."

"Who was it that you visited, and what was the nature of your business?" Segal asked, putting a little edge in his voice.

"I would rather not get into the details if I don't absolutely have to," Belincort said. "It had to do with an investment opportunity which is highly sensitive. It would be very costly to my company and to others if details were made public."

"Mr. Belincort, this is a murder investigation," Segal said.

This did not have the desired effect. Instead, John Belincort got a crooked smirk on his face. "Well, someone seems to have done some damage to me, but I'm still alive. I don't think you can exactly call that murder."

"We have reason to believe you visited Adrien Koll Friday evening," Segal charged.

This clearly took Belincort by surprise. At length he did answer. "I did meet with Adrien Koll, but that is all I'm prepared to say. Even that fact could be disastrous if it became public."

"Adrien Koll was murdered Friday night, so you see, this is a murder investigation." Segal let the statement hang there for a moment while Belincort seemed to process the information with genuine surprise. Then the expression on his face changed.

"You can't possibly believe I had anything to do with that. Koll was perfectly all right when I left him."

"And what time was that?" Segal asked.

"Around nine at night, I think. It was getting dark."

"Was there anyone else there?" Segal asked.

"No, there was no one else in the meeting. But just as I was leaving I saw someone else come up and talk to him. I don't know who it was, possibly someone in Adrien's rifle club. He told me he had a private shooting range there."

"You didn't know who the third person was?" Segal asked.

"No, like I said, it was getting dark and I was pulling out. I didn't get a very good look, and the guy was dressed in dark clothes."

"And what then?" Segal asked.

"Nothing," Belincort said, "I came back to the Grove and I went to bed."

Segal made a mental note to have someone check out the security camera recordings from the Grove Park Inn to confirm this.

"OK," Segal continued, "you went to bed Friday night, fairly early. What about Saturday morning?"

Bell furrowed his brow. "I remember I was supposed to go to a breakfast meeting. I had an address, but when I got to the address I couldn't see anything that looked like a restaurant. It was just an old rundown building down by the river. I remember getting out of the car."

Belincort stopped talking and looked away from Segal. He looked around the room again as if he might find some clue to a memory there.

"After that, I can't remember anything."

Segal was disappointed, but he believed him; at least, he believed the part about not remembering the most recent events. He also knew from experience that this could change when the drugs were completely out of his system and his mind had some distance from the trauma.

"Are you familiar with the White Hog Militia?" Segal asked. Sometimes a quick change of subject could get interesting results in an interrogation.

Belincort immediately answered, "No."

A little bit too immediately? Segal wondered.

Segal quickly fired off another question. "Have you ever met Julius Hargrove?"

"The painter?" Belincort answered. "No. I've heard of him, but I don't believe I ever met him."

Segal thought it was not unusual that he had heard of Hargrove. A lot of people had.

"I think that's all for now," Segal said. "They'll probably release you soon. I assume you'll be going back to the Grove Park Inn."

Belincort's eyes got wider. "What day is it anyway?"

"Tuesday," Segal said.

Belincort shook his head in disbelief. "Yes, I guess I will. The conference lasts through Friday."

Segal handed him a card. "Call me if you remember anything else, and please don't leave town before I talk with you again."

Belincort looked at the card and nodded.

Segal left the room and looked for Dr. Tina May on his way out. He didn't see her and when he asked at the desk the receptionist said she was in the middle of a procedure. He handed her a card and asked that she pass it on to Dr. May.

"Ask her to call me if there is any change in Mr. Belincort's condition," he added.

"I'm sure she'll be happy to have this," the receptionist said with a little smirk on her face.

He did a double take and walked out, thinking for the thousandth time that the women around him seemed to know everything while he knew nothing.

BY THE TIME Segal got back to the station he was feeling tired, bruised, and disjointed. The adrenaline rush which had carried him through his close call with the wrecking ball had worn off leaving him to pick up the mental and physical pieces of the mess unaided.

He stopped for a moment by the door of the break room where someone had taped up a picture of Dinah in her roller derby uniform. It was cut from a newspaper story under the headline *Roller Girl Phenom*. So, Shirley Dawn had published the story she had told him about. In the photo, Dinah was standing with most of her weight on one skate, making the opposite hip jut out a little. She had removed her helmet and she held it pressed against that hip with her hand gently curling around it. It reminded Segal of the pose struck by Joan of Arc in the Hargrove painting. Just switch out the type of armor and helmet, and, of course, the girl.

He moved on to his desk. He would read the story later when he had more energy. He closed his eyes for a second and exhaled, and when he opened them, Gina was placing a thick folder on the desk in front of him. Gina, as efficient as ever.

"What took you so long?" he said.

She smiled and said, "You should take some ibuprofen. I'll get you some."

Segal realized that she must have heard about the wrecking ball adventure. In any case, Segal knew she could read him like one of the books he carried around in his pocket.

He turned his attention to the folder, City of Asheville and Buncombe County documents pertaining to the building which, by this time, was no more than a pile of bricks and mortar dust. The first document he saw was a permit for demolition which referenced the current owners, Tangent Holdings. Segal recognized the name from the news. It was the development group working on a renovation of part of the River Arts District. Some would say they were going to renovate it beyond recognition. Segal didn't know enough about the project to have an opinion one way or another. *Good topic to discuss with Shirley Dawn someday*, he thought.

Gina came back to his desk with a couple of ibuprofen tablets and a paper cup of water.

"Did you see it yet?" she asked.

Segal popped the first pill into his mouth and took a sip of water and repeated with the second pill.

"Did I see what? I just opened the folder," he said.

Gina leaned over his shoulder.

"This folder has copies of everything I found, but I

flagged the pages I thought you would find especially interesting.

Segal could see the hot pink sticky notes peeking out from between the pages.

"OK, the property is currently owned by Tangent Holdings," she said, tapping the page with a finger. Segal noticed that the pink color of her nail polish matched the sticky notes and wondered if the color coordination was intentional.

Gina next flipped the sheets back to the first sticky note.

"This form deals with the most recent transfer of ownership. Check out who the seller was." She tapped the hot pink fingernail on a name halfway down the page.

"Tectonic Plate Properties," Segal read. "Interesting."

"OK, but go back one more."

Segal flipped to the next pink note. He couldn't believe it. "Julius Hargrove? Julius Hargrove was a previous owner?"

Gina nodded and smiled. "I thought you'd like that."

Segal flipped back to the next sticky note.

"That's the transfer of ownership before the last one."

Segal ran his finger down the page. "OK, Hargrove is listed as the buyer." He ran his finger a little farther down. "And the seller was Continental Drift Holdings, whoever that is."

Gina nodded.

Segal repeated his motions, learning that the owner prior to Continental Drift Holdings was an individual named Lewis Jackson. When he flipped back to the last sticky note the appearance of the form was totally different.

"Jackson owned the building for a long time. You have to go back over forty years to find the previous transfer. Did you notice the dates and sales prices on the other transactions?"

Segal flipped back through the relevant forms and jotted the numbers down in a notebook. When he completed the list he leaned back to look at it. Gina came around and sat in the chair across from him at his desk.

"Let me make sure I have this straight," he said. "Lewis Jackson owns the property for almost forty years. Then Continental Drift, whoever they are, buys the property for two hundred and twenty-five thousand dollars."

Gina nodded.

"Then, three months after they buy it, they sell it to Julius Hargrove for one point one million. Then, a little over a year after that Hargrove sells it to Tectonic Plate Properties for one point three million dollars. Then one year later Tectonic sells it to the current owners for one point five million."

"Pretty interesting, huh?" Gina said.

Segal sat back.

After a moment he said, "Thanks, Gina, really good work," then, more to himself he said, "I've got to tell Walter about this." He knew that Walter was much better than he was when it came to business and investments. Unlike himself, Walter actually followed what was happening in the stock market. Walter would stand a much better chance of working out the implications of this new information.

He didn't have long to wait. He barely had time to get a cup of coffee and reread the forms when Walter came in like a kid returning from a class field trip.

"How did it go?" he asked after Walter hung up his coat and got a cup of coffee himself.

"It went OK. Of course, we didn't find a body, since we already had our missing person accounted for, but Phil did seem to pick up the guy's scent, which confirms that he had been there." Phil, or as most people called him, Sergeant

Phil, was one of the department's oldest and most reliable German Shepherds—also Walter's favorite.

"OK," Segal said, "That's consistent with what we thought and with what John Belincort told me."

"So Belincort came around enough to answer some questions?" Walter asked.

Segal realized then that he hadn't talked to Walter since his visit with Belincort at the hospital, so he delivered a quick debrief.

"And you believe him when he says he doesn't remember anything after pulling up to the building?" Walter asked.

"I'm not sure. He was still pretty fuzzy from the incident and the drugs, so it's definitely possible. We'll revisit it when he's had a little more time to recover."

"Well, I brought in some of the pictures from the house like we planned," Walter said. "I'll get Gina to make copies."

"Gina's already been busy today," Segal said. He lifted the heavy folder Gina had prepared and quickly went through the history of property transfers.

"Damn," Walter said, scratching the back of his head. "That is some kind of spicy investment action going on. We need to follow up on this with the State Department of Commerce."

"I'm going to follow up with Margery Hargrove tomorrow. See if she can fill me in a little on Julius's finances. Maybe see who gets all this money now that he's gone. Can you deal with the State Department of Commerce?" Segal asked.

Walter nodded and smiled. Segal could tell he smelled blood on this one.

"On second thought, why don't we hold off on the Secretary of Commerce for a while. We already have the governor's office involved here. I'm not sure how much state level action we should bring in before we understand what's going on," Segal said.

"What was the name of Koll's company?" he asked after a moment of reflection.

Segal flipped through some notes. "Continental Drift Financial Planning."

"And the investment company in these transactions was," Walter paused as he thumbed back through Gina's folder, "Continental Drift Holdings."

"Are we seeing a bit of a geological tectonic plate pattern here?" Segal said.

"Like the coast line of Africa matching up with South America," Walter said.

They let that sink in for a few moments.

Walter began flipping through the pictures he brought back from Koll's house. He stopped at the third one and held it up for better light.

"You told me John Belincort had not heard of the White Hog Militia, right?" he asked.

"That's right, never heard of it," Segal said.

"Well, I think Mr. Belincort just lied to you." Walter handed the picture to Segal.

Segal looked closely at the picture which showed a number of men, including John Belincort, lounging around a camp fire. Many guns were evident. They were all wearing camo fatigues of one kind or another, and they all, including Belincort, wore the patch of the White Hog Militia.

Segal continued to look at the picture as he said to Walter, "It hurts my feelings when people lie to me. Does it hurt your feelings when people lie to you?"

"If by hurting my feelings you mean does it piss me off, then yes, it hurts my feelings a lot."

IT WAS LATE afternoon by this time. As Segal sat for a moment and thought about the revelations of the day, he realized how tired he felt.

"Why don't you come over to dinner tonight?" Walter said. Apparently he could read the fatigue in Segal's face. *Why is everyone reading me like a book today*, Segal thought.

Actually, what he felt was an edgy combination of fatigue, restless nerves, and mental fog. He knew the best way to deal with it was physical exercise, the kind that left all the toxic stuff behind in a pool of sweat.

"Thanks, Walter, but I think I need to hit the gym."

"Hit the bag with your own wrecking balls," Walter said, holding up his two fists.

"I'll see you in the morning. Make that late morning. I'm going to pay Mrs. Hargrove a visit first thing. See what she knows about this financial stuff."

He started to pick up some of the folders on his desk to take home, but changed his mind. This evening was about recharging his batteries.

He checked the trunk of his car to make sure the gym bag was there. That's where he usually kept it so it would be handy when the opportunity presented itself, as on this occasion.

He drove south and turned off the highway near the airport and onto a small connector that took him to a metal industrial building with a sign bearing the name of gym. There were a lot of gyms closer, but he liked this one for its eclectic combination of characters and the martial arts they practiced. The instructors there were all previous or current competing athletes, and the people they trained ranged from up-and-coming pros to people working on medical rehab, to eight-year-old's getting their first taste of this kind of discipline. That, and they were just plain good people and they made him feel like part of the family. And they played good music on the PA system.

Segal's chosen martial art was boxing. Most of the guys at the station thought it was old-fashioned. The general consensus was that other forms like judo or karate were more useful in self-defense situations. But Segal liked boxing. Boxing was built on rhythm and speed with a deep connection to the mechanics of the body that all felt right to him when it was working.

He changed and started his workout by stretching and jumping rope. They always had a timer going, two-minute rounds separated by thirty second rests: simulating a boxing match. In the main ring the head boxing coach was working with one of the best new prospects in the area, a kid who reminded Segal a little bit of the young Ali, the way he was built.

They were well into their workout and the young guy was soaked in sweat. The coach was moving plenty too, but he seemed fresh as he always did. Motion seemed to be his natural state of existence. He talked to the young guy continuously during the round calling out punch combinations constantly, correcting the guy's movements, demonstrating moves in slow motion, checking with the guy to see if he understood. The coach was wearing a protective vest and hand pads and the kid was firing punches into both with a crisp snap. As Segal knew from his own training, the coach had a goofy teasing way about him, but the moves he was teaching were no joke, and often what seemed like subtle and trivial adjustments paid big dividends. Between rounds the coach looked around the gym and called out to various people.

"Hey Segal, did you bring your crossbow with you today?" he called.

The young boxer and a couple other guys working out seemed to get a real kick out of this, and Segal could only shake his head, smile, and accept the ribbing. Once again, he thought of Shirley Dawn; she did know how to write a catchy headline.

Segal did one more round of jumping rope and then switched to the heavy bag, working through some of the standard punch combinations. He did one round slowly, working on form, then a second round for speed and power.

In the ring, the young boxer finished and the coach gave him a hug and sent him off to the showers. Segal was breathing hard and covered with sweat by this time.

The coach looked at him and said, "Segal, come on in here for a round or two, let's see how you're holding up." Segal nodded and ducked under the top rope and stepped over the bottom one. He faced the coach who slipped the pads back onto his hands to receive Segal's punches. The bell sounded and the coach started a circling motion in the ring.

"Follow me," the coach said.

Segal moved with him, counter circling him and in the process moving in a little and dragging his right foot.

"That's right," the coach said with a grin. "You're cutting off the ring on me."

It was something Segal did unconsciously.

The coach started calling out combinations of punches, simple and repetitive at first. This allowed Segal to concentrate on snapping the punches out there with speed and power. He was glad he was already warmed up. The punches made a satisfying pop against the coach's hand pads when they landed.

As the round moved on the punch combinations got longer and more complex. He tired and the sequences grew long enough as to be a challenge just to execute. But the sequences were not random, they were structured for a reason. Each punch or dip or roll set up the next punch or movement. Eventually he made a mistake and got lost in a sequence. The coach called it again and had him move through the sequence over and over again until he could remember it, not just with his mind, but with his body too. This was exactly the point: to incorporate the feeling of the sequence so well that his body would know what to do even when his brain was tired and even when he was barely conscious because someone had hit him.

Just when he thought he couldn't keep his gloves up another second, the bell sounded. Segal bent at the waist and put his gloves on his knees, sucking in deep breaths of air. The coach pulled the pads off his hands and patted him on the back. He leaned in close and talked to Segal in a low voice.

"Good work. You were a little distracted there for a minute but your body remembered. Trust it, man. Don't overthink things."

Segal just nodded and smiled, not yet able to speak. He gave the coach a fist bump, his glove to the coach's bare knuckles.

"You're a good man, Segal," he said still in a low voice. Then in a louder voice intended to include the whole gym, "Even if all these other guys think you're an asshole." This brought a round of laughter to the rest of the gym and a smile to Segal's face.

The coach leaned in one more time for a confidential word. "Now go out there and rain down some freaking justice on the criminal element. Make sure everyone gets exactly what they deserve."

Segal showered and dressed back in his street clothes. He pulled out his phone and saw that he had a text from Dinah:

—McCormick Field. Large water balloon hurled over the stands, landed in shallow left field. Nobody hurt.—

As he passed the gym office on his way out the coach motioned him in. The coach was writing in a check book on the desk in front of him.

"I need to refund you some money," he said. Segal looked surprised. "You prepaid for the jujitsu class for your cousin, Tommy, but he dropped out. He hasn't been coming."

Segal sighed. This was disappointing news. One more thing that wasn't working for Tommy. "That's all right. Keep it coach. Maybe I can get him to come back."

He walked out into the cool air of the evening. It felt wonderful and he felt drained. He was not going to let this piece of bad news spoil his mood. He would go home, eat something quick, and get some rest. As he drove with the wind in his face the words of encouragement from his coach kept repeating in a loop in his mind. *Pretty good therapy.*

FOURTEEN

Bath Robe

THE NEXT MORNING Segal considered calling ahead, but decided this time an unannounced drop-in on the widow, Margery Hargrove, might be more interesting. He knocked on her door at 8:30. He could hear her voice and some movement, and it didn't take long for her to open the door, still tying her robe in place. It came to just above the knee and was a shiny silk material with an interesting print that was probably meant to look oriental. With the belt pulled in at the waist it did a good job of accentuating her figure.

"I'm making some coffee, Lieutenant, would you like some?" she said. Her hair was messy and her eyes were still puffy from sleep, or possibly lack thereof. The coffee smelled amazing.

"Sure," Segal said, and he followed her on into the house. Although it was not large, it had high ceilings, giving it very satisfying and comfortable proportions. As he expected, the walls were nearly full of art work of various kinds. There were a few which Segal thought to be Hargrove's, but the majority were clearly from different artists. While Segal stopped to take in the living room Margery went on through to the kitchen. He watched her back as she reached up to the cupboard and pulled out a couple of mugs, and then into a drawer, looking for teaspoons he assumed. Meanwhile, the machine on the counter made mechanical clicking and hissing sounds which Segal associated with the age of steam engines.

She stepped out of sight and then Segal heard the sound of the refrigerator opening. "Milk in your coffee?" she asked. Segal told her yes. "How are you doing with the investigation?" she called out.

Segal thought she was trying to sound nonchalant, but the attempt was not very successful. There was something there below the surface. He knew from experience that grief came and went in waves. She was holding it together now, but he wondered how she would do when he started asking questions that would bring her attention back to her dead husband and the details of his last days and hours.

"It's ongoing," he said. "I actually came here to see if I could get some more information." He continued his examination of the art in the living room, feeling like he was touring an exhibition in a museum. He stopped in front of a photograph of a younger Julius and Margery in hiking clothes, Mount Pisgah in the background.

"That must have been taken fifteen years ago," Margery said. She had come up behind him and when he turned she handed him the cup. He took it and they both took careful first sips. Segal sat on the couch when she motioned him in that direction and set the cup on a coffee table.

"What I want to ask you about this morning is your husband's financial and investment activities, especially with regard to real estate." Segal withdrew a pen and a small moleskin notebook from his pocket as he said this.

Margery had just taken in a mouthful of coffee, and Segal thought she might just spit it back out when she heard the question.

She put the cup down and found a napkin to pat her mouth, laughing as she did so.

"I'm sorry, Lieutenant," she said, "but the thought of Jules going around wheeling and dealing in stocks and bonds and real estate or anything like that is pretty rich."

Now that the danger of spewing coffee all over the place had passed she took another smaller sip, smiled, and shook her head.

"It's not that he didn't have money," she continued. "He and his sister inherited a pretty good chunk from their parents. Not jet set kind of money, but a healthy chunk. And then Jules always made a good income from his work. Even back before he had a lot of recognition he just worked so hard and seemed to always have some kind of income flowing, graphic design, anything it took. He wanted his work going out and money coming in."

She paused to take another drink of coffee. From the look on her face Segal could see that the question had transported her back to happier days.

"So were you the money manager of the family then?" Segal asked.

"I was always the one who paid the bills and balanced the check book. That's about as far as I went. When it came to investments and things like that Jules had a financial guy who handled all of that stuff. Jules had zero interest in any of it. He would just glance at the statements once a month and then say something like, guess we're doing all right, and that was it."

"Do you have the name of the money manager?" Segal asked.

"It was someone his sister put him on to. Someone downtown," she said as she put the coffee down and got up. She walked into the next room where Segal could see her rummaging around an old wooden desk, moving papers around on the top and opening and closing a few drawers. Apparently she didn't find what she was looking for there, so she moved her attention to an olive drab filing cabinet standing beside it. She pulled out a file folder, plopped it onto the desk, and opened it.

She picked up the first paper she came to and said, "Here it is, last month's statement. Tectonic Shift Financial Planning, Adrien Koll."

She brought the paper over and handed it to Segal who was experiencing the sensation of a puzzle piece sliding into place. He knew there had to be some link between the two murder victims and here it was.

"Have you ever met Adrien Koll?" he asked.

"Koll?" Margery said. "I did meet Adrien Koll once. He commissioned the Joan of Arc Postmodern painting, but I never realized he was with the investment company. He said the painting was for the meeting room of some club he's with. Pretty sweet offer, I thought, but after a while Jules got mad at him for some reason.

"Wait, you're saying Adrien Koll commissioned the painting? Was this common knowledge? Did the Marks brothers know?"

"I wouldn't say it was common knowledge even now. A week or so ago the Marks brothers found out about it. They had met Koll and they didn't like him much, so they were concerned. At least Henry Marks and Mark Morrison were. I don't know about the kid, Engel."

"Did your husband meet with Koll very often?"

Margery thought for a moment. "Not that I know of, but they could have met at the studio. I mean that would probably be the most natural place for them to meet since that was where Jules was most of the time and that was where the painting was."

Segal nodded. Made sense. That would be his next destination.

"Would you mind if I took this to make a copy?" he said, holding up the monthly statement. "I'll get it back to you."

Margery made a hand gesture showing her consent, like she was brushing the paper away.

Segal got up and took a step toward the door.

"Thank you, Mrs. Hargrove. I know this is not an easy time for you," he said.

She shrugged. "Fortunately, I have friends that are helping me through it."

As if on cue, Segal heard the footsteps of someone descending the stairway. The footsteps stopped at a landing and Segal found himself looking face to face with Henry Marks. Henry was wearing a bath robe too, only his was thread bare and faded blue in color. It took him a second to fully open his eyes and realize that Margery was not alone in the room below. When he did meet Segal's eye he looked down and said nothing.

Segal looked back to Margery who gave him a sheepish smile.

"We'll be in touch," Segal said and made his exit without further comment.

As HE DROVE to the studio in the River Arts District, Segal ran possible scenarios in his mind.

Hargrove finds out that Koll is using his name and his money in some kind of illegal real estate dealings and threatens to publicize it? Koll kills him, but then who kills Koll?

Hargrove kills Koll because he finds out Koll got him mixed up in this stuff, but then who kills Hargrove?

Maybe there's another person, call him person X. X is in on the dirty dealings too, maybe even the one in charge. Something has gone wrong with the deal and he needs to eliminate anyone who knew too much.

And how does this insurance guy, Belincort, fit in? He could be in it as an investor or as an insurer of the property, but in either case, he would probably be in a position to know what was going on. He could fit in to the player X theory, too. We need him in an interrogation room sooner rather than later.

And what about Henry Marks and Margery Hargrove? Probably had nothing to do with the crime, but you couldn't eliminate it, not yet: love triangle and all. On the other hand, it could support Henry's alibi; that he didn't come home from the party the night Hargrove was killed.

There's something here, but we just don't have enough of the picture yet, Segal thought as he pulled up to the studio building.

He put the key in the lock to Hargrove's studio but before he could pull the door open someone called his name. It was Mark Morrison, the red-haired apprentice.

"Lieutenant," he said. "I was hoping it was you. I've been working next door and I need something from the main studio. I was hoping you could let me come in and get it."

"I guess it depends on what you want," Segal said with reluctance, but he nodded his head toward the door and said, "Come on in."

"Thanks, Lieutenant, I just need some rabbit skin glue. We made a batch of it and we haven't put it in smaller jars yet." He proceeded to a work bench on the right-hand wall and picked up a white plastic container, about a gallon capacity. He brought it over to Segal to show him.

"Rabbit skin glue?" Segal said. He was looking at a gelatinous off-white mass, a little like custard.

"Yeah, we use it to prepare a canvas before painting, among other things," Morrison explained.

"And is it really made out of...?"

"Real rabbit skin? Yeah, it really is. You can make it from other animal hides, but the old man was very strict. Not my favorite preparation job, but if you want to stick to the authentic renaissance techniques, it's the only thing to use," Morrison explained, and gave Segal a grin. He had clearly been asked that question before.

"Sounds like a messy process," Segal said. He visualized killing a creature and pulling off the bloody hide and then boiling the thing down followed by some kind of messy, smelly process to separate collagen or whatever constituted the basis of the glue.

"You got that right," Morrison said. "Fortunately, I don't have to do that anymore. That job, at least the messiest part, is traditionally assigned to the most junior apprentice."

"In this case, the most junior being Mark Engel," Segal said.

Morrison grinned and nodded. "He doesn't seem to mind though. He set up to do it out at his dad's place near the Forks of Ivy, out in a barn so he doesn't have to stink this place up."

Segal took another doubtful look at the stuff and then nodded. "I guess it's all right. You can take it."

Morrison took a step toward the door. But Segal held him up.

"Before you go, is there any place in the studio that Hargrove kept papers? Business papers?"

Morrison pointed to a desk on the other side of the room. "You might find something over there, but I think he kept most of that sort of thing at home."

Segal nodded, then asked, "Where is Mark Engel? Is he here too?"

Morrison got a funny look on his face. He hesitated as if trying to decide how to answer the question. "No, he's not here. I haven't seen him for a couple of days. He might have gone out to his dad's place to get away from all this. He's done that before."

Segal raised his eyebrows and Morrison continued, "He's taking this all pretty hard. You know, he lost his father about a year ago, and had a bunch of hassles dealing with the estate. We all liked Jules, but Mark idolized him. Maybe Jules kind of filled in for his father. He probably needs some time to himself."

Segal nodded. "Good to know," he said. "If you see him remind him I still need to talk to him again. I'll probably need to talk to all three of you again."

Morrison nodded his mop of red hair. "You know where to find me. I'm not too sure where Henry is right now."

Segal looked at him and tried to gauge the truthfulness of that statement and couldn't tell. But then, he supposed, ratting out your friend for sleeping with your boss's wife wasn't something he would expect most guys to do.

"By the way, I heard you and Jules had an argument a few days before he died. What was that all about?"

"Who told you that?" Morrison spat out. The flash of anger took Segal by surprise. Morrison seemed to realize his overreaction and calmed himself down. "He waited until I was done with a painting and then told me the perspective was off."

Segal gave him a questioning look.

Morrison took a deep breath and explained. "He could have corrected me when I first showed him the drawing of the scene, but instead he waited until I put all the time into the painting to bring it up."

Segal let it hang there for a minute, but Morrison just looked down. "What are you guys going to do now that Hargrove is gone?" Segal asked.

"I've got a couple of projects to finish up here. After that, I don't know. Henry is trying to find the people who offered to pay for the Joan of Arc painting to see if we could make some bucks finishing it up for them."

Segal nodded and Morrison took off. Segal went to the desk, which looked like an antique, maybe Civil War time period. He could well imagine it standing in Lincoln's law office in Springfield. He folded down the cover, seeing that it formed part of the writing surface and also exposed a number of slots in the back which could hold letters, papers, and any number of objects. In front of those slots was a pile of papers. Segal leafed through them finding mostly bills, requests for donations, and offers from credit card companies. Beside the stack was a brass protractor, stainless-steel ruler, and a magnifying glass that looked like it came off the cover of a Sherlock Holmes book. The slots themselves held a number of notes and objects, but nothing that looked relevant to the case.

Folding the cover/writing surface back up he took another look at the structure of the desk. He noticed a single shallow drawer just under the hinge of the lid. Inside it he found a manila file folder containing a number of monthly reports on Hargrove's investment portfolio at Tectonic Plate Investments. Quickly leafing through, he saw that the file went back over at least two years, so it should provide Walter with everything he needed to analyze the situation.

He tucked the folder under his arm and headed out. In the hallway, he took out his phone and switched it off silent mode. He had silenced it earlier as he generally did before an interview. He saw that he had missed a couple of calls, one from Gina and one from a number he did not recognize. He called Gina back.

"Hey, Segal," she said. "We got a call from a Doctor May at the hospital. She tried to call you earlier. She asked if you could stop by the emergency room. She's there for another hour or so. She sounded a little upset."

WHEN HE GOT to the hospital Dr. Tina May was still in her scrubs, but she had traded her white lab coat for a light sweater. Her shift had ended, and she was ready to go. She was talking to one of the admitting nurses but looked up when he walked through the door of the ER. A look of relief filled her face.

"Good to see you," she said. She came around the desk and looked at him for a moment as if trying to decide how to proceed.

"I'm just getting off my shift, maybe we could talk outside."

Segal motioned her ahead and she went through the door. He glanced back at the admitting nurse who watched with unconcealed interest. He followed Tina May outside and they found a bench and sat down.

"Listen," Segal said, "Before we get started, I want to say I'm sorry about the roller derby thing, about leaving in the middle of it."

Tina lowered her eyes and smiled. "It's sweet of you to say that, but you really don't have to apologize. Believe me, I know something about dealing with emergencies." She nodded her head back at the hospital.

"Maybe, when we get through this case, we could…"

Tina nodded and smiled.

There was a moment of awkward silence and then she spoke. "I have some news for you about your patient, Mr. Belincort."

"How's he doing?" Segal asked.

"Last time I saw him, much better. We got the results back on his blood work. For one thing, the electrolytes were all out of whack. That was no surprise since he was dehydrated. The lab also found traces of sedatives in his blood."

"That was expected, too. Right?" Segal asked.

"We expected to find sedatives, yes, but it was the particular ones that we found that were surprising. We found traces of ether and scopolamine."

Segal wrinkled his brow. "Ether used to be used to knock people out for operations, didn't it?"

"Yes," Tina said. "Used to be is right. No one uses it anymore because we have much more reliable drugs with fewer side effects."

"What about the other one, scopolamine? I never heard of that one."

"That's another kind of old-fashioned drug. It used to be one of the drugs given to women for childbirth. They gave it to help deal with the pain and anxiety, but it also has the side effect of inducing amnesia. Your guy is likely to not remember much about recent events."

Segal took out his notebook and wrote down the names of the drugs.

"Maybe I should go in and question him now to see what he does remember."

Tina shook her head. "That's the other thing I wanted to tell you about. He's not here anymore. Two men came for him and checked him out. One was a big State Trooper."

"Let me guess," Segal said. "The other was a thin creepy little guy in a gray suit."

Tina nodded. "He said they were from the governor's office." She handed Segal a card.

"J. Davenport, chief of staff," Segal read aloud.

SEGAL AND WALTER were in the chief's office. They had just brought him up to speed on the case, including the crazy real estate deals and the governor's office springing Belincort before he could be questioned further. Segal thought their next move should be to go up to the Western Residence and demand an explanation from the governor.

The chief sat back and thought for a moment, then shook his head.

"Let me put out some feelers. See if I can figure out what's going on before we go charging in."

"I know where I'd like to put some feelers," Segal said.

"That's exactly why I don't want you going up there," the chief said.

Segal started to protest, but the chief held up his hand. "Let me remind you, Segal, that the governor has the power to take this whole investigation out of our hands and give it to the SBI if he wants. Then we may never know what's going on."

Segal sat back, still fuming, but knowing his boss was right.

"It sounds like you guys have plenty to follow up on in the meantime. Let me see what I can find out."

When they left the chief's office Walter let Segal stew for a couple of minutes. Walter picked up the folder of financial statements Segal had given him and said, "I guess I could go through these, but I don't really feel like it right now."

Segal was quiet for a couple of seconds, still deciding what he should do next. He turned to Walter and asked, "Feel like taking a ride?"

"Sure. Where we going?"

"Ever been to the Forks of Ivy?"

FIFTEEN

The Forks of Ivy

SEGAL AND WALTER pulled off the highway at an exit called The Forks of Ivy. There was so little evidence of human activity that it was difficult to see why an exit ramp had been built there at all.

"Maybe one of those, if you build it they will come, kind of scenarios," Segal suggested when Walter made a comment to that effect.

"Doesn't look like they've come yet," Walter said and punctuated it with one of his little snorting laughs.

Segal drove on, allowing his path to be guided by the directions from the app on his phone. It was a two-lane road that twisted and turned so much that it was easy to totally lose orientation. They crossed a bridge and saw a creek below which Segal presumed to be Ivy creek that gave this place its name. They turned and for a while the road followed the stream.

After a few minutes the mechanical female voice of the app said, "In two hundred feet your destination will be on the left."

"She always knows," said Walter.

"You have arrived at your destination," the app said.

"I always feel proud when she says that," Segal said.

"She makes it sound like such an accomplishment. We have arrived."

He turned onto the gravel and dirt driveway and stopped for a moment to take it in. To the left of the drive and ahead thirty yards or so was a modest old farmhouse. It was painted white with green trim and shutters. Its roof was steep by modern standards and was clad in slate. Segal put its age at a hundred years or older. It seemed reasonably well cared for although the sparse lawn needed mowing. The driveway continued past the house and then bent around behind it. They could just make out a couple of outbuildings and an old silo. An old Chevy van was parked in front of the first building. Segal let the car roll forward and pulled up beside it.

When they got out Segal could hear a rhythmic pounding sound coming through the open door of the barn. They approached the doorway where they could see into the room. He recognized what he saw inside very well since he had grown up in the country himself. This was the repair shop you found on every farm since there was so much equipment and the equipment was always breaking down. The floor was of rough boards, stained from years of use and oil spills but otherwise it was swept surprisingly clean. Two walls of the shop were lined with work benches and a third with shelves. There was the usual equipment, a couple of vices, a drill press, a welder, and boxes of tools. There was even a small forge and an anvil which appeared to be very old indeed. Just the kind of place you could deal with all the usual problems of the heavy farm equipment.

In the depth of the shop Mark Engel stood with his back to them. He had a pair of headphones on and he was pounding a pipe up and down in a five gallon bucket. Something about the way he held his head to one side made him look fragile and vulnerable, or so Segal thought. The acrid smell of black walnut husks filled the air. It was clear that he was completely oblivious to their presence, and Segal stood for a moment trying to figure out how to get his attention without scaring the shit out of him. Before he could figure that out Engel turned toward them, and jumped back.

Segal raised his hands and said, "Sorry about that."

Mark Engel exhaled in relief, took the headphones off, and pulled out his phone to stop whatever it was he had been listening to. Segal could hear a faint sound of music coming from the head phones. *Reggae*.

"It's all right. We don't get many visitors out here these days. I mean, I don't," he said.

"That's right, I heard your dad passed away recently," Segal said. "Was it just you and your dad living here?"

Engel looked down and nodded. "For the last few years, yes. My mother has been gone almost ten. I got an apartment in Asheville when I started working with Jules and taking classes at UNCA, but there are some things it's better to do out here."

"What you making?" Walter asked. He had walked on over to the five-gallon bucket and looked at the mashed up brown mess inside.

Engel turned toward him, apparently glad to get off the subject of his family.

"Ink," he said. "I'm making walnut ink."

Segal could remember ruining a pair of jeans and a shirt when he was a kid with the brown stains from walnut husks. "How do you make walnut ink?" he asked.

"It's pretty easy," Engel explained. "You just mash up a bunch of walnut husks and simmer them in water for a while. Then you filter the solids out and maybe evaporate some of the water off if you need to make it more concentrated. Add a little alcohol to help preserve it, and you're all set."

"Is this one of the messy jobs they give the low man on the totem pole, like making the rabbit skin glue?" Walter asked. Segal knew he was really asking if Mark Engel resented his status in the group.

Engel seemed to understand that. "I don't mind. It's all part of the tradition. Jules said it's never a good idea for an artist to be too far from the materials he works with. It's part of the training."

Segal noticed a propane burner and cooking stand out the back door which presumably is where he simmered the ink as well as rabbit hides for glue.

Every time Engel referred to Julius Hargrove, Segal could sense the reverence in his voice. It must be true, what they heard, that Engel idolized him, or at least he had.

"We had a few more questions for you," Segal said. "First of all, let's go over the night Jules died."

A shadow came over Engel's face. This was much more difficult to talk about than how to make walnut ink.

"You said you had dinner with some friends?" Segal asked.

"That's right," Engel said. "Sort of a group meeting."

"I assume there are people there who could confirm that," Walter said.

Engel nodded, but looked uneasy. He pulled out his phone and looked up a couple names and numbers and Walter noted them down.

"And this was what time?" Segal asked.

"Six to seven o'clock, something like that."

"And you went straight to the party at Hargrove's house after that?" Segal continued.

Engel nodded.

"When I questioned you and the other apprentices before, Mark Morrison said he and Henry Marks were at the party. He didn't mention you."

"I wasn't there long," Engel said.

"Why not? Sounds like it was a pretty good party if the other guys stayed there all night." Segal said.

Engel said nothing and looked around the shop as if he might find something there to help him out.

"Let me guess," Walter said. "You were looking for Jody Mare, and when you found out that neither she nor Julius Hargrove were there you left."

Engel looked surprised at first and then he just nodded. Segal thought, and not for the first time, about how good Walter was at seeing through the fog of things and spotting the shining flicker of truth.

"Did you see Mrs. Hargrove there?" Segal asked.

"I looked for her. I at least wanted to speak to her and to let her know that I didn't just ignore her invitation. I looked all over, but I couldn't find her, so I left."

"And you didn't speak to the other apprentices either?" Segal asked.

"I didn't see Henry at all. I saw Mark Morrison across the room, but he was in a big serious conversation with a girl, so I didn't want to interrupt," Engel explained. "Then by the time I was going to leave, I couldn't find him either."

Segal paused for a moment. What Engel told them seemed plausible enough: plausible and interesting since it called into question the alibis for Henry Marks and Margery Hargrove. Maybe they weren't at the party the whole time after all.

"When you came to the studio after you left the party, were you hoping Jody would be there?" Walter asked.

"I thought maybe that's why she wasn't at the party, maybe she and Jules were working there."

"And were they?" Segal asked.

"I guess so. I could tell there was a light on in the main studio, Jules's studio, but when I tried the door it was locked. He doesn't usually do that unless he wants to be left alone, so I left him alone. I went to our studio and did a little work."

"Did you hear any sounds coming from the room, either when you were standing outside the door or when you were in your studio?" Segal asked.

"I could hear some low music. Jules liked music on when he worked. And I heard talking, but not enough to hear what they were saying. And I heard Jody laugh."

"You're sure it was Jody Mare?" Walter asked.

"Yeah, she has a unique laugh. You don't forget it."

"And after that, did you hear anything else? No sounds of a struggle or anything?"

"No, nothing like that. I was kind of listening for the door when I was in my studio. They must have left very quietly because I didn't hear the door and when I left around nine the light was off."

And by that time Julius Hargrove was dead, Segal thought.

After that they walked outside. Segal took in the pastoral scene, farmhouse, field, forest and mountains in the distance.

"Are you planning on holding onto this property, keep it in the family?" he asked.

"I'm trying to but it looks like I'll probably need to sell. My father ran up a lot of medical bills in the last year of his life. I spent half my time in the hospital and the other half with the insurance company. It looks like the insurance company isn't covering what we thought they would. That, and he lost money on some investments." These words were spit out, and it was clear his mood had taken a sudden turn from contrite to angry. "It's ironic since my dad was a country doctor himself. He just did a little farming on the side as a hobby. He inherited this place from his father. Seemed like half the medical work he did was for free, then to be pretty much ruined when he got sick himself," he added.

"Too bad," Segal said. "It's a nice place." He looked at Mark Engel who was gazing out at the property, too. This was clearly another loss that he was feeling, and Segal was sorry he brought the subject up. What Engel had said about the insurance company was a story he had heard many times before, including how his cousin's health insurance was or was not covering Tommy's issues. Lots of fine print in those contracts. He couldn't help but feel sorry for the kid. It was a lot to deal with, especially for someone his age.

SEGAL AND WALTER drove back toward Asheville in silence at first.

After a while Walter said, "Just when you think you know where everybody was, they all start moving around on you."

"Yeah. We had Jody Mare gone from the studio before time of death, now it looks like she could have been there. And we got Henry Marks and Margery making a love triangle and they may or may not have been at the party when our man was crossbowed to death," Segal said in disgust.

"And the same for Mark Morrison," Walter said.

Segal's phone sounded. He handed it to Walter to answer.

Walter answered and said, "Yeah? Yeah? No shit...we'll be there ASAP." He hung up.

Segal looked at him and Walter said, "Montford Avenue."

SIXTEEN

White Duck Taco

OFFICER DINAH RUDISILL pulled her cruiser over to the White Duck Taco on Riverside Drive. She was hungry and she was by herself. Today it suited her: being alone. She knew about the theory of how different people built up their energy. An introvert needed to be alone to recharge her batteries. An extrovert needed to get energy from other people. This description did not help with her self-analysis. Sometimes she needed the energy of other people, sometimes she needed to be alone. What did that make her, fifty-fifty? Felt kind of wimpy, like she was afraid to take a stand. Right now sitting down alone and not needing to talk to anyone felt like a relief.

That, and she was really hungry. She had worked out early in the morning, come on shift at eight. It was now noon and all she had taken in was a cup of yogurt and a couple coffees. She walked into the building that looked like a Quonset hut and checked out the menu. She chose the Bangkok Shrimp Tacos, nachos, and a cola, got her tray, walked out, and settled down on one of the picnic tables by the river.

The first bite of the taco was amazing: just what she needed. She gazed out at the river, alternating bites of taco and sips of cola and the occasional nacho for good measure.

She ate faster than she would have in polite company. She was thinking about that artist's studio, and the puzzle of how he was killed, why he was killed, and especially why he was killed in that particular way.

It was intriguing. She was thinking about Segal, too. There was something different about him—a more open and direct way of being than most cops possessed. Word around the station was he was super smart, if a little odd, but since she was new to this area, looking for a direction and learning the ropes, she thought this could be an interesting direction to go. She had seen all she needed to see of macho men in the army. Plus, he was good looking without the attitude that most good-looking guys revealed. Also, there was none of the artificial distance that a lot of the senior officers cultivate. She found him both open and mysterious at the same time.

She suddenly realized she was through the taco and most of the nachos as well. So good. Her mind wandered back to the coconut macaroon pie with salted caramel topping she had seen on the menu board, but before she could reach a decision, her radio came to life.

"Officer Rudisill. Dinah, come in. Over."

"Rudisill here," she answered.

"Please answer a call on Montford Avenue," the dispatcher said, and gave her the address as well. The number sounded familiar.

"What have we got there? Over."

"Incident with a Miss Jody Mare," the dispatcher said. After a brief pause filled with static she added, "She asked for you by name, Dinah."

MONTFORD AVENUE FORMED the heart of a neighborhood that had gone through a rebirth in the past few years. It was filled with Arts and Craft style houses dating from the early nineteen hundreds when they had been built by the same craftsmen who had created the Biltmore estate. It accommodated a cross section of society, the size of houses ranging from small cottages to large mansions and even a handful of medium-size apartment buildings. Like most cities, Asheville had seen a period in the midcentury when many people moved to the suburbs leaving places like Montford Avenue to deteriorate from neglect. Recently, some of the more astute buyers found they could obtain these architectural gems for next to nothing, put some money and sweat into them, and end up with a really special place.

When Dinah pulled up to the house she could see Jody sitting in a swing on the wide front porch. Dinah took it all in, thinking how pleasant it was. Porch and swing. Oak tree in the yard. She had spent the last few years in college dorms, then army barracks, then tents overseas. Now she stayed in a little one-bedroom apartment, part of a cheap modern complex, the main material of construction being particle board.

Jody stopped swinging and came over to wait for her at the top of the porch stairs. The way she was standing with most of her weight on one leg made Dinah think of the pose of Joan of Arc in the unfinished painting in the studio of Julius Hargrove. However, right now her face didn't show that radiant confidence. She looked like she had been crying.

Dinah climbed the stairs to the porch and stood beside her, waiting a moment for Jody to tell her why she called.

"You OK?" Dinah asked.

Jody looked at her a moment then shook her head no and started to cry. Instinctively, Dinah gave her a hug. She held her for a moment until she could feel Jody's body relax and then backed away a step.

"I've been robbed," Jody said, "someone broke into my room."

"Show me," Dinah said.

Jody led her through the screen door into a large living room.

"Is this all yours?" Dinah asked. She couldn't help but continue the comparison to her own lifeless place. The room was neat and clean and had a homey comfortable vibe to it.

"We share this," Jody said, "my housemates and me. This and the kitchen. There's no one in the second-floor room right now, we're kind of between housemates since the last one moved out."

She led Dinah on through the living room and into a hall on the right. They passed a wide doorway that led to the kitchen which took up most of the back of the house. It looked like heaven to Dinah. Down the hall were two doors. The one to the right, Jody said, led to one of the other bedrooms, the one to the left led to hers.

They entered Jody's room. Dinah stopped just inside and checked it out carefully. The bed was unmade. She saw a desk and a chest of drawers, both with most of the drawers pulled open. On the other end of the room was a closet with the sliding door also open: clothes and shoes strewn in front of it, boxes on the floor where they had apparently been thrown after clearing them off the top shelf. To the right Dinah saw a door.

"Where does that lead?" she asked.

"To a screened-in porch," Jody said. She opened the door and led Dinah out.

The porch was not very wide. A few pieces of wicker furniture faced out over a shaded yard. There was a flimsy screen door leading to the back yard that would have been little barrier to entry. Dinah examined the outside of the wooden door which led back into Jody's room. Marks from a crowbar were clearly visible.

She nudged the door back open with her elbow. "Don't touch the door knob until we have it checked for finger prints," she told Jody.

"Have you figured out what's missing?" she asked Jody when they were back inside.

Jody sat down in the chair by the desk. She retrieved a large portfolio from a niche between the desk and the book-case and opened it on her lap. It contained a stack of draw-ings done on different sizes and weights of paper.

"Is this your work?" Dinah asked, drawing near for a better look.

"Some of it is, but mostly its drawings that other artists have given me," she said. "When I came in earlier this was laying open on the bed and some of the drawings were gone."

"Do you remember which ones specifically?" Dinah asked.

"They took anything that was drawn by Jules and a few by the Marks brothers, too," she said. "They can draw so much like Jules sometimes it's hard to tell them apart, at least in the rough sketches, which is what all of these were."

"And that's all that's missing, just these drawings?" Dinah asked.

"As far as I can tell. I don't have a bunch of money or jewelry or anything like that."

Dinah looked around the room again at the mess the thief had made. There was a laptop on the desk. If it were a crack head looking for something to pawn that would be gone for sure. If the thief was looking specifically for those sketches, why tear up the rest of the room?

"Those drawings, the missing ones, did they have any-thing to do with the Joan of Arc painting?" she asked.

"No, but Jules did give me a few that do," Jody said. "He told me to keep them under wraps until the painting was done."

"Are they here?" Dinah asked.

Jody led her back to the front room where she opened a backpack and pulled out a sketch book. She opened the book and there, pressed between the pages, were three small sketches done in sanguine chalk. To Dinah they looked much like some of the drawings she had seen in Hargrove's studio.

"I had the backpack with me," Jody said.

Dinah keyed her radio mic, and when the call was picked up she said, "I need to talk to Lieutenant Segal."

TWENTY MINUTES LATER Segal and Walter pulled up. Dinah and Jody were back on the front porch, Jody in the swing and Dinah sitting in a rocking chair writing in her notebook.

"You look right at home here, Officer Rudisill," Segal said.

"I wish," Dinah answered looking around again at the porch and the rest of it, "it's a lot nicer than the place I'm living." She proceeded to give Segal and Walter a quick rundown on what she had learned as she and Jody showed them the room. She knew that ordinarily they would not send an evidence team out on a case of petty theft, but this was clearly an exception, considering the possible tie-in to the murder investigation.

Segal took Dinah aside. "You said you had seen something specific that you thought could be relevant to the murder."

She took Segal to the living room where Dinah had left her backpack. She withdrew the book and showed him the sketches pressed inside.

"Holy crap," Segal said under his breath. He laid them out side by side on the coffee table in front of the couch and sat down to study them. "Walter, come in here and take a look at this," he called. Walter and Jody both came in.

"It seems to belong with the Joan of Arc painting," Walter said, "but it's hard to tell what they mean."

They all looked at them a moment longer and then Segal reached down and rearranged the sequence and pushed them together. They all crowded around and looked in silence.

Viewed in this way they showed a scene which told a story. There was a figure with horns, cloven hooves, and a tail ending in a trident. Clearly a depiction of the devil. He was handing a handful of coins to another figure who looked over his shoulder as if checking to make sure no one was around to see. A third smaller figure watched the transaction with a smile and hands clasped together. It was clear that the man receiving the payoff had the face of Governor Price and the smarmy little figure watching them was Davenport.

Walter got on his phone to arrange for the forensic team to come. Meanwhile, Segal continued to look at the sketches.

"Do you mind if I take these to make copies?" Segal asked.

Jody nodded. "If you think it might have something to do with Jules' death, I'm probably safer without them, at least for now." She went back to her room to get him a folder to protect the sketches.

Segal and Walter walked out onto the porch and Dinah followed.

"Good work," Segal said to her. "Do you think you could hang out with Miss Mare until forensics gets here? That way Walter and I can get back to the station and get to work on some other leads."

Dinah smiled and said, "Sure."

He and Walter headed down the stairs, but on the sidewalk he turned and said, "And send me a copy of your report."

She gave him the thumbs up. She and Jody sat on the porch swing to wait for the forensic team. They pushed against the floor with their feet to make the swing go back, then released to let it glide on its own.

After a couple of swings with only the creaking of the chains to be heard, Dinah asked, "So how much would it cost to rent that room upstairs?"

"SO THAT'S INTERESTING," Walter said when they were back in the car. He had the folder with the sketches in his lap, looking at them again.

"Yeah, it means we know for sure someone was willing to commit an act of breaking and entering to get those sketches. Presumably, the motive would be to keep the contents from becoming public. And what you're wondering is, would the same people be willing to kill Julius Hargrove?" Segal said.

"Yeah, and I'm also wondering what exactly the sketches refer to?" Walter asked, scratching the back of his head. "I mean Hargrove obviously thought something evil was going on with the governor, probably something that involved money, but what exactly would that be? If it had something to do with the weird real estate deal, then it looks like Hargrove was right in the middle of it himself, so why would he expose it in the painting? And for that matter why use the painting to expose it at all? If he thought or knew something unscrupulous was going on, why include it in a perfectly good painting. Why not just report it? I don't get it."

"He wouldn't be the first artist to sneak messages into his paintings. The guys at the wine bar told me all kinds of stories about painters. Like this artist, Guido Reni. He was commissioned to do a painting of the archangel, Michael, crushing Satan. He was offended by a Capuchin cardinal, so he put the cardinal's face on Satan in the painting. At least people thought that's who it was. The painter couldn't come right out and accuse the cardinal of anything. He would never have another commission if he did. What he could do was drop this little hint and let people speculate about it on their own. Maybe Hargrove was doing something like that," Segal said.

"I don't like where this is headed," Walter said. "Too close to the governor's office and that is some dangerous ground."

"I told you what Margery Hargrove said when I asked her about Julius's finances. She said he didn't pay any attention to his investments. They were all managed by Tectonic Shift Financial Planning. As long as he could put his card in an ATM and get a few bucks out he was a happy man. So that could explain some of it. Maybe he didn't know he was part of a squirrelly deal until it was too late."

They fell silent for a minute.

"I wonder, are there ATMs in heaven?" Walter mused. After a couple of beats he realized that Segal had not started the car yet. Segal just sat at the wheel and stared forward, his keys in his hand. Walter cleared his throat. "We taking off, Segal?"

Segal snapped out of his trance and started the car. "I was just trying to put the pieces together," he said. "I was also thinking there's no particular reason to believe this guy is done killing people."

"Could be time to divide and conquer for a while," Walter said.

"Maybe."

"I'm thinking that the financial angle is looking more and more important. If we're going to have to go after some powerful people we had better understand exactly what was going on. Suppose I take the financial mess for a while."

"Yes. You can get with Gina, she looked up the documents I showed you, and you could get some help from Joe Adamski," Segal added.

Walter gave a little laugh. "Oh, man. He's gonna love this shit."

Segal knew that Joe Adamski, the accountant assigned to the police department, relished the few times he was asked to help them out with financial details of a case. It gave him a break from expense accounts and invoices and the other routine elements of his job.

"That leaves me time to check in again with some of the other players. I want to talk to Margery Hargrove some more and the other Marks brothers as well," Segal said.

"And maybe Alexa Price, too," Walter said. "Seemed to me she wants to talk to you, like there's something she wants to tell you but she just hasn't opened up yet."

Segal gave Walter a look and said, "That one I'll have to think about, but I'm going to have to talk to her sooner or later. You're not worried about the flying monkey thing?"

"Just be on your guard."

Segal's phone buzzed for a message. Walter picked it up for him. "Says here, *May 27, 1917, Vincent Price was born*," he read.

"I've got to get rid of that history app," Segal muttered. "It's always sending messages at the worst times."

Walter snorted and scratched the back of his head. "Old Vincent would have fit in perfectly in Asheville," he said.

Segal put his key in the ignition but before he could turn it, his phone sounded. Walter noticed it was from a lady they both knew in Social Services. Walter closed his eyes, knowing it was not good news, and certainly not the kind of distraction Segal needed in the middle of a case like this. Tommy must have been in some kind of trouble again.

He listened while Segal made sounds of acknowledgment and asked a couple of short questions and ended by saying, "OK, I'll be there in fifteen."

Segal started the engine and pulled away from the curb. "I'll drop you at the station and then see if I can get this straightened out."

"It's OK," Walter said. "Don't worry about it. I'll dig into the financial mess and you do what you need to do."

Segal nodded and drove on.

SEVENTEEN

Capulet's Tomb

SEGAL PARKED HIS car at the station. Walter went in, but Segal walked over to Pack Square where the social worker suggested they meet. It would be better than having Tommy hanging around the social services office or the police station, she said. Better for Tommy and better for the people who worked in the offices, too.

He saw them sitting on one of the benches as soon as he rounded the corner, Tommy and the social worker. This was not their first meeting. He knew the social worker. He judged she was around sixty, but she dressed in a younger fashion which was something he always admired about her. She had a calming way about her that helped de-escalate situations like this. A lot of people barked out orders. Yelling at Tommy when he was wound up only confused and frustrated him more. It was like spraying gasoline on a camp fire.

Segal could tell at a glance that Tommy had backed away from that emotional tipping point that could lead to the worst of the scenes he was capable of. His attention seemed to be fixed on a hot dog vender who had his cart set up about half a block away.

Tommy turned when Segal approached and his face

broke into a big grin. He stood up and gave Segal a hug, hanging on just a little too long. It gave Segal a chance to face the social worker over Tommy's shoulder and mouth the words, "Thank you."

When Tommy released him, Segal pulled out his wallet and gave him a little money. He said, "Why don't you go over and get us a couple of hot dogs and something to drink." He motioned to the social worker to see if she wanted anything but she declined.

As soon as Tommy stepped away Segal sat beside her on the bench.

"Tell me what he's been up to," Segal said.

The social worker smiled and exhaled slowly. "The station got a call from the grounds keepers over at River Side Cemetery. Some people complained about a guy acting strangely. I don't think he did anything too outrageous, but they said he just didn't seem right. When the patrol officers got there he told them he was looking for the crypt of the Capulets. I guess they had met Tommy before so they persuaded him to come and see us before anything else developed."

Segal bowed his head and exhaled. "*Romeo and Juliet*," he said. Giving Tommy that paperback was looking more and more like a huge mistake.

"Yes," the social worker said. "And you remember what happens when Romeo goes into the tomb."

Segal nodded.

"That's what I'm worried about."

"I don't think Tommy would ever purposely hurt himself."

The social worker looked at him now more with pity than anything else. "He told me he went to see his girlfriend, a waitress over in West Asheville, but she wasn't there. He was afraid she had died. I called the place she worked and they said she just had the day off. And they said she was definitely not Tommy's girlfriend. I'm afraid he is becoming delusional."

"I still don't think he would hurt himself."

"You don't know that for sure, Segal. You really don't," she said, almost in a whisper. "When you and his mom are ready, see me and we can talk about some options."

Segal sat back and faced forward, looking away from her, perhaps away from the truth. He tried to imagine himself having that conversation with his cousin. He couldn't do it. He couldn't pull up a convincing mental image of it and he couldn't summon the words he would use either.

He looked over at Tommy. Tommy had the hotdogs and was in the process of accepting change back from the vender. He put the change in his pocket and picked up the drinks as well. He headed back to the bench, bringing all of it with him. He looked so happy in that moment. It was almost impossible to believe he could be so troubled at times.

The social worker rose as Tommy approached. "I will leave you gentlemen to your gourmet meal," she said.

"Thanks again," Segal said. He reached out and held her hand for a moment.

"Think about it, Segal," she said, and then she was gone.

Segal turned back to Tommy who had devoured half the dog already.

"So you were looking for Capulet's tomb, huh?"

Tommy smiled and nodded.

"And what were you going to do if you found it?" Segal asked.

Tommy just smiled and looked blank, like the question didn't make any sense.

"I wasn't going to do anything. I was just looking for it to make the story, you know, more real."

Segal gave a laugh. Suddenly the darkness of the moment passed.

"You're a knucklehead, you know that?" Segal said, and he gave Tommy a push on the shoulder. Tommy spilled a little of his cola and laughed too.

"No, Segal, you're the knucklehead," he said and pushed him back.

They finished the hotdogs and Segal walked him over to his car to drive him home. Before he got into the car Tommy took the slim paperback edition of *Romeo and Juliet* out of his hip pocket and tossed it onto the console between the front seats.

Segal glanced at it and smiled. It was even more worn now than when he had given it to Tommy. *Just like a good paperback should be*, he thought. He picked it up and found a card slipped between the pages like a bookmark.

He pulled it out. It was a black card with the outline of a pig in white, a pair of assault rifles, and a radiant cross. Under that block letters spelled out the name, White Pig Militia. At the bottom in smaller letters was a quote, "Tolerance is the Enemy of Truth." In smaller letters still was the address of a website.

"Tommy, where did you get this?" Segal almost yelled.

Tommy pulled back at Segal's sudden change of mood. "Some guy was handing them out at Prichard Park. I always take stuff people are handing out 'cause I don't want to hurt their feelings."

Segal knew this last bit to be true, but he was still shaken. "Don't ever have anything to do with these guys."

"OK, Segal, I promise."

EIGHTEEN

War Room

THE ACCOUNTANT, Joe Adamski, was a very thin man in that plateau of middle age where nothing seemed to change. He had thinning black hair and was seldom seen without a white shirt and thin dark tie. He wore heavy glasses of vintage plastic and carried just enough tension in his face and body to convey intensity. So far as Segal could tell, nothing gave Joe more pleasure than finding a mistake and assigning that mistake incontrovertibly to a specific individual. In his day-to-day job these were generally small mistakes of arithmetic or transcribing. To Joe, such mistakes represented fundamental moral failings. This case offered him transgressions orders of magnitude beyond the mundane and Joe's enthusiasm exceeded even Segal's expectations.

Walter texted Segal that Joe had sequestered part of a storage room in the basement below the accounting department for the project; a war room as he put it. When Segal walked in he felt intensity in the air. An old metal conference table with a rubberized top occupied the center of the room. A few unmatched chairs surrounded it. On the table were stacks of files and documents. It didn't look exactly neat, but there was evidence of some well-ordered logical system in progress. Stacked against the far wall were several cardboard file boxes with even more raw fodder for analysis. On either side of the table were two large white boards. One was covered with numbers and diagrams, the other with sticky notes.

Walter sat on one end of the table in front of a laptop and on the opposite end Joe sat with one hand glued to an adding machine while the other ran an index finger down a long list of figures. It reminded Segal of a scene in an old movie with a couple sitting at different ends of an impossibly long dining table, only in this case they were chewing on numbers and names instead of asparagus and roast beef. Walter appeared to enjoy this almost as much as Joe.

"Hey Segal," Walter and Joe said in unison. Neither of them looked up and Segal had the good sense to not distract them before they were ready. Instead, he approached the white board to study the diagrams.

The first diagram to catch his eye looked like an organizational chart. At the top of the chart was the name Continental Drift Holdings. Below that was a short vertical line connected to a long horizontal line. Spaced along this line were a series of six connectors, and under each connector a different name. A couple were names of people while the others looked like names of other companies: Pangaea Corp, Magnetic Alignment Strategies LLC, Wegman Capital Inc, and Permian Partners.

Under each of the company names were more connectors and lines with other names.

"That's the ownership chart," Walter said, "At least as much of it as we have so far."

Segal studied the diagram more closely.

"So, Continental Drift Holdings is owned by these two people, whoever they are, and these four companies. And the four companies in turn are owned by other companies."

"That's right," Walter said, "and the ownership of those companies, we don't have a complete picture on yet, but we're working on it."

Segal stepped back and shook his head. "What a rat's nest."

"It is a festering, stinking rat's nest plastered with shit! That is exactly what it's designed to be," Joe said, springing from his seat.

Segal recoiled. He had never seen the accountant quite so energized.

"But you know how to deal with a rat's nest?" Joe continued. "One freaking rat at a time. See those boxes over there? Those are documents filed with the secretary of state to create corporations and this set of boxes has filings to dissolve corporations."

Segal looked at the diagrams and notes and boxes. "That's a lot of rats," he said.

"Maybe. Or maybe there are a few really big rats making it look like a lot of smaller rats," Walter said.

"Yeah," Joe said. "It's called Smurfing, as in Papa Smurf organizing all the little Smurfs. Already we know that this guy, Koll, was a shareholder in at least half a dozen of them."

Segal walked around the table and took in the scene again. All this in just a few hours and with just two guys working on it and using only public documents. It was turning into the snowball of all snowballs.

"Legally speaking, what are we looking at here? What laws do you think are broken?" Segal asked.

"It looks like the possibility of tax evasion, money laundering, bank fraud, possible SEC violations," Joe said.

"And don't forget insurance fraud," Walter added.

The mention of insurance fraud brought to Segal's mind the man who was nearly dispatched by a wrecking ball.

"What about John Belincort?" he asked.

Joe wrinkled his forehead. "That doesn't sound familiar," he said. He looked to the left on the table and located the paper he was looking for. "Here's my list of names," he said more to himself than to anyone else. Running his finger down the list he stopped halfway down the page. "Nope, haven't come across him yet."

"What you didn't ask about was John Belincort's insurance company, Bell Tower Insurance. That name does appear in these papers a lot. I mean *a lot*," Walter stressed.

"Does that mean he was in on the schemes?" Segal asked.

"If you're going to get bank loans on buildings and so forth you have to have insurance," Joe said. He stood up and came over to join in the conversation. "Of course, that doesn't prove that he was in on the shady side of their dealings, but it sure would be convenient to have someone in the insurance business who would write you policies without asking too many questions."

Segal nodded his head. A picture was beginning to emerge from the chaos and it wasn't a good one.

"It could take us a while to get our arms around all of this," Walter said.

"I think there's too much here to get our arms around the whole thing. Anyway it's off our beat. Eventually we turn it over to the IRS, FBI, SEC, whoever. What we need to focus on is who had motive to kill Julius Hargrove and Adrien Koll, and John Belincort. I think that means we concentrate on the transactions surrounding that building in the River Arts District that was just knocked down. We learn everything we can about that, or at least enough so we understand who's who and what's what."

Walter nodded. "The chief called. He wants us to update him. You think we should go to his office or ask him to come over here so we can show him this stuff."

Segal scanned the room, trying to imagine how this would look to his boss, or anyone else seeing it for the first time. He blew out a deep breath. "Let's go to his office. We'll blow his mind a little bit at a time instead of all at once."

"So LET ME get this straight," the chief said. He shifted his weight from leaning forward on the desk, listening intently to their story, to leaning back in his chair in a position better suited for pondering. "You've got these sketches of the background of Hargrove's painting which show the governor and his people in a bad light, suggesting some kind of payoff. We don't know what the basis of that is, but it seems to give the governor a motive to get rid of Hargrove, or at least stop him from completing the painting. You've got a robbery which you believe was an attempt to retrieve those sketches, but you don't have a suspect yet. You have this investment guy, Koll dead at a shooting range where he hosted gun training for a right-wing vigilante group called the White Hog Militia. You have an insurance exec who was almost killed by a wrecking ball who lied to you about knowing Koll or the Militia. Then you come across evidence that ties Hargrove to Koll through this weird looking real estate deal."

"The real estate deal concerning the same building in which the insurance exec was almost killed," Walter filled in. "And that particular deal looks like it's only the tip of the iceberg of shady deals."

"And we haven't thoroughly questioned the insurance exec because the governor gave him permission to leave town, against my instructions," Segal added. "Even facilitated it."

"Right," the chief said. What he didn't say, what he didn't have to say, was this could not possibly be a coincidence. "So, this is all going in the direction of some squirrelly-ass business deal which may or may not come dangerously close to the governor of the state of North Carolina, and Hargrove being killed to silence him."

Segal and Walter nodded.

The chief leaned back even farther in his chair and seemed to ponder for a moment.

"What else?" the chief asked. "Are there any other angles you're working?"

Segal took a drink of coffee to get his thoughts collected.

"We're looking closer at the Marks brothers," Segal said.

"Hargrove's three apprentices," Walter explained before the chief asked.

"It looks like Henry Marks, the most senior apprentice, has been hooking up with Hargrove's wife, Margery," Segal said.

The chief raised his eyebrows. "Finally, something I can understand. Good, old-fashioned sex and lust. Simple yet powerful. I like this angle."

"Then there's Mark Morrison, second in seniority. He apparently has a bad temper, has some violence in his record. Plus, we know he had a loud argument with Hargrove shortly before the killing. He seems like the kind of guy that could fly off the handle and shoot someone with a crossbow if one was handy. Either that or unload a full clip into someone else," Walter said. "Also, the alibies for those guys are not airtight."

"Are there any more Marks brothers?" the chief asked. "So far I like the first two."

"There's a third, Mark Engel. He's just a kind of intense guy, young, fanatically devoted to Hargrove. Seems like he had a crush on the model, Jody Mare, which was not recip-rocated. He's the one who borrowed the antique crossbow from the Biltmore. His alibi is even shakier than the others."

"Any way to confirm what the guy from the Biltmore said? I mean, are we absolutely sure this old crossbow was not the murder weapon?" the chief asked.

"I'm seeing a guy tomorrow," Walter said. "Guy that runs that shooting and archery range out toward Candler. I'll see what he says, but the guy at the Biltmore seemed pretty sure."

"Anything from forensics or the autopsy?" the chief asked.

"No fingerprints except the ones you would expect," Walter said. "We sent the crossbow bolt to the SBI like you said. They confirmed the blood type on the tip and shaft matched the victim. No big surprise. But they did say they found something else. It's what they're calling organic resi-due on the string end of the bolt by the feathers. They did their DNA extraction on the residue and sent the bolt back already. They're sequencing the DNA now and they'll let us know. If we're lucky it could be from the shooter's fin-gers or hand."

The chief leaned forward again in his chair and covered his face with his hands and blew out a slow breath. "I don't need to tell you this, but I'm going to tell you anyway. You have got to be careful about this angle with the governor. If anything goes public it will be a disaster."

"He would have the ways and means to take this whole case from us and give it to the SBI," Segal said.

"To say nothing of the fact they already may have killed two people over this and tried to kill a third," Walter added.

"I don't want to see anything in the papers about this. Nothing other than 'Crossbow Murderer Arrested.'"

Segal and Walter both nodded.

"Is there any way you can sort of unofficially probe a little around the governor angle without having a formal interview? Just throw a couple pieces of bread on the water and see what comes back?" the chief mused.

"I think it's time for me to have another talk with Alexa Price," Segal said.

Walter just closed his eyes.

"But first, Dinah and I are going to hunt down Mr. Belincort and see why he lied to me."

THE SOUND OF the ball slamming against the front wall was loud, sharp and hollow, even from outside the racquet ball court. It reminded Dinah of the sound gun shots made in some of the narrow streets of Baghdad. It was one of the outside courts in a park in Winston-Salem. Belincort's secretary had disclosed his whereabouts to Dinah and Segal after considerable persuasion. It turned out Segal could present a very no-nonsense presence if he wanted to. You couldn't really call it intimidating, it just seemed to cut through any intermediate bullshit and convince the person, human to human, the way things were going to be.

On the way over Diana reviewed the notes on what they knew about Belincort. It was ten in the morning. Walter had stayed behind to continue his work with Joe on the paper trail.

"So this guy gets paid to play racquet ball and golf?" she asked.

"Not just racquet ball and golf," Segal said. "Don't forget the eating and drinking at the finest restaurants. He gets paid for that, too. And taking people to football and basketball and baseball games. It's called entertaining the customers."

Dinah took a quick peek through the little window in the door and saw Belincort. He was warming up, waiting for his opponent/customer to arrive.

"He's alone," Dinah whispered to Segal.

Segal nodded. She pulled the door open and entered, her fingertips resting on the pistol at her waist. She and Segal had discussed strategy on the way over. She went in first because Segal wanted her uniform to be the first thing he saw.

He had just pulled his racquet back to make a side-armed serve and he froze in that stance for a second when he saw her.

"John Belincort?" she said. She took another step into the court and identified herself. "I'm Officer Dinah Rudisill with the Asheville Police Department."

Belincort relaxed, lowering both hands and standing up straight.

"You're a little far from home aren't you, Officer."

Segal appeared through the doorway and took a step to stand beside Dinah.

"Not so far away that we couldn't come down and have a talk about what happened to you earlier this week," he said. He withdrew his ID and held it up.

Belincort scowled. "Yes, I remember you from the hospital."

"Do you also remember I asked you not to leave Asheville until we had a chance to talk?"

Belincort turned from him in a dismissive gesture. "Yeah, well, I had business I had to attend to. I'm meeting an important client here. In fact, he's a little overdue, so if you don't mind, I would prefer if you weren't here when he arrives. You can make an appointment with my office."

He bounced the ball and swatted it against the front wall with his racquet. The ball retuned in a lazy arc and he slammed it with a powerful forehand. It streaked to the front wall and seemed to rebound off even faster, speeding straight for Dinah's head.

If he had intended to make Dinah or Segal jump and duck he was sorely disappointed. Dinah put her hand up and caught it, stopping it dead in the middle of the air without ever taking her eyes off of Belincort.

There was a moment of stunned silence.

"Your client isn't coming," Segal said. Belincort gave him a curious look.

"Your secretary called him and postponed the game," Segal explained.

Belincort looked confused and then mad. "You have no right to do this," he shouted.

"Let me tell you about some of the things we have the right to do," Segal explained in a calm voice. "We have the right to arrest you for impeding a police investigation. We have the right to handcuff you, put you in our car, and take you back to the Asheville police station for questioning." He stopped to think for a moment.

"Anything else you can think of, Dinah?"

"We have the right, actually the obligation, to make arrest records public," she said.

"Yes, and we could also stand back and let the person who tried to drop a brick building on your head have a second shot at finishing you off," Segal explained.

"Yeah, well, I'm not too worried about that," Belincort muttered.

In the end, the inconvenience of being hauled back to Asheville seemed to be the most compelling threat to the man. They moved the discussion to a picnic table nearby. Segal began the questioning.

"It turns out that you did not tell the truth, the whole

truth, and nothing but the truth when we first spoke in the hospital," Segal said.

Belincort began to explain but Segal stopped him by raising a hand.

"I'm willing to put any inaccuracies down to the drugs and your weakened and confused state of mind. But now we need the truth."

Belincort exhaled, nodded, and looked down. He glanced over at Dinah who was sitting beside Segal, watching and listening. She had a notebook in her lap and the blue racquet ball in front of her on the table. She caught his glance and let a Mona Lisa smile curl her lips. She could tell he was dying to pick up that ball, just to have something for his hands to do in the awkward situation.

"Let's start with this," Segal said. "Do you know who it was that tried to kill you?"

"No, not exactly," Belincort said.

"And what does 'not exactly' mean?" Segal asked.

"When you're in the insurance business as I am there are often people who feel like they were wronged in some way."

"What do you mean by wronged?" Dinah asked.

Belincort looked at her. "Could be a number of things. The most common is when a claim is denied. A customer or relative of a customer feels that the payment should have been made, or a payment should have been higher. People never read their contracts."

"So you think it was some disgruntled customer?" Segal asked.

"Could have been," Belincort said, but he looked away, making Dinah think his answer was disingenuous.

"Did you kill Adrien Koll?" Segal asked.

That made Belincort sit up straight.

"Is that what you think? You think I killed Adrien Koll?"

"As far as we know, you were the last person to see him alive," Segal said.

"Adrien was fine when I left him that night. In fact, after what happened to me, I thought maybe he was the one who set me up."

"What do you mean, 'set you up'?" Dinah asked.

"I mean I thought it might have been Adrien who arranged a breakfast meeting with this guy down by the river in Asheville. But then I heard Adrien himself had been killed, so I don't know what to think. Maybe what happened with me was just supposed to be a warning."

"A warning about what?" Segal asked. "What are you not telling us?"

Belincort looked away again.

"A warning about what?" Segal repeated. Belincort sighed and did a quick scan around as if to make sure no one was watching.

"Adrien Koll was the head of an investment company," he said. "They mostly did real estate deals as far as I know. I've been insuring properties for them for several years. At first it was pretty straight forward. Then Adrien started asking me to push the envelope a little. Not exactly fraud, things like agreeing to appraisal values that might be a little on the high end. Then the appraisals got higher and higher, but there was still no outright fraud. I mean he wasn't insuring buildings then burning them down or anything like that. I started to feel uncomfortable with some of the things they were doing."

"Did you tell Koll about it?" Dinah asked.

"Not in so many words," Belincort said, "but I think he was picking up on it anyway."

"What about the White Hog Militia?" Segal asked.

Belincort sat back. "The White Hogs! That was the

straw that broke this camel's back. Adrien invited me to go camping for a weekend with what he called his 'gun club.' I didn't really have any great interest, but I went anyway. I figured it was entertaining customers, just like playing golf or racquet ball, or a fishing trip." He glanced back at the blue rubber ball in front of Dinah, then he continued.

"Turned out the 'gun club' was the White Hog Militia. These guys are crazy, the political and religious stuff they believe, and my God do they love their guns. But I was in an awkward position, surrounded by these guys for a weekend. I more or less had to play along, but I knew then I was done with Adrien Koll."

"And that's what you talked to him about Sunday night?"

"I told him one more deal and I was out. He was pissed at first, then he calmed down and seemed to accept it. I went to that meeting to see a property down by the river in Asheville the next morning. I remember going into the building. I remember someone grabbing me from behind, and after that a blank."

"And what about Julius Hargrove? Do you think Koll or any of this gang killed him?"

"I doubt it. I certainly didn't hear about it, and besides, he was the governor's brother-in-law. They have some very close political ties that wouldn't stand for that."

Segal and Dinah let that sink in for a moment. Then, Segal asked, "Can you give us the names of anyone else involved with Koll's company or with the White Hogs?"

Belincort hesitated. Dinah gave the racquet ball a little push that rolled it across the table top to him.

"No, I'm not going there," Belincort said, shaking his head. "You don't understand what you're dealing with here. This is a group that has wealth, they have political connections through the governor's office and higher, and with the White Hog Militia they have more guns than Fort Bragg. I'm not messing with them and if you know what's good for you, you shouldn't either."

NINETEEN

Gala Event

THE NEXT DAY Segal drove his old Volvo up the winding hill to the Grove Park Inn. He had phoned Alexa Price to see if he could meet with her at the Western Residence, but she was not there. She was meeting with some of the staff at the Grove Park Inn concerning arrangements for a fund-raising event for her husband's re-election campaign. She suggested he meet her there.

He flashed his badge and let the valet crew park his car. He walked through the front doors of the classic old inn and into the enormous cavern of the lobby he loved. It always felt great walking into that space. The scale of the thing, the enormous rocks, the mission style furniture, all came together to let the history of the place resonate.

He scanned the seating area and the bar for Alexa. He figured she shouldn't be too hard to find, but he didn't see her. He walked across to the terrace doors which gave him a view out over the city and the mountains on its western side. When he turned back to the room, he saw Alexa walking briskly down the hall with a couple of people wearing staff badges, followed by the large state trooper. Heads turned when she entered the room. She was that kind of woman.

Alexa spotted him immediately and smiled as she altered

her course toward him. She was dressed in a white blouse and light tweed skirt that hugged her hips perfectly as she walked. Her outfit was completed by navy blue hose and black shoes with short heels. A woman perfectly attired for a business meeting.

"Good to see you, Lieutenant Segal," she said. She approached so close that Segal wasn't sure if she was going to hug him or shake his hand. After a pause he extended his hand and she pressed it between both of hers and held it for several long beats, looking him in the eye as if searching for something she had lost.

She turned to the trooper/bodyguard who was keeping his distance behind her and said, "It's OK, Gerald. You can return to the residence now."

The trooper looked uncomfortable and cleared his throat and started to protest, beginning with the word, "Ma'am—" but Alexa cut him off.

"I'll be fine, Gerald. Lieutenant Segal here is a police officer so I'm sure he'll see that I'm well protected." She gave the trooper a look which clearly communicated that he should disappear with no further discussion. That is exactly what he did, but not before giving Segal a glare of disapproval.

Alexa said, "Let's have a drink," and began walking toward the bar before he could respond.

She ordered a glass of Chardonnay and Segal asked for a ginger ale.

"Oh, yes," she said. "This is an official visit, isn't it? Sometime we need to have a drink just to have a drink." She brushed a fingertip across the back of his hand.

Segal felt a wave of response move through his body.

There weren't many people in the sitting area so they easily found a place out of earshot of the other guests. She sat on a couch and he on a chair with wide arm rests in the Mission style. He watched her as she crossed her legs and sat back and took a healthy sip of wine.

"Tough meeting?" he asked.

"Just tedious," she said. She swirled the wine in the glass a little. "You wouldn't believe the number of details."

Segal took a drink of his ginger ale. It was made on site and was way hotter with ginger than the common bottled varieties. It stuck in his throat and nearly took his breath away.

"Does the name Tectonic Plate Investments mean anything to you?" Segal asked. He watched her face closely for signs of emotion or surprise, but if there were any they passed quickly.

Alexa furrowed her brow and slowly took another sip of her wine. The pause was just long enough to make Segal wonder if she was stalling for time while composing an answer. If she was trying to deceive, her big problem would be that she didn't know what Segal already had.

"It does kind of ring a bell," she said, "but I'm not sure."

"How about Continental Drift Holdings?"

She frowned and shook her head. "I don't think so."

"Have you met a man named Adrien Koll?" he asked.

"Now that name does sound familiar," Alexa said. "I believe he was a contributor to my husband's campaign among other things."

"Among what other things?" Segal asked.

"Things like being a bore. I believe he's in some kind of finance or investments, something like that."

"Was," Segal said. That got Alexa's attention. "Mr. Koll is dead. Murdered. Near the Western Residence, actually. That was the crime scene you saw me at when you were out running the other day."

Alexa just sat with her mouth open. Segal thought she was either truly upset or the best actress he had yet run across.

"We haven't released that name publicly yet pending notification of next of kin, so please keep that to yourself."

Alex recovered enough to shake her head to indicate that she would.

"What about John Belincort?" Segal pushed forward.

"Is he dead, too?" Alexa said this a little too loudly and looked around to see if anyone had noticed. She leaned toward Segal and continued in a lower voice. "That name I do know a little. He's in the insurance business, I think. He and his wife live around Winston-Salem. We see them in Raleigh from time to time." She took another sip of wine and seemed to study Segal's face when she put the glass down.

"Do these names have something to do with your investigation into what happened to my brother, Lieutenant?"

"That's one of the things we're trying to figure out," Segal said. "Is there anything you know of that would tie these men to your brother?"

She continued to look Segal in the eye. "So far as I know they traveled in completely different circles."

Segal took a sip of his ginger ale, this time ready for the bite. He waited for her to continue, knowing that most people abhorred gaps of silence in their conversations. He watched her face closely.

"Do you think we're in danger, my husband and I?"

"Do you have reason to think you are?" Segal asked. He found this a very interesting question.

"I just mean with all these things happening..." she said, her voice trailing off.

Segal decided to let it lay there for a moment.

"Are there any developments in your investigation of my brother's case?" she asked.

"Well, interesting that you should ask," Segal said. "There was a break-in at the home of one of the models who worked with your brother."

"A break-in?" Alexa said. This time Segal couldn't tell if she was genuinely upset or not. "Was anyone hurt? Anything taken?"

"Thankfully, no one was hurt," Segal said. Then he hesitated and leaned forward and looked around the room as if to make sure no one was within earshot. "Some of your brother's sketches were taken," he said in a whisper. "Please don't tell anyone about that part. That part we didn't release to the press."

"Have you found out who the thief was?" she asked.

"Not yet, but we will. He left some pretty good evidence at the crime scene," Segal said.

Alexa sat back and drained the remainder of her wine. Segal's last statement seemed to take her by surprise. It took her a moment to recover her usual composure, then she said she had to go. They both stood up and she took an envelope from her hand bag. She handed it to him and said, "I have an invitation for you to our little party. I really *really* hope you can come." She said it with an intensity well outside her usual playful flirtation.

Segal took the envelope from her and she gave him a quick kiss on the cheek and left. He sat back down, took another sip of the hot ginger ale and watched her walk away, enjoying the show.

BACK IN HIS CAR, Segal was on the phone to Walter.

"How did you do with your crossbow expert?" Segal asked.

"Like I told you, he's the man when it comes to this stuff. They got a couple of models of crossbows there and he had a catalog with a lot more they could order. I asked him how many he sold and he said probably twenty or thirty so far this year."

"You've got to be kidding, that many?" Segal said.

"They have a very gun-like feel, Segal. Appeal to the same kind of people."

"Like, what do you get the gun enthusiast in your life who has everything?"

"Exactly," Walter said. "He let me shoot one. It was pretty cool. I shot one of those compound bows, too. What you said about them was right. It would take some practice and training to hit anything with the regular bow, but the crossbow, any fool could do it."

"What did he think of the antique one from the Biltmore?" Segal asked.

"Yeah, I took the picture with me but I didn't even have to. He knew all about it and all about the rest of the Biltmore collection too. This guy is really into weapons. Anyway, he confirmed what the curator told us, that thing couldn't be the murder weapon."

"What about getting a list of people who bought the crossbows from him?" Segal asked.

"Nothing doing. This is a cash only business and they definitely don't keep a list of people who buy weapons."

"What about the bolt? Did he have anything to say about that?" Segal asked.

"Now that was interesting. According to this guy everyone uses carbon fiber arrows and bolts now. Before that steel or aluminum. No one has used wood like this one for years. He thought it was handmade, very authentic to traditional ones. Even the tip was hand forged. Very high-quality craftsmanship."

Segal let that sink in for a moment.

"What about you?" Walter asked. "Did you meet up with your girlfriend?"

"As a matter of fact, we just had a drink in the lobby of the Grove Park Inn."

"You get much out of her?"

"I got an invitation to the big fundraising gala at the Grove tonight," Segal said.

"Anything relevant to the case," Walter asked.

"I gave her a lot more information than I got, to tell you the truth," Segal said.

"That's what I was afraid of," Walter said. "I was afraid you would go up there and get all beguiled. Are those some monkey wings I hear flapping in the background?"

"She's plenty beguiling all right," Segal admitted. "But I look at giving her a little information like tossing a stone into a pond. Let's see how far the ripples go and what they bounce off."

"Yeah, and who gets pissed off at you when they feel their boat rocking," Walter said.

"Yeah, that, too."

"What are you wearing tonight?" Walter asked. Walter took it upon himself to act as Segal's fashion consultant. It was part of the symbiosis of their partnership.

"You think I should actually go to this thing?" Segal asked.

"You got to go," Walter ordered. "You got this ball rolling. If you're getting people nervous, it will drive them crazy when you show up there. Besides that, I'm picturing a roomful of beautiful women and bowls of steamed shrimp on ice and a full buffet. You've got to go."

"So, I can't just show up in my sport coat?"

"You're not getting the picture here, what this thing will be like," Walter said.

"So, the dark blue suit?" Segal asked.

"Not unless you got the mustard stain out of the elbow," Walter scolded.

"The charcoal suit?" Segal asked.

"Perfect."

SEGAL CHECKED HIMSELF in the mirror and straightened his tie. Walter was right as usual. The charcoal gray suit looked like the right thing to wear. In the universe of suits, he probably liked it better than the others he owned. The real problem was that he just didn't like wearing suits all that much. He tried putting a paperback in the pocket, but it made the jacket bulge unsymmetrically. When he took it out he felt unarmed.

For the second time that day he pulled up to the Grove Park Inn, this time for the fundraiser. He showed the staff his invitation rather than his badge, but the badge was there just in case he needed it. They directed him down the hall to the left where there were some meeting rooms and ballrooms. He took a quick look into the cavernous lobby again as he passed by. It had a different vibe in the artificial light, but it was no less magical.

As soon as he entered the wide hallway in the new wing of the hotel he saw the big state trooper standing guard outside a set of double doors leading to one of the rooms. Segal recognized him even though he wore an ill-fitting suit instead of his uniform. The way the guy was built reminded Segal of something. He couldn't quite put his finger on it, but something.

As he walked in that direction he passed several pedestals, each displaying a sculpture or other piece of artwork. The pedestal nearest the door guarded by the trooper held an enormous Chinese Urn. The decorations on the urn struck Segal as gaudy and overly complex in contrast to the other pieces which were simple and well balanced. He paused for a moment to look at it. It bothered him. He headed to the door, but the trooper stopped him by putting a hand on his chest when he attempted to walk into the room.

Segal pulled out the invitation, and he could feel the big man glaring as he passed on into the room.

Segal scanned around. To the left, a bar attracted a number of well-dressed people. In the far-left corner a string quartet played softly. In the back of the room were several round tables with four to six chairs each. People were sitting there eating and drinking or just talking. On the right was a long buffet table loaded with food. Everywhere were groups of people standing and talking, holding flutes of champagne or other drinks. His eyes searched the room for Alexa but he didn't see her or the governor.

As he scanned the room again he felt a hand on his right arm. He turned and smiled when he saw who it was. Shirley Dawn.

"You hanging out with a better class of people now?" she asked in a teasing voice.

Segal looked around the room. "I don't know if I'd call it a better class, but I do have a personal invitation from the first lady of the state." He slid the corner of the envelope out of his pocket as evidence.

"Very impressive, Segal. She must really like you. You even put on a suit and everything. Very impressive," she said, giving him a look up and down.

"You don't look so bad yourself," Segal said, checking her out in return. She was wearing a dress of shimmering silver material. She looked like a pixie. He felt relieved to be with someone he knew and no longer standing awkwardly alone.

Shirley Dawn pulled on his arm. "You can fill me in on all the latest news about the crossbow murders and that little incident with the wrecking ball in the River Arts District, but first, let's hit the buffet table. I'm starving."

Segal did a quick scan of the table. He found a plate and put a few carrot and celery sticks on it plus a dinner roll and some kind of creamy chicken dish and a few green beans. Then he saw exactly what Walter had prophesized: a huge, iced bowl of steamed shrimp.

He lost track of Shirley Dawn but soon found her with a plate stacked high with food. He motioned for her to meet him at one of the round tables.

"You on a diet or something?" he asked, nodding to her overflowing plate.

"Saving room for dessert," she said. "They've got a good-looking chocolate cake and some banana pudding."

"Have you seen the governor or his wife?" Segal asked.

"Oh, they'll make a grand entrance later," Shirley said. She checked the time on her phone. "I would say in about sixteen minutes."

"I take it you've been to this sort of thing before."

"Part of the beat, Segal," she said between bites. "I've timed them. The governor and his wife show up twenty-five minutes after the posted hour. That gives time for stragglers to get in and for people to have at least one drink to loosen up. Then any jokes the governor tells seem funny. My strategy: hit the buffet table early while everything is fresh, then I can concentrate on the action once the main act takes the stage."

Segal nodded in admiration of a well-thought-out plan. Shirley Dawn could be a pain sometimes but she knew her way around. He considered asking her about some of their recent findings without giving too much away.

She beat him to the punch.

"Tell me about the break-in on Montford Avenue," she said.

"Why do you want to know about a little break-in?"

"Because it was in the home of Jody Mare, who is, or was, a model working with Julius Hargrove," she said.

Segal raised his eyebrows. "Who told you that?" he asked.

Shirley Dawn made a face. "No one told me that," she said. "I put it together for myself. I heard the address on the police scanner and thought it sounded familiar. I just interviewed her a few days ago." Shirley stabbed a chunk of beef stroganoff with her fork as if for emphasis.

"And I suppose you want to know if we think it's connected with the crossbow murders, as you call them?" Segal asked.

"It would be a pretty big coincidence if it wasn't, don't you think?" Shirley asked, raising her eyebrows at Segal.

He looked back at her and raised his own eyebrows, stalling for time, deciding what to tell her. After a beat he just said, "I agree that would be an extremely low probability coincidence."

"So does that mean Officer Dinah Rudisill, aka Dinosaur Rudisill, is working with you on the crossbow murder cases?" she asked.

"I would say her contributions have been very much appreciated," Segal said, "and don't go pumping her for information, she's just a rookie."

"I make no promises, Segal. She's in the big leagues now. But you know I always play fair."

Segal frowned, but he had to admit this was mostly true.

"I already did the story about her as a roller derby star, but it wouldn't hurt if her talents extended to her job on the police force as well."

Segal started to comment, but there was some commotion near the door. He turned in that direction along with everyone else. A man he did not recognize stepped up to a microphone and announced, "Ladies and gentlemen, the governor and first lady of North Carolina."

The string quartet began playing a few bars of *The Old North State*. Governor Price entered with Alexa on his arm. They were both smiling and waving as the roomful of admirers applauded. The governor was wearing a charcoal gray suit nearly identical to the one Segal had on, and Alexa looked stunning in a perfectly fitted dress of pale yellow.

They proceeded into the room. Segal couldn't take his eyes off Alexa as she released her husband's arm so he could walk to the microphone. Segal was vaguely aware that the governor was speaking, thanking people for coming and for supporting him and the state of North Carolina, subtly implying those two things were one in the same.

In Segal's mind, the man's voice faded into the background as he watched Alexa calmly look around the room. She didn't seem to listen to her husband's speech much either. She occasionally acknowledged a person with a nod or a wave. When her eyes met Segal's he did not look away and she blew him a kiss. Segal smiled and nodded back to her. When her eyes moved on with their scan of the room Segal glanced across the table where Shirley Dawn looked at him with her mouth hanging open.

He became aware that the people around him were sitting down and resuming their conversations and the governor had stopped speaking.

"I'm going to get some of that chocolate cake and when I get back you're going to tell me how you have the first lady of the state blowing kisses to you," Shirley Dawn said.

Segal sat and watched Alexa and the governor move

away from the microphone and begin working the room. They took a couple of steps side by side and joined a small group of people with animated greetings. Another man approached and broke into the group, vigorously shaking the governor's hand. Alexa smiled at the others and moved away on her own, smiling and shaking hands and greeting people as she went. In spite of himself, he felt a little nervous and excited as she worked her way toward his table. He pushed his chair slightly away from the table so that he could cross his legs, relax, and watch the show unfold.

Shirley Dawn returned with two plates in her hands. One held a variety of cookies and candies and nuts and a cup of banana pudding. The other held a wedge of chocolate cake that barely fit on a dinner plate. It looked rich and moist and it was covered with creamy icing, also chocolate.

"Damn," Segal said. "That might be the best-looking chocolate cake I've ever seen."

Shirley Dawn appeared to give the statement serious consideration. "You could be right, Segal."

They both grabbed forks and took bites. Segal closed his eyes for a second to savor the taste. When he opened them he saw Alexa approaching their table. He shot to his feet, cleaning his teeth with his tongue so he wouldn't have a chocolate icing smile.

Alexa smiled and took his hand in both of hers. "I'm so glad you could come this evening, Lieutenant," she said in her official loud party voice. Then, before she let go of his hand she leaned in and whispered, "Maybe we could have that drink together after this circus is over."

Before he could answer, Alexa turned her head and smiled. "Mrs. Price, this is Shirley Dawn with the Asheville Citizen-Times," Segal said.

Alexa extended her hand and Shirley shook it. Shirley

started to ask her a question, "Mrs. Price, what do you think of your husband's—"

She was cut off when Alexa's attention wandered to the table. "Good God," she said. "That might be the best-looking chocolate cake I've ever seen."

She reached down and took Segal's fork off the table and helped herself to a bite. She smiled as she savored it, nodded, and put the fork down. "I don't know how we'll do on contributions tonight, but at least we'll know we gave it our best shot." She extended her hand to Shirley Dawn again and said, "Nice to meet you, Shirley. I enjoy your work. Keep writing." She turned and smiled at Segal as she walked away. "I'll see you later, Lieutenant."

He watched for a long moment as she walked away, moving smoothly in the perfectly fitted dress. When he turned back to the cake, Shirley was staring at him.

"All right, Segal, off the record, background only, what is going on with you and Alexa Price?"

Segal held his hands up, palms out. He was about to protest his innocence when he noticed movement at the door.

TWENTY

Chinese Urn

AT THE DOOR they saw a woman trying to step around the oversized trooper acting as door guard. She appeared frantic and frustrated. She stepped right and he mirrored her move. She stepped left and he blocked her again. His problem was that with each step of the awkward dance she backed him a couple of inches into the room. He was reaching a point where he could no longer keep this from becoming a major spectacle in front of his boss's guests.

She pushed him which had no effect at all. She might as well have pushed against Mount Pisgah. The second time she pushed, he grabbed her wrist, turned her around, and hustled her out of the room, and out of sight of the guests. It wasn't until Segal heard the sound of her voice rising in protest that he realized the woman was Margery Hargrove.

Segal glanced around the room. Most of the other guests seemed not to have noticed the little ruckus. Or maybe they just chose not to.

"I'd better see what's going on," he whispered to Shirley.

Segal walked with an exaggerated calmness to the door. No one seemed to take much notice of him or the unfolding drama outside the door. By the time he was out of the room, the door guard and Margery Hargrove were thirty feet down the hall, far enough away that her voice did not rise above the music and background of voices in the banquet room. The last time Segal had seen her she was wearing a bathrobe. This time she was a little more formal in dark jeans and a light jacket. Under the jacket was a tight-fitting black knit shirt. Clearly not dressed for the formal reception. She had made an effort to apply some makeup, but it could not cover up the damage that crying and stress had done around her eyes.

She was still agitated and the trooper still held her wrists. The trooper was turned away from Segal, and Margery was barely visible on the opposite side of him. Then, Margery leaned to the side and spotted him. For some reason his presence seemed to settle her. The look in her eyes and the way she held her head to one side told Segal she was on some kind of medication, prescribed or otherwise. When she stopped her struggle the trooper let go of one of her wrists and turned to see what she was looking at. He did not seem pleased to see Segal.

"Can I help?" Segal asked. This time he pulled out his badge instead of the invitation.

"I know who you are," the man said.

"I want to see her." Margery said, taking her appeal to Segal.

"Who?" he asked, though he had a fairly good idea.

"I want to see Alexa, my sister-in-law." She said the last part with mock affection in her voice.

The trooper moved his free hand to his belt while still holding on to Margery's wrist with the other. His hand found a pair of handcuffs and withdrew them.

"Wait a minute, officer," Segal said. "Do you think that's necessary?" He was thinking of his boss's words. "We don't need to see this in the paper."

At that point a voice down the hall called out, "Margery!" They all turned and Segal recognized Henry Marks. He trotted up the hall and put a supportive hand on Margery's back when he got there.

Segal didn't think much of the young man, but if Margery could be persuaded to leave peacefully with him it might provide the best way out of the current dilemma.

Perhaps the same thought occurred to the trooper because he let go of her wrist, although he did not put the cuffs away. Segal leaned toward him and said in a whisper, "I know it's your job to protect the governor, but it is not going to look good if you arrest the first lady's sister-in-law a few days after her husband was killed."

The trooper seemed about to speak when Segal saw his head snap around toward to door to the banquet hall. Alexa was standing there with her arms crossed, smiling with her mouth but not her eyes.

"You!" Margery yelled, pointing toward Alexa. Segal was amazed at how much rage she could pack into that one word.

Alexa walked slowly and calmly toward them. "This is really not a good time, Margery," she said.

"No, it's a really lousy time, Alexa," Margery said. "Know what makes it a lousy time? My husband just got killed and now you and your husband, the *governor*, have managed to get the court to put a freeze on our assets."

"We'll talk about it tomorrow, Margery. At the lawyer's office."

"You mean the lawyer you hired to write Jules's will? We could go in and get him right now. I'm sure he's in there, being one of your local supporters. Probably all the judges, too."

Alexa did not respond. She just stared at Margery for

a moment. Then, she nodded at the trooper and turned on her heel. "Tomorrow, Margery," she said.

The trooper reached for Margery's wrist again, bringing the handcuffs up with his other hand. Margery moved with surprising speed. She did a little ducking and stepping move that took her out of reach of both the trooper and Henry Marks. Just as quickly her hand went into the pocket of her jacket and came out with a small twenty-two caliber automatic pistol.

"We wouldn't want to upset your guests now would we? Maybe this will get your attention," she screamed. Alexa turned around, her eyes wide when she saw the gun. The three men each reacted by instinct before there was time to think. The trooper and Henry both jumped away. Segal did the opposite. He lunged toward Margery and the gun. As he moved, she pointed the gun well away from Alexa and pulled the trigger.

It amazed Segal how much sound the little gun made, but it was also the sound of the Chinese vase exploding into a million pieces.

In the ringing noise and the smell of burnt gun powder, confusion reigned for a second, but only a second. Segal grabbed Margery's arm immediately after the shot. He had no problem removing the gun from her hand.

The trooper recovered his wits and lunged back toward Margery.

"I've got the gun," Segal yelled so the big man would not tackle her. Instead, the trooper made use of the hand cuffs which he still had at the ready.

Segal checked toward the door. Alexa was OK but gulping for breath. If it was Margery's intent to bust up Alexa's cool exterior, she had accomplished her goal.

Further toward the door he saw Shirley Dawn. She was

holding up her cell phone taking a video of the scene. She panned from him to the shattered fragments of the Chinese urn and back over to Alexa. Segal wondered how long she had been recording. Would there be a photo of Margery with a gun in her outstretched hand on the front page tomorrow? Segal thought again about the chief and his warning about how important it was to keep any connection with the governor's office out of the press.

He looked back and saw the trooper marching Margery down the hall with Henry Marks trailing a few feet behind. The trooper had a cell phone to his ear. Segal assumed he would be calling the Asheville police as the rules of jurisdiction required.

Shirley Dawn came up beside him and watched too, no longer recording video.

"This is exactly why you hit the buffet table early, Segal," she said

NEARLY AN HOUR later Segal stood in the parking lot watching two patrol cars move away into the night, one carrying Margery Hargrove, the other with Henry Marks. The officers had responded right away, but it took that long for them to get the basics of the incident written down. Margery would, without doubt, spend the night in jail while she came down off whatever combination of drugs she had ingested. It would also give the officers time to think about what charges to bring against her. Henry would probably be released after questioning.

Segal had his phone to his ear, filling Walter in about what had happened.

"No reason for you to go in tonight, Walter," he said. "Nothing's going to happen till the morning. You could fill Dinah in for me though."

"I told you it would be good for you to go to that party. Look at the excitement you would have missed," Walter said.

"Yeah," Segal said. "You were right about the shrimp, too."

"I told you," Walter said, and he signed off.

Segal's mind drifted as he strolled. He knew there would be some blowback from the governor's office, but he couldn't get up the energy to worry about it. He told himself to stay focused on the case. Resolving the two murders was the best way, the only way really, to answer any charges from the bureaucracy that would come his way. Then let the chips fall where they may.

Patches of fog drifted in as they so often did there in the mountains. He wasn't paying much attention to the other people as they left the inn and headed to their cars. Alexa and the governor had departed in a black SUV some time ago. Alexa gave him a little smile and a wave that was not much more than a ripple of her fingers. *Guess that intimate drink will have to wait for another night*, Segal thought. It seemed that the last of the people from the gala and probably from the restaurants were heading toward their cars and he supposed he should do the same. But for the moment he stood there, hands in his pockets, looking out into the night, thinking about the case.

He became vaguely aware of a presence behind him and he stepped a little to his left, thinking that someone wanted to get by. Instead, he felt a vicious push to his shoulder which sent him stumbling into the small, darkened section of the lot outside of the ring of light surrounding a lamp post. He nearly lost his balance but caught himself against the stones of a retaining wall. He remembered what his boxing coach had told him once: "Lose your balance and you could lose a fight before it even gets started."

He spun around to face his harasser and saw the big state trooper guard glowering over him. The guy was huge. He had a good six inches and at least eighty pounds on him. He had a crew cut and a red face. He had no discernible neck between his barrel chest and his cement block of a head. *Minotaur*, was the first word to jump into Segal's head. That's what the guy reminded him of. All he needed was a set of horns and he could have been a perfect Minotaur. He also looked like he might be drunk. Segal thought that was quick work, or maybe the guy had been sipping a little on the side all evening.

Segal reached for his badge to show the guy. Flashing the badge almost always diffused the situation of a drunk out looking for trouble in the wrong places. He held the badge up to the guy and said, "I'm Lieutenant Segal, Asheville Police."

Instead of backing down the Minotaur made a clumsy swing with his right hand, trying to swat the badge away. Segal easily dodged. The momentum of the guy's crude swing pulled him off balance like a batter missing a pitch.

"I know who you are," the Minotaur said.

Segal took a step back so the guy wouldn't fall on him and said, "All right, you know who I am but who are you? I know you're a state trooper even though you're not in uniform. I know you work for the governor, but what's your name?"

"Leave them alone!" the Minotaur bellowed.

Segal wondered for a second how much of this was professional and how much was personal.

"Leave us alone," the Minotaur said again, with a voice that sounded like the bawling of a large calf.

"Calm down, Trooper." Segal held his hands up, palms out, but the Minotaur's response was to take another swing, this time with his left.

"I might not be a trooper after tonight. I could lose my job over this."

Segal took a step back and easily parried the blow with his right hand. This time the Minotaur did not lose his balance as much. He stumbled forward and tried to grab Segal by the neck.

Segal definitely had no interest in a wrestling match with this side of beef. He took a step back and clipped the guy on the chin with a snap of a left jab.

"What is your name?" he asked.

The Minotaur stopped for a moment and seemed to think about it and then just bellowed again, "Leave us alone. Leave us all alone!" He took a huge swing, this time with a clenched fist aimed at Segal's head.

Segal ducked under the punch and realized in that instant that he was backed up almost to the retaining wall, losing room to maneuver. Not a good feeling.

Instincts took over and the boxing drills kicked in. Since he was in a crouch from ducking the last high swing he let his body twist and load up for a savage hook to the Minotaur's ribs. The Minotaur grunted and dropped his hands to guard his midsection. Segal twisted back to the right and delivered another hook, this time to the jaw.

The Minotaur staggered back and gave Segal the chance to circle to the left where he was no longer trapped against the wall. The Minotaur turned to face him.

Big men were not used to people hitting back, so the Minotaur looked more confused than hurt. He put his fists up and came at Segal again. This time Segal had plenty of room to move. He flicked out a combination of two left jabs and a straight solid right. The Minotaur stumbled back, stunned and confused but not badly hurt. He squared up again and this time caught Segal with a glancing blow. Even though it did not land squarely, Segal felt the guy's strength in it and realized time was not on his side. If he didn't end this quickly he might be in big trouble.

He came back fast with two right-left combinations followed by a right hook with all his might to the Minotaur's jaw. He pulled back before delivering another blow and stood at the ready as the big man collapsed against the wall and slid to the ground.

Segal watched him closely. After one small, aborted motion to get to his feet, the Minotaur made no further attempt to stand up.

"Do you want us to call the police?" someone called from the direction of the entrance to the inn. Segal and the Minotaur both looked in that direction and saw that a group had gathered.

"We are the police," they both said in unison. Segal held up his badge. "It's OK," he said. "Just a training exercise. You can go now."

The people dispersed, muttering their disappointment that the show seemed to be over.

Segal looked back at the trooper sitting against the wall. The guy had a little blood trickling from his nose, and still had a little of that drunk stare in his eye, but now it seemed more regretful and ashamed than malevolent.

"You OK?" Segal asked, coming closer.

The guy nodded, but still made no effort to stand. Segal found a tissue in the pocket of his jacket and handed it to him.

"You want to tell me what's going on?" Segal asked in

low voice. He looked back at the entrance to the inn. They were alone.

"He asked me to scare you, to warn you. Get you off their backs," the trooper said. He would not look directly at Segal. "I can't afford to lose my job."

"You mean the governor told you to do this?" Segal asked.

The trooper shook his head. "No, not the governor. I mean Davenport." He said the man's name like it was a dirty word.

That figures, Segal thought. *Keep this at arm's length.*

"How was that supposed to work?" Segal asked. "You beat me up in a parking lot and then I just drop a double murder case?"

The big guy looked at him.

"What? You were supposed to do more than beat me up?"

"The governor and his wife didn't have anything to do with the murder, so maybe you don't drop the murder case, you just stop looking into things that could look bad for them," the trooper said. "Mrs. Price really is upset about her brother. This was just to get your attention. I wouldn't really have hurt you too bad." He looked down, not willing to meet Segal's eye again.

"Well, you got my attention," Segal said. He shook his right hand which was throbbing. It felt like he had punched an oak tree. "But why should I believe you? If they would send you to do this why wouldn't they send you to kill me?"

"I don't kill people for money, but there are people who do," the big man answered. His jaw was beginning to swell and it was difficult for him to speak clearly.

"Why didn't they send the White Hog Militia?" Segal shot back. He really wanted to see if the trooper even knew who they were.

"Because you can't really control the Hogs," the trooper said. "Davenport thinks he can, but the governor is smart. He knows better. Those guys are crazy. Believe me. You don't want them looking for you."

He looked at the big guy again and in spite of the attack a few minutes earlier Segal couldn't help but feel a little sorry for him. He had the feeling someone was telling him the unvarnished truth for a change.

"How the hell did you get mixed up in a thing like this?" Segal asked.

"My job is looking out for the governor. You start by doing little things for them and getting rewarded with little things back. You figure it's the governor telling you to do it, so how bad could it be? It gets to a point that you're in so deep it's hard to say no."

Where have I heard that before, Segal thought.

Another thought flashed into Segal's mind. "It was you who broke into that house on Montford Avenue, wasn't it?"

The big guy looked astonished. "It was just to get some stupid drawings, which really kind of belong to Mrs. Price anyway. They were her brother's and she would be keeping them in the family. I would never have taken anything else or hurt that girl. No way."

Segal checked his inside pocket and pulled out a collection of pictures of people associated with the case, the ones they used when questioning suspects.

"Have you ever seen this man visiting the Western Residence?" he asked, holding out the photograph.

The Minotaur man studied the picture a moment and then nodded his head. "Yes, a couple of times," he said.

"His name is John Belincort," Segal said. "We checked your log book and we didn't see his name there. Did he give you some other name?" Segal asked.

Minotaur looked extremely uncomfortable with this question, but Segal looked at him intently and the guy apparently saw no way out. "Sometimes we override the protocol. Sometimes Davenport tells us to let people in without a log entry. Sometimes he goes in and out without a log entry himself."

Segal straightened up when he heard this and thought about the implications. They would have to recheck some alibis.

"What about this guy?" Segal asked, holding up a picture of Adrien Koll.

This time the Minotaur nodded right away. "I think maybe he's a big donor. At least we gave him the VIP treatment when he came the last time."

"VIP treatment?" Segal asked.

The Minotaur went on to describe how certain people were given the best parking spots and were shown directly into a private lounge adjacent to the governor's office, with drinks and snacks and even a cigar on the back patio sometimes.

"And when was the last time he visited there?" Segal asked.

"About a month ago."

Segal thought again. Davenport and the governor, and possibly Alexa, had lied to him about Belincort and about Koll, and the presence of the Minotaur here showed they were willing and able to influence people around them to carry out some less than legal actions.

On the other hand, he would have to do some rethinking about Margery, too, given her little stunt with the pistol.

The big man broke his reverie. "What do we do now?" he asked.

"What do you mean?" Segal asked. He was so wrapped

up in the case he didn't understand what the guy was talk-ing about.

"I mean this," he said, holding up his arms to encom-pass everything around them. "Are you going to arrest me or what?"

"Oh, that," Segal said. He imagined a couple of scenes. One was hauling this guy in when he might not pass a breathalyzer test himself and staying up half the night deal-ing with the paperwork. The second scene was of him ex-plaining to his boss how he got into a fight with a State Trooper in the parking lot of the Grove Park Inn. He de-cided he did not want to be a part of either one of those scenes.

"No, I think we arrested enough people tonight," Segal said. He offered the guy his hand and helped him to his feet. "Only next time you want to have a boxing match, let's go to the gym."

Segal insisted the guy call a rideshare car even though he protested. The car pulled up to the entrance to the inn almost immediately.

The guy took a step toward it and then turned and looked back at Segal.

"What do I tell Davenport?" he asked.

"Tell him you did your job. Tell him he won't have to worry about me very much longer."

TWENTY-ONE

Dinah's Jeep

DINAH THREW THE last of the boxes into the back of her jeep. She was dressed in jeans and a T-shirt and running shoes instead of her uniform. Her wild shock of dark curly hair was pulled back and tamed into a ponytail and an Asheville Tourist ball cap was clamped on top. She returned to her tiny apartment and did one last walk through to see if she was forgetting anything.

She found a flat, rectangular box in a drawer of the night stand. She flipped it open to see the military medal inside, a silver star on a tricolored ribbon. It brought back a flash of memory of Afghanistan. What she had done there on that day had been based purely on survival instinct, survival for herself and for the soldiers around her. The memory included a lot of noise and screaming and the smell of munitions. She quickly shut the box and that train of thought along with it.

She shook her head. *Did I forget it or was I subconsciously leaving it on purpose*, she wondered. But she was not the type to dwell on such thoughts. She scanned the one-room habitat once more and then she was gone. This place would not be missed.

She tucked the medal into a duffle bag in the back seat

and climbed behind the wheel. She glanced back at the bags and boxes. Everything she owned in the world fit in there with room to spare. As she turned the key in the ignition she felt light and happy, like she was headed into a fresh new part of life.

Dinah was moving into the upstairs room of the house on Montford Avenue; the one where Jody Mare lived. She couldn't help but smile. After years of dorms and barracks and tents she would be living in a real house with real normal people. Being with the police, she was still a member of a group, but it wasn't like the military. Here she would have her own identity and life while not on duty. In this house she would not have the threat of constant danger hanging over her head.

When she pulled up in the driveway Jody came off the porch and grabbed a box to help unload. The two other housemates were off at work or school. It didn't take long to complete the transfer.

Her room was square with four dormer windows, one set into each facet of the roof. The floor was made of wide wooden planks, dark brown, matching the trim around the windows and doors. The windows let in a pleasant level of light filtered by the leaves of the oak trees in the yard. The room already included the basic furniture she would need, a bed, dresser, night stand, and one easy chair. Anything else, she could get later. For now, she liked the feeling of free open space.

"You can fix it up any way you want," Jody said. "Hang up some pictures, rearrange things, get some more chairs maybe."

Dinah nodded. She hadn't thought about things like that for a while.

"You have some nice views out of your windows," Jody

said. "Especially this one." Jody moved to the window that looked out over the front yard and the street.

Dinah moved to check it out. Above the trees and houses she could just make out a little of the downtown skyline with the mountains behind.

Her gaze dropped and she noticed a guy climbing into a blue van across the street. She thought he looked familiar.

"Is that one of the Marks brothers?" she asked, pulling back the curtain a few inches.

Jody looked out just in time to see the blue van disappearing down the street.

"Mark Engel," she said. "He texted me that he was dropping some Annigoni paper off."

Dinah gave her a confused look.

"Annigoni is really nice paper for drawing," she explained. "I didn't really need it here, I think he just wanted an excuse to come by."

Dinah gave her a curious look.

"I guess he's got a kind of thing for me, which I've done my best not to encourage. But on the other hand, I haven't been mean to him either. He got kind of protective of me after what happened to Jules."

"Protective in a creepy way?" Dinah asked.

"No. He's a good guy, does most of the grunt work around the studio. Give you the shirt off his back if you asked him. He's had a pretty tough year. Lost his father. Now, losing Jules. He's taking it pretty hard. I think Jules was like a father figure to him."

"Maybe," Dinah said. She had heard this before. She shrugged it off for the moment and toured around to check out the view from the other windows. They were all pleasant enough, but the front one was definitely the jewel.

The minute she backed away from the window her phone sounded. It was dispatch calling.

"I know you're off duty, but you asked to be called if anything came up on that truck with the APB. They just reported it over at the hospital in the emergency room parking lot."

"Tell them I'll be there in ten to give them some backup," Dinah said. She thought for a second about changing into her uniform but didn't want to take the time. She grabbed her gun and her badge and headed out.

As PREDICTED, she pulled up to the ER within a few minutes. She recognized the two cops standing by their cars near the entrance. On her way over she saw the truck in question, a big blue Ford diesel. A tarp covered a large shape in the back. No doubt, this was the truck from the APB and the one which had coal rolled soot in her face. She unhooked one of the bungee cords at a back corner and peeked under. The contraption she saw matched the description from Segal and Walter. She replaced the bungee and went to speak with her fellow officers.

"We got a call from the security guard," one of them said. "There are three guys inside. One of them has scratches all over his face and hands. They asked him if he had a fight with a bobcat, but the guy said, 'No, Maine Coon.'"

"Let me guess," Dinah said.

"Yeah, 911 got a call from a lady over in Albemarle Park. Said she heard this awful screaming and crying from an animal and when she checked it out there were three guys trying to force a large cat with long hair into something mounted in the back of a pickup. I guess it scratched the shit out of at least one of them."

"So what's the next move?" Dinah asked.

"The question is how to take them with the least chance of them hurting anyone in there. We don't know if they are armed or what they'll do. We need to be careful given the setting."

"I'm not in uniform," Dinah said. "Let me go in and get a lay of the land."

The others nodded. She asked them for some handcuffs, which she slipped into her pocket as she turned toward the entrance.

Inside she approached the admission desk and leaned over, discreetly showing the attendant her badge. In a low voice she explained what she wanted. The attendant motioned her to a side door with a nod of her head.

A woman of about forty wearing a lab coat and scrubs came up and introduced herself. "Hello, I'm Dr. Tina May." When Dinah introduced herself and showed the doctor her badge, the doctor smiled and took a step back. "You're the new jammer for the Asheville roller derby team, aren't you?"

Dinah smiled. She was surprised to be recognized. It felt kind of good, a little boost to the ego, but she didn't let herself get carried away with it. "I hear you have an unusual patient."

"Yes. We all got the feeling there's something off about this guy," the doctor said. "He seemed very nervous when a security guard came by so we thought he might be someone of interest to the police."

"Can you let me borrow one of those lab coats and a clipboard?" Dinah asked.

When Dinah opened the door she saw the guy on the bed. The headrest was cranked up so he was nearly in a sitting position. His head was bandaged and one eye was covered with cotton and bandages as well. His face, what she could see of it, was nearly covered with blotches of the reddish-brown stain from an antibiotic wash.

"Mr. Stank?" she asked, looking at the medical form on the clipboard.

"That's Frank," he said. "Garth Frank. I knew I shouldn't let Lewis fill out my paperwork."

Dinah approached and looked at him more closely.

"Looks like that cat really got you."

"You should see my ears," he said. "She almost ripped them off."

"It says here the doctor is discharging you. Can I have the full names of the men who will be taking you home?"

Garth complied.

Dinah stepped into the hall and found a wheelchair.

He started to speak when she wheeled it in, but she held up her hand and said, "I know, everyone says they don't need a wheelchair but it's the rules."

He got in and Dinah said she needed to get a blood pressure. When he offered her his arm she clamped a handcuff on his wrist and quickly on the other wrist as well. He began to stand, but she sat him back down with a push to the chest.

She pulled out her badge and read him his rights, beginning with, "You have the right to remain silent."

It was a right Garth chose not to exercise, protesting throughout the little speech required by the Miranda Act.

When she finished he stopped talking, too, but only for a second.

"Can I have my ball cap?" he asked with the closest he could come to dignity.

Dinah looked around the room and then in the closet where she found a foul and greasy ball cap. She picked it up with the tips of her fingers. The letters Patriot were embossed on the front together with a pair of crossed muskets. A tag in the back said Made in China.

She held it out to the guy who took it from her. When he realized he couldn't put it on his head with his hands cuffed, he held it out to Dinah and asked, "Would you mind?"

She took the filthy thing and placed it on top of his head. She couldn't really pull it down properly due to the thick bandaging, but he seemed pleased enough.

Up front the admission clerk motioned the other two over to her desk.

As Dinah had instructed her, she told them their friend was being released and they should bring their vehicle to the door to pick him up. As soon as they complied Dinah came out wheeling the patient in front of her. He still wore the hospital gown, but he carried his crumpled T-shirt in his lap, the one that read WHM—Be the Pig. His two friends got out of the pickup and walked toward them.

"Garth, you look like a damn mummy!" One of them said.

"They arrested me, Lewis," the patient said. He raised his hands from his lap to show them the cuffs.

"Actually, you're all under arrest," Dinah said. She held up her badge and the two other cops walked up behind them and applied cuffs to them as well. It was a seamless operation.

Dinah was about to shut the door to one of the cruisers after they were all loaded when the one named Lewis leaned toward her and asked, "Who's going to take care of my truck?"

"I'll take care of it myself," she said.

Lewis looked at her with renewed interest and a wide grin formed on his face. "You're Dinosaur Rudisill, aren't you," he said. "Hey Garth," he called to the newly released patient in the other car, "We just got arrested by the Dinosaur!"

Any lift she had felt when the doctor recognized her was deflated when she realized that these clowns were fans, too.

She held up one of the plastic bags which contained the items the other officers had confiscated. She fished out his truck key, but continued to look at the bag for a moment. There, along with his wallet, pocket knife and loose change, was his cell phone. It gave her an idea.

She walked back to the other cruiser and leaned down to look into the window of the back seat at Garth. He seemed to be a little star-struck by her presence.

"Is it true you boys threw a watermelon with that catapult in the back of the truck?" she asked sweetly.

Garth nodded his head.

"How far did it go, like fifty feet or so?" she asked.

Garth snorted. "Fifty feet? You're not even close."

"What, a hundred?"

"Farther, much farther," he said shaking his head.

"What then?"

Garth leaned back in his seat. He and the other boys had discussed this before. "At least two hundred yards."

Dinah pulled back. "No way," she said.

"I can prove it," Garth said.

On the down low she motioned the other officers to come closer so they could hear too.

"How can you prove it?" she asked.

"I got a video on my phone."

"Can I see it?" she asked.

"Hell, yes, you can see it," he said.

She pulled it out of the bag with his personal effects.

"I'm not allowed to give it back to you. What's your password?"

Garth motioned her closer so he could give her the password in a whisper.

"And it's OK with you if we look at the videos on your phone. You don't have to let me if you don't want to."

"Sure, go for it."

She looked over at the other cops who smiled and gave her the thumbs up. They were confirming what they just heard. The suspect had just freely granted his permission for her to view the contents of his cell phone.

"What's your password?" Dinah asked.

"White pig," he said, "One word."

TWENTY-TWO

Vortex Doughnuts

SEGAL PARKED OUTSIDE of Vortex Doughnuts. The meeting with his boss later that morning at the station would not be an easy one. He wanted to put it off for a few minutes and fortify himself with caffeine and sugar.

He stood in front of the case judging the relative attraction of the cake doughnuts verses the yeast doughnuts when he caught a movement out of the corner of his eye. There, across the room at a table, sat his boss, the chief. He was reading the morning paper. As he turned the page he looked over and caught Segal's eye. They nodded to each other. Segal would rather have had his breakfast in peace before their meeting. He suspected the chief felt the same way, but there they were.

Segal made his selections and joined the chief at the table. He sat down without invitation. Such was their relationship. He shoved a chocolate cake doughnut with salted caramel icing in the chief's direction: a symbolic request for absolution and a reminder of the core values they shared.

"I'm done with the front section if you want to take a look," the chief said without looking up. He slid the section in Segal's direction, face down. On its return trip his hand pulled the offered doughnut closer to his cup of coffee. The gesture was not dramatic enough to signal absolution, but perhaps that absolution was at least a possibility.

Segal picked the paper up and muttered, "Shirley Dawn," when he turned it over. He said it like he was swearing, slowly and under his breath. The bold headline read, "Crossbow Widow Seeks Revenge." Under that was a photo of Margery Hargrove with the small pistol in her outstretched hand. In the foreground Segal could be seen reaching out and diving toward her. The photo did a good job of capturing the smoothness and intensity of his action, like a defender diving to block a wide receiver. The photo also showed the State Trooper and Henry Marks jumping backward in different directions. All their ungainly panic was perfectly captured as well. Margery's face, which formed the focal point for the tableau, was the only calm element in the picture.

Segal had to admit that Shirley Dawn was a master of news as drama. With a picture like this the written story was almost superfluous, but of course, Shirley had managed a few column inches anyway.

Shirley included a brief description of the fundraising party and what she saw of the incident in the hallway, which wasn't much. She concluded by reporting that, "Mrs. Hargrove was charged with discharging a firearm within city limits and reckless endangerment, and destruction of property, possibly a felony depending on the assessed value of the Chinese Urn. Further charges are pending as the incident is under review. The urn is thought to date from the Ming Dynasty."

"Ming Dynasty my ass," Segal snorted. "Try the Dung Pile Dynasty. I'm pretty sure she made that part up."

The chief finally folded his part of the newspaper and looked at Segal for a long moment.

"I guess I'll let you slug it out with the art historians over the origin of the urn, Segal. Right now I'm a little more interested in exactly what happened last night and how it impacts our murder investigation. I already have calls in from the governor's office, the newspaper, the TV station, and a couple of attorneys. This guy at the governor's office, Davenport, is especially pissed," the chief said. "They want to send some people over later to be briefed on this and on the Julius Hargrove investigation. He's threatening to have the state take over the case."

"They can't do that. They have no standing, especially in light of the financial stuff and the family connection," Segal protested.

"I know that, but you better believe they have a whole boxful of wrenches they can throw into our gears if they decide it's in their best interest."

"This had nothing to do with Walter or Dinah or me. Margery Hargrove came there on her own all frustrated and looking to pick a fight."

"Wait," the chief said, holding up a palm, "You can start by telling me what *you* were doing there in the first place." The chief took a sip from his coffee and waited.

Segal explained about his earlier interview with Alexa Price and how she had given him an invitation, and how he thought it might be a good idea to accept based on what he might learn and observe. He didn't realize how lame it all sounded until the words were actually leaving his mouth.

"They also claimed their guard, who, by the way, happens to be a member of the State Highway Patrol, would have had Mrs. Hargrove in handcuffs if you had not intervened."

Segal started to explain that he was concerned about the appearances of handcuffing the bereaved widow and sister-in-law of the first lady, but this time he sensed the lameness of his explanation before he said it out loud. He just nodded. Sooner or later the chief would work it out for himself.

"The DA wants to talk to you about charging Mrs. Hargrove with attempted murder. Alexa Price was standing right there. He's asking if Margery Hargrove just missed her mark," the chief said.

"That would be a big mistake. The urn she shot was nowhere near Alexa. I don't think anyone there would testify she was trying to shoot Alexa, not even Alexa herself. Not even the guard," Segal said.

"You seem pretty sure about that guard," the chief said.

Segal just nodded and looked away. He really didn't want to explain the boxing match in the parking lot if he didn't have to. "We don't have to worry about him. There was some friction there, but we ended up having a pretty good talk. He's the one who went into Jody Mare's place and took those sketches, by the way."

This clearly surprised the chief. "Was it the governor or the governor's wife who told him to do that?"

Segal shook his head. "It was Davenport, his chief of staff."

The chief nodded. "Which means the governor and his wife may or may not have been in the loop." He looked down for moment and moved the chocolate doughnut a little closer to his cup like a chess master moving his rook.

"Look, Segal. Best case scenario is you solve this quickly. Worst case is someone else gets killed before we figure out who's doing this. All the flack in the news and from Raleigh is irritating, but the real danger is more killings. The clock is ticking"

"Right," Segal said. It was the same thing he had been telling himself and he was glad to hear his boss was on the same page.

"At the very least this incident last night has to move Margery up on the list of suspects. If she can lose control and shoot off a pistol in the Grove Park Inn, why can't she lose control and shoot her husband with a crossbow? And then you've got her affair with Henry Marks. That gives her motive. Actually, it moves Henry Marks up on the list, too."

Segal nodded his head. "But this financial stuff has to come into it, too. We can tie Koll and Belincort to Julius Hargrove with it. That can't be an accident. Then we have the attempt at stealing the sketches from Jody Mare. They show the governor and his trained rat, Davenport, paying off the devil. That ties in the governor, or at least the governor's office. That, and the fact that his personal State Trooper bodyguard was the one who stole the wrong sketches. The only thing left to do on that is to tie the governor into the screwy financial deal with Koll and Belincort."

The chief exhaled slowly. "I think it's a good angle. I think Walter and what's-his-name in accounting should stay on that. But the governor's office is going to want Margery Hargrove's head on a platter. If she's in the clear you at least have to prove to them why she's not on the suspect list."

"That's basically what Walter and I planned before the fiasco at the Grove," Segal said. "Walter will concentrate on the financials while Dinah and I follow up with the rest of the field, beginning now with Margery. She supposedly has an alibi for the night of the murder. But her alibi, at least for some of that time, is Henry Marks. I'll start by following up on that and try to get some kind of confirmation."

The chief nodded.

Segal mused for a moment, finishing off his own doughnut. "All the financial stuff aside, there's something about how these murders and the attempted murder were done. They're dramatic and it seems the killer wanted people to know about them. He knew that the bodies would be found, and the bizarre aspects would become public. I even saw a closed-circuit TV camera in that old building that was taken down by the wrecking ball, just in case the body was lost in the rubble. If it was all business, why not just kill those guys quietly and make them disappear or attempt to make the deaths look natural. This killer did almost the exact opposite, like he wanted to make a very public statement."

The chief nodded again. "Or tell some kind of story."

Segal stood to go when his phone pinged with the message tone. "At least it looks like the catapult case is wrapped up," he said after he read it.

The chief's phone pinged, too. "Three guys are locked up and the DA's office is figuring out what all to charge them with. Is there any statute against discharging a catapult within the city limits? Arresting officers include Dinah Rudisill."

Segal smiled. "Pretty impressive."

"I'll call the college to let them know we recovered the catapult. They'll be happy, mostly because of the liability thing," the chief said.

"Can we take it back to them?" Segal asked.

"Not yet. I want to check with the DA's office to see if they need it for evidence. We'll release it to them in time for the music festival in Lake Eden. That was their big deadline."

Segal nodded and left. Looking back through the window he saw the chief pick up the chocolate doughnut and take a bite.

SEGAL SAT IN the interview room of the jail waiting for the guards to bring Margery Hargrove in. He checked his email on his phone and saw a message from the SBI lab in Raleigh. The DNA found on the upper shaft of the arrow had been identified as belonging to a rabbit. The lab tech asked if it were possible the arrow could have been used for hunting before the murder? But Segal was not thinking about hunting, he was thinking about the pot of rabbit hide glue Mark Morrison had picked up from the studio. Pretty good stuff to stick the feathers on to a homemade crossbow bolt.

His train of thought was interrupted when Margery Hargrove was escorted into the interview room. He thought she looked relatively good considering she had spent the night locked up. Her hair was combed and her eyes were clear and her demeanor was considerably more positive than the last time he had seen her. There was something different about her face, something less edgy.

"I brought you some coffee and breakfast," Segal said. She sat in a metal chair across the table from him. He set the paper coffee cup and a small bag in front of her. She grabbed the cup immediately and brought it to her lips.

That's it, Segal thought. *No lipstick*. He had only ever seen her with heavy red lipstick before. He liked her better without. She looked younger.

"Wow," she said as she opened the bag, "Vortex. How do you know you're talking to an Asheville Cop? He's eating gourmet doughnuts."

If there was any sarcasm intended it did not show up in her voice. She seemed genuinely happy to be there with him. For the second time that morning the power of chocolate and salted caramel seemed to work in his favor.

"You're in a good mood considering what you've been through," Segal said.

"Believe it or not I got the best night's sleep since Jules died. Maybe shooting that stupid vase was cathartic. I don't think I ever believed in that concept before, but I don't know how else to explain it. Yesterday I felt weak, like I couldn't breathe. Today, I'm still upset. I'm still missing Jules, but at least I feel like I can move on. I should be bailed out in a little while," Margery said, "Soon as my lawyer gets the paperwork through the system. Then, I have a funeral to plan."

"How did you manage that, if you don't mind me asking? I mean making bail. I thought you said last night they had frozen your bank accounts."

"They had. My lawyer got in touch with Alexa's lawyer yesterday and he wouldn't budge. In fact, he implied I might be the one who killed Jules. That's one of the things that got me going." With the word "going" she made a circular sign with her finger in the air.

"What lawyer are they using?" Segal asked. He knew most of the local lawyers, at least the ones working criminal cases.

"It's that flip-weasel, Davenport." She took a bite of the doughnut and a sip of coffee.

"Davenport? I thought he was chief of staff."

"Yes, but being chief of staff includes fending off anything that might cause any trouble or embarrassment to the governor or his family."

"Like you, for instance," Segal suggested.

"Like me, like Jules, like Jules' paintings, like anything. Anyway, when he got nowhere with Davenport I told my lawyer to go to Alexa directly. I gave him her cell number. We've never been exactly best friends. She's always had the typical little-sister syndrome. No one was good enough for her big brother. But we both loved him and we both knew that."

"So, she cooperated?" Segal asked.

"She didn't even know Davenport had done it. She told

him to reverse it immediately before it leaked out publicly. I mean, how would that look for the governor's image?"

Segal wondered if Shirley Dawn had heard that part of the conversation last night, but since it was not mentioned in the article this morning he guessed not.

Segal leaned forward, elbows on the table while Margery took another bite of doughnut and another sip of coffee to go with it.

"Listen, I don't want to mess up your catharsis or anything, but I have to ask you again about the night of…let's say the party."

"The night of the murder," Margery said, letting Segal know it was all right to discuss it.

"Right," Segal said. "We're trying to nail down exactly where everyone was between the hours of nine at night and six in the morning."

"Like I told you, I was at home the whole time, first with the party, then in my room." She looked down when she said this last thing.

"The trouble is, this thing between you and Henry, it gives you two a possible motive to want Jules out of the way," Segal said.

"I can explain about Henry," Margery began, but Segal lifted his hand to make a stop sign.

"You don't need to explain that to me. I'm not making a moral judgment. I'm just telling you how things are and how things look. There's a problem with Henry being the only alibi witness for you and for you being the only alibi witness for Henry."

Margery looked down.

Segal leaned back in his chair. "You have plenty of people at the party until midnight or so who can vouch for you.

Is there anyone else who can verify that you were home between twelve and six?"

Margery took another sip from her cup. "Mark Engel," she said. "I didn't want to get into this because it was such a pathetic scene. About two or three in the morning, he came back to the house. The party was still going on downstairs, at least to some extent. I had come upstairs with Henry. After a while we had fallen asleep. I heard some kind of commotion that woke me up. I put my hand on the other side of the bed, but Henry wasn't there. I put on my robe and came out into the hall. Mark Engel was just coming up the stairs. He asked me if I knew where Jody was. Then Henry came up the stairs behind him and pushed by him in the hall. He put an arm around me and looked back at Mark. I think he did it just to gloat. Just to make Mark mad. Henry can be a prick like that sometimes."

"What did Mark Engel do?" Segal asked.

"He literally collapsed, just leaned on the wall and slid down to the floor. I felt sorry for him, and I was pissed at Henry. I think all the stuff he had been through with his father dying last year and everything and now Jules was just too much. I think Jules and I were like a surrogate mother and father for him for a while. He wants to be like the others, but he's really still a child in some ways."

"Was there any particular reason he was looking for Jody in the middle of the night?" Segal asked.

"I don't know. I guess he thought she'd be there," Margery said. She popped the last of the chocolate and salted caramel doughnut into her mouth and chased it with the remainder of the coffee.

DINAH SAT ON the desk while the computer tech occupied her chair, leaning in toward her monitor. He looked from the screen down to the cell phone which was hooked to her computer by a thin white cable.

"That should do it, Miss Dinah," he said. He unplugged the cable from the phone and the computer. He handed her the phone and scrunched up his nose. "This thing smells terrible."

"Snuff," Dinah explained. She took the phone in two fingers and slipped it into the plastic evidence bag with the rest of Garth's belongings.

"You sure you got all the videos?" she said. "Let's watch one to make sure."

Dinah was no stranger to technology, but she wanted to make sure they got this right.

The tech keyed in a few strokes and brought one up on the screen.

The video was unsteady at first but settled down to a scene of the Ford diesel truck. It seemed to be on top of a hill above a parking lot associated with a shopping complex of four or five big box stores.

The catapult was in the bed of the truck. The tarp was off and one of the other guys was cranking the throwing arm into position. The microphone had picked up mostly wind noise so far. Garth stepped into the frame with a watermelon in his arms.

"OK. This is watermelon test number six," he said into the camera in the style of a news reporter. He placed the medium sized melon into the throwing basket and backed off. "We will be attempting to precision drop this watermelon onto the roof of the office supply store yonder."

He pointed to the target which was vast. Dinah questioned the precision needed to hit it. Garth bent down out of the frame and reappeared with a rope in hand.

"Count it down, boys," he said and voices off screen

complied. "Ten, nine, eight, seven, six five, four, three, two, one."

Garth pulled the rope and the arm swung with a speed and force that surprised Dinah. As the melon flew up and away it quickly became apparent that the boys had miscalculated. The arc of the melon was very high and at least a hundred feet short of the target. It came down on the hood of a late model Mustang and exploded as if it had been spiked with gun powder. The Mustang bounced on its suspension, the air bags inflated and the burglar alarm went off all at the same time.

"Oh, shit," they all said at once. The video showed a few seconds of two of the guys scrambling to get the tarp back over the truck bed, presumably so they could beat it out of there.

The computer tech laughed and stood up to relinquish the chair to Dinah.

"I hope they're all as good as that one," he said. "Let me know if you need any help uploading some to YouTube."

"Before you go, show me again how to find the time and date stamp in the metadata for the videos," Dinah said. The tech did so and took off.

Dinah leaned in toward the computer screen and watched a few more. The boys had experimented with some different fruit and vegetable combinations, but nothing compared to the watermelon for the dramatic impact explosion.

The most recent video showed the incident with the Maine Coon cat. Dinah could hear the cat screeching and Garth yelling out in pain. She could hear the other two guys laughing, but the picture was unsteady and she could just make out the cat repeatedly swatting and dragging its claws along the sides of Garth's head. She wondered how they expected to load the cat into the basket of the catapult and keep it there until the catapult was fired. She would have to ask them that question.

She found one video in which they had attempted to make a flaming ball as described in accounts from the Middle Ages. They had rolled up some rags into a ball and doused it with charcoal lighter fluid. Dinah thought it probably would have worked, except that they made the mistake of lighting it before they put it in the catapult basket. The video showed them trying to pick it up with a couple of sticks but, fortunately for them, they abandoned the idea before they ignited the fuel tank of the truck or caught their clothing on fire. The rest of the video was just them watching the thing burn on the ground like boy scouts around a campfire.

There were a lot of videos and Dinah realized it was going to take a while to go through all of them. She had started with the most recent and was working her way backward. She had the idea of jumping back to the day that the catapult was stolen. It would be great if they had actually videoed the theft itself.

She looked on the calendar for the date of theft, which was also the date of Hargrove's murder, of Koll's murder and the date of the infamous birthday party that had gone on all night, at least for some of them. She found no video with that date. She scrolled backward in time to a couple of days prior to that and found a video there.

The video did not show the theft of the catapult. Instead it seemed to be a meeting and she quickly realized it must be a get-together of the White Hog Militia. Garth must have been taking the video because she soon saw the other two knuckle heads walk by. Each of them had a gun in one hand and a barbeque sandwich in the other. They stopped, apparently waiting their turns to shoot on the line of a firing range. On the line several other men stood with a variety of firearms raised and ready.

Someone yelled, "All clear," and another voice said, "Fire at will," then all hell broke loose. After several seconds the gunfire tapered off to a moment of silence followed by a loud cheer.

"You'd think they just won the Battle of the Bulge," Dinah said to herself. She'd seen too much of the real thing to be impressed by any of this.

The video was nearly at its end. The guys who had just fired lowered their weapons and turned to make way for the next group. She caught a glimpse of the guy closest to the camera as he brushed by. She gasped. She thought she recognized his face, stopped it, and carefully backed it up, freezing the instant when the face pointed directly at the camera. It was Mark Morrison, the red-haired Marks brother.

TWENTY-THREE

Black Pug

SEGAL AND DINAH tried looking for Mark Morrison, first at his apartment, then at the Hargrove studio. No luck at either place.

Dinah had showed Segal the video and he had told her about the rabbit skin glue; the same stuff he let Mark Morrison remove from the main studio.

Segal pulled out his notebook. "That girl that Morrison was with at the party, she works at one of the potteries around here, right?" He turned back a few pages and found the entry. "I think it's downstairs and around the back."

They proceeded down the stairs, outside, and around to the back of the building where a large kiln was fired up under a metal awning. They could see the bright glow between the cracks around the bricked-up door. A woman wearing an apron smeared with clay removed a round plug in the door with a pair of tongs and peered in for a second then replaced the plug. Dinah asked her about Morrison's girlfriend and she motioned to a door at the back of the building.

Entering they found themselves in a large, well-lit room. To the right, was a table with a roller attached to a large crank wheel which Segal surmised was used for rolling out slabs of clay. Much of the room was taken up with shelves full of clay cups and pots and vases in all stages of preparation and also numerous plaster molds and jars full of glaze materials. Several tables for hand work and glaze application occupied the center of the room.

On the left wall, a number of pottery wheels could be seen, some powered by foot and some by motor. A girl sat at one of these with her hands shaping a spinning cone of wet clay. Mark Morrison himself sat behind her reaching around and placing his hands on hers while nuzzling the nape of her neck like Patrick Swayze did with Demi Moore in the movie *Ghost*. *I'll bet that's a must-do reenactment for anyone that works in this trade*, Segal thought.

They hung back a second then Dinah moved a chair a little to make some noise. The couple looked up and Morrison removed his arms and sat back. He did not seem especially glad to see the detectives, but he didn't seem especially upset or worried either. They both stood up, first Morrison, then his girlfriend. They hesitated for a moment with their hands held a little away from their bodies, fingers spread and covered with wet clay. They nodded to the detectives, then washed in a nearby sink.

Morrison walked out with Segal to a picnic table under the awning by the kiln. The girlfriend stayed inside with Dinah.

Morrison took out a pack of unfiltered smokes and lit one up.

Segal got right to it. "Tell me about your relationship with the White Hog Militia."

Morrison frowned and blew out a stream of smoke. "Man, I don't really have anything to do with those assholes."

Segal took out his phone to confront him with the video, but Morrison raised his hand.

"I did go to one meeting. This guy I know, lives in the same building as me, said he belonged to a gun club. I told him I had never shot a gun and he said I should come to a meeting with him, so I went."

"And where was this?" Segal asked. Morrison went on to describe the location and appearance of the place which left no doubt it was Adrien Koll's.

"The so-called meeting was just a bunch of guys sitting around drinking beer and eating barbeque and taking turns shooting their guns on a target range. Pretty soon there were no more targets and they were just shooting to shoot. I have to admit, it was pretty fun shooting a gun. My friend lent me a pistol. A thirty-eight."

"But you said they were assholes," Segal prompted.

"When the sun was going down they lit a campfire and started talking politics. Not politics really, not like most people talk, it was more conspiracy theories, only it started getting through my head that they really believed this stuff."

"Like what kind of stuff?" Segal asked.

"Like they think Washington is run by satanic people who eat children, stuff like that. My favorite was a website they talked about where you could order children online. You order pieces of furniture like chests or cabinets and the children come packed inside of the furniture."

"And they believe that?" Segal asked. He had heard similar stories but never really considered that anyone would really believe them. Not really.

"I swear to God," Morrison said. "One of the Hogs said he knew for a fact that the guy running for governor had ordered children that way."

"Wait a minute, our present governor, Price?" Segal asked.

"No, the guy running against him. The Hogs seemed to think our current governor is OK."

Segal paused to let this sink in. After a moment Morrison started talking again.

"The guy that told that story was older, he seemed to be in charge. I thought he looked familiar and then I realized where I had seen him before. It was the financial guy who used to come and visit Jules once in a while, the one that was buying the Joan of Arc painting. I hadn't recognized him without his business suit."

"Did you talk to Jules about it?"

"I was telling Henry and Mark Engel at the studio about it and Jules overheard us talking. Later on he asked me to tell him more. He really blew up about it. He got really pissed and said it couldn't be. He accused me of making the whole thing up. That was really what we were arguing about that day you asked me about. After a while I think he believed me and he was pissed at the investment guy."

BY THE TIME they finished at the pottery it was nearly five so they decided to compare notes at the Wedge Brewery.

"She confirmed what he told us about the night after the party. They were together all night in the spare bedroom at Margery's. Sounds like she was in better shape than Morrison was, sobriety wise. She said she didn't think he could have made it out the front door even if he had wanted to. I believed her," Dinah said.

Segal filled her in on his interview with Morrison.

"And you think he was telling the truth?" she asked when he finished.

"Seems right. Everything fits, so yeah, I believe him.

"So, what's next?" Dinah asked.

Segal looked around. "Maybe a Pilsner."

"Well, I've got to bounce. They're making me fill in a graveyard shift tonight."

Segal shook his head. "Part of the price of being a rookie."

IT WAS A little after eight in the morning when Dinah opened the front door and walked into the living room of the house on Montford Avenue, her home, now that she had moved in. One of her new housemates, Lucy, was sitting on the couch working on a laptop. She looked up from the screen, gasped, and put her hand to her mouth.

"Oh, Dinah, it's you!" she said, and gave a laugh of relief. "I just looked up and saw a uniform. I didn't recognize you at first.

Dinah smiled. "Yeah, that's what a uniform does. People see it and not you." She reached behind her head and released her hair out of the tight ponytail where it had been constrained during the night shift she had just finished. It billowed out and she started looking and feeling less official right away. This house was going to be the place where she would leave the uniform behind and just be herself. That was the plan anyway.

She trudged up to her room and looked out the front window. She realized she was scanning the street for signs of trouble or danger. She shook her head. *You don't have to be a soldier or a cop in your own home*, she told herself.

She changed into shorts and a T-shirt and went out for a short run. She stuck to the streets and sidewalks of her new neighborhood, exploring, learning the details, observing streets as well as all the small connections and paths and alleys that old neighborhoods always have. She could tell herself she didn't need to be a cop or soldier at home, but certain parts of the brain just didn't shut off so easily.

When she got back she showered and put on jeans and

a light blouse. She sat on the bed and thought about breakfast, but before she took action she let herself fall back on the bed where she quickly drifted off into a nap.

She awoke in a state of slight confusion. She had not intended to fall asleep. For a second she didn't know where she was nor what time of day it was. It came back quickly. Her new room, her move. She had worked the night shift. The digital clock by her bed showed 11:30 in the morning.

There was a tapping on her door. That was what had woken her up.

"Dinah, it's Lucy," her housemate called. Dinah noticed some anxiety in her voice.

Dinah sat up and told her to come in. She sat there on the end of the bed rubbing sleep from her eyes. "Must have dozed off a little," she said as Lucy rushed in.

"I'm a little worried about Jody," she said without preamble.

Dinah recalled the advice of one of her trainers, a tough old police sergeant: "When a person tells you they're a little worried it usually means they are very worried."

"Jody was supposed to meet me here to go to brunch, but she hasn't showed, and I haven't heard from her. Jody is never late for anything, ever. She doesn't stay out all night either."

"I assume you tried to call her?" Dinah asked.

"That's the thing. I called a while ago when I was out on the porch, and she didn't answer. I called again just now, and I happened to be in the living room. I could hear her ring tone coming from her room. I tried her door, but it's locked."

Dinah stood up. There could be any number of explanations for a person being late, even a person who was "never" late. But for a young woman in the twenty-first century to leave home willingly without her cell phone? That was a red flag waving in the breeze.

Dinah made for Jody's door, followed by Lucy.

Lucy asked as they ran down the stairs, "Do you know how to pick locks? Do they teach that in police school?"

Dinah didn't answer. She had switched into focus mode. She tried the door for herself and found it sturdy and locked.

She ran through the front door and down the steps and around to the side of the house where she remembered the screened porch which led to Jody's room. The screen door was open and the door from the porch to her room was ajar as well.

She ran in and knew instantly that Jody was not there. A room felt different when no one was in it, but she checked anyway just to confirm. No Jody. The cell phone was on the desk, her backpack with laptop and books was on the floor. Her purse hung by a strap from the back of the desk chair.

She scanned the room again and sniffed the air once, and then again.

Lucy came to the door behind her.

"What's that odor?" Dinah asked. "Kind of a chemical smell."

Lucy came in beside her and took a deep breath through her nose. "I know what that is," she said. "I remember it from chemistry lab. That's ether. Used to be used as an anesthetic for operations."

Dinah went back outside. She quickly reconstructed in her mind how this could happen. *Pull up all the way in the driveway on the other side of the house. In fact, if you cut your wheels you could swing a vehicle behind the house and completely out of view of the street. Sneak in the back door through the porch. Knock Jody out with some ether, load her up and pull out. The whole thing could be over in a minute or two.*

She called Segal.

SEGAL WAS IN his car, arranging and rearranging the facts of the case. Morrison had seemed like such a solid suspect with his history of violence and temper and his connection to the White Hog Militia and the rabbit skin glue. Segal was just visualizing him standing in the studio with that tub of white gelatinous stuff when Dinah's call came in. She gave a quick account of the situation at the house on Montford.

"Stay there," Segal said, "I'm on my way."

Segal phoned Walter and filled him in as well.

"You want me over there?" Walter asked.

"No, I'll check it out and call you back. How are you and Joe coming with the documents?"

"It's starting to make sense. We were stuck for a while until Joe thought of checking the other properties nearby. Most of them were bought up by Tectonic Plate companies in the last couple of years. That little maneuver with the building where you played tag with the wrecking ball? That was done to drive up the apparent value of the other buildings around it. When a real estate appraiser estimates the market value of a building they go a lot by the most recent selling prices of similar properties nearby. Drive up the price of one and you drive up the value of them all."

"Finally, something that makes sense. Pure everyday greed and dirty dealing," Segal said.

DINAH CAME OUT on the porch when Segal arrived. He was surprised to see her out of uniform.

"You're not on duty?" he asked.

Dinah shook her head no. "Remember, I pulled the double shift yesterday."

"How did you find out Jody was missing?" Segal asked. He was totally confused.

"I moved into the room upstairs," Dinah said. "I live here now."

"Oh," Segal said. Somehow it seemed strange, like getting involved with a suspect in an investigation. But then, who was he to talk about that.

"Show me what you found," he said.

As Dinah led him back to Jody's room Segal saw the house in a new light. It was a nice place. This time Jody's door was open when he turned the handle. Dinah had unlocked it when she came in through the door to the porch. She explained that all to Segal.

"When I saw that she left these, I really got worried," she said, indicating the backpack and the cell phone.

Segal did not need any explanation of what this implied.

"And, you may not smell it now, but when we first came into the room we got a slight whiff of ether."

"Ether?" Segal said. "That's the second time ether has come up in the last couple of days. They found it in the blood analysis of our buddy, Belincort. I know it was used as an anesthetic, but that's way out of date. Who would even have that around anymore?"

"Chemistry labs have it," Lucy said. She had wandered into the room when she heard their voices. "That's how I knew the smell, from organic chemistry lab. It wouldn't be that hard to get."

Segal took that in and thought for a moment. Ordinarily a college student missing for a few hours would not raise any red flags, but these were not ordinary circumstances, and he did not like where the other details pointed.

"You haven't been contacted by anyone about this have you?"

"Are you thinking of a ransom demand as in kidnapping?" Dinah asked.

"It's a possibility," Segal said.

Both young women shook their heads.

"Have you checked email, phone messages, texts?" Segal asked. "Is there a landline in the house?"

"There's no landline," Lucy said, "but we can check email."

She and Dinah both left the room checking cell phones for emails and messages. It gave Segal a chance to think for a moment. He was genuinely concerned for the girl. He would file an all-points bulletin at the station, but he knew he couldn't really count on that getting results. He couldn't report it as a kidnapping without a ransom demand. Besides, that's not what he thought it was anyway. Not in the usual sense.

Lucy and Dinah came back and reported.

"Nothing but junk mail," Lucy said.

"No luck here either," Dinah added. "What about her parents?"

Lucy shook her head. "They live pretty close and they have my number. If they heard anything they would have been over here or at least called me."

"Are they especially wealthy?" Segal asked.

"I don't think so," Lucy said.

For a moment they were all silent.

Then Segal spoke up. "We should track down the Marks brothers and see if they know anything."

"I already talked to Henry Marks and Mark Morrison," Dinah said. "Neither one has seen her."

"How about Mark Engel?" Segal asked

"Just tried. No answer," Dinah said. "You think he could be in trouble, too?

"It's possible," Segal said, "Mark Engel was next on my list to talk to anyway. I'll go over there right now."

"I'll come with you for backup," Dinah said.

After seeing her in action a couple of times now Segal realized she was exactly the kind of person he would want for backup in a dangerous situation. But this was not that kind of situation, and anyway someone needed to cover the home base. Jody might just turn up yet, or a ransom demand might come in.

"I'll get Walter if I need someone," he said. "I need you to stay here. Keep an eye on things. Especially watch for any sign of contact about a ransom. Get her phone out of her room and answer it if it rings. Let me know immediately if anything happens.

Dinah nodded.

Segal called Walter and filled him in on what had just happened. "Mark Engel wasn't at the studio and he isn't answering his cell phone. I'm going to try his apartment."

"You want me to meet you there?"

"I'll call if I need you," Segal said.

"You think this is a serious situation?" Walter asked.

"If by serious you mean the possibility that someone else could die in some bizarre fashion, then yes, I think it is a serious situation."

Twelve minutes later Segal found the address: a small house on a side street in West Asheville with a ratty looking yard, a little grass, a lot of weeds and some bare ground. No sign of the blue van or any sign of life inside.

He knocked and got no answer. He tried calling Mark Engel's cell phone as he listened carefully with his ear to the door. He tried looking in the window but saw no one.

"Can I help you?" asked a voice behind him. It was a lady who looked to be in her seventies. She had long gray hair which didn't seem to be brushed in any particular premeditated fashion. She wore a long loose dress, and running shoes. Beside her was a black pug on a short leash. The pug sat down and made soft snorting sounds.

Segal showed her his badge and introduced himself.

"I'm looking for Mark Engel. Do you know him?" Segal asked.

"I knew his father. He was my doctor, even when I couldn't really afford one, so I'm happy to let Mark use this little house while he's going to school," the woman said. "I own this house and I live across the street. Is he in trouble?"

"He might be a witness to a crime. I need to talk to him," Segal said.

"Let's go in and see if he's there." She took a set of keys out of her pocket, unlocked, and pushed the door open.

Segal raised his eyebrows and said, "Great." He was thinking, *lucky break. No warrant needed. She invited me inside.* The landlady stepped aside, and the pug watched him with no sign of genuine interest. The lady said she would take the dog for a short walk and be back in a few minutes.

He walked into a neat, clean living area. Most of the space was one unbroken room, kitchen area to the right, bed to the left. In the back a door stood open to a bathroom. On the opposite side of the kitchen there was another door. Segal guessed it was a storage room or perhaps a laundry room. Everything was simple. In the middle of the room was a small table with two chairs. Segal wondered if Mark Engel ever had anyone over. There were a couple of books on the table along with a notebook which Segal assumed was for sketching. The bed was made, clothes hung neatly in the closet, kitchen clean, and dishes put away.

The guy lives like a soldier, Segal thought, *or a monk.*

There was no sign of violence or disruption. He continued to circle the room slowly, looking for any clue as to where Engel might be.

He came to the notebook again. He flipped it open and leafed through a few of the pages. There were some sketches of anatomical details, hands, eyes, knees. There were a couple of Jody. He must have been sketching while the master was working on his painting because she was wearing her armor. There was another of her sitting in one of those canvas director's chairs in the studio with her legs crossed and her sword leaning against the arm of the chair.

He flipped another page. There were sketches of radiant crosses, assault rifles, and knives. Segal recognized them as elements of the insignia patch of the White Hog Militia.

Segal flipped another page and saw a sketch of a catapult. The sketch was executed in sanguine colored chalk. It had enough mechanical detail that you could probably actually build one based on this drawing alone. It reminded him of some of the drawings in da Vinci's notebooks, designs for fanciful engines of war. He realized it was not just a catapult, it was *the* catapult. The one from the university.

At the bottom of the page the date, May 30, 1431, was written in brown ink.

He took out his phone and got a photo of that page and the one with the insignia.

"Looks like Mark is not here," the landlady said, sticking her head back into the room. "Are you ready to leave?" Beside her the pug snorted as if he, too, wanted an answer to that question.

Segal placed the notebook back on the table and followed the old lady out the door. He knew very well that he had been pushing the limits of searching without a warrant and he didn't want to push it too far.

"When did you last see Mark?"

"I saw his van pulling out late last night," the landlady said.

On the way out he noticed a picture taped to the end of the kitchen cabinet. He didn't know how he had missed it before. It was Dinah, the picture from the newspaper article. The same one that was taped up down at the station. Only in this one Engel had sketched in armor over her roller derby pads to make her look more like Joan of Arc. It made the hairs on the back of his neck stand up. He pulled out his phone to call Walter.

TWENTY-FOUR

Porch Swing

AT THE HOUSE on Montford Avenue, Dinah did her best not to pace, but every time she let her mind wander, she found herself walking back and forth across the living room again. All her training and experience had prepared her for action. Waiting was making her nuts.

She glanced at Lucy, sitting on the couch trying to do something on her laptop. Dinah realized she must be driving the poor girl crazy, so she went out on the porch to release her nervous energy on the swing. This was successful, at least to some extent, in calming her rattled nerves. Soon her breathing slowed down to match the gentle rhythmic sound and motion, and the slow deep breathing had a magical effect on her mood as well. She reviewed what she knew about the situation, trying to remember anything that might be useful.

She thought back to the very first time they had met, when she had given Jody a ride home from the studio and talked with her about the Marks brothers, and what Jody had told her about each one. Jody had admired the older two, at least she admired their work. On the personal level they were too full of themselves for her taste. They had never asked her out or hit on her sexually, assuming, like some other people, that she had a thing going on with Julius Hargrove, an assumption that Jody denied. Mark Engel seemed immature and a little pathetic, but he was nice to her.

Jody had insisted that his excuses for stopping by her house were harmless. She drifted back into the house and into Jody's room for another look.

The room seemed cold and empty to her now as if no one had ever lived there, or more accurately, as if the person who had lived there was now a part of history. It gave her a chill down her back.

She leafed through the drawings in the large standing folder again. *People with this kind of talent live in a different world*, she thought. She went over to the desk and rummaged through the drawers, this time examining each item more closely. She found nothing of note in the wide flat drawer in the center, just the usual collection of pencils, pens, paper clips, rubber bands, and loose change.

She opened the top drawer on the right and saw a stack of mail which she placed on the desktop for closer inspection. It was the usual stuff that you might find in anyone's desk drawer: bills, advertisements, and other junk mail. On the very bottom of the pile she found an invitation to a barbeque dated last fall. It was from the fine arts consortium, the group to which several artists, including all the ones associated with Hargrove's studio, belonged. She couldn't tell from the invitation whether Jody had gone or not, but it was the location that caught her eye. It was held at the Engel family farm in the Forks of Ivy, and it gave the address.

Dinah thought for a moment. She wondered if she should call Segal. It was one more place they might look for Mark Engel.

The sound of a cell phone made her jump. For a second,

she was confused. It was not her usual cell phone ring tone. Then she realized it was Jody's phone, in her other pocket.

She found it and checked the screen. It said the call was from Mark Engel. She answered immediately. It was Jody's voice, frantic and hushed at the same time.

"Who is this?" Jody asked.

"It's me, Dinah. Where are you? Are you all right?" Dinah could not seem to get the questions out fast enough.

There was a pause for a moment with just heavy breathing. She thought she could hear music playing faintly in the background.

"I'm not sure where I am," Jody said in the heavy whisper she had used before. "I woke up a few minutes ago and I have a terrible headache and I'm feeling sick. I think I'm going to throw up."

There was another pause, with the music faintly in the background, just enough to tell the accent on the back beat.

"Jody, where are you?" Dinah called. She was trying to keep the panic out of her voice.

She waited a moment hearing only rapid breathing on the other end. Then came a man's voice, though not distinctly. It was clear he was somewhere else in the room. She thought she heard the word, "Hey!" and then something else spoken rapidly, then nothing. The call was ended.

Dinah just looked at the phone, trying to think what this meant—what she should do next. Was it a kidnapper offering proof of life? Maybe Jody had been kidnapped and managed to get to a phone. It was Engel's phone so he might be a victim as well, like Segal said. Maybe Jody just got drunk at a party last night and passed out and that's why she had a headache and nausea. But those were all also side effects of ether.

Dinah pulled out her own phone and hit Lieutenant Segal's number. It went to voicemail. She tried the station and transferred to dispatch when he did not pick up there. Dispatch told her that Segal had checked in from West Asheville and that he and Walter were with the chief.

Dinah put her hand on her hip and looked around the room as if searching for something that would tell her what to do. She snatched up the invitation she had looked at before and made her decision. Segal had told her to stay put, but the situation had changed. "Tell Segal I'm going to the Engel place at the Forks of Ivy."

She ran upstairs and got her gun and badge and then out to the porch where she told Lucy about the phone call and the invitation. Dinah copied the address from the invitation into the map program on her phone.

"You're sure you can stay while I'm gone?" she asked Lucy. Since she was acting outside of orders, she wanted to make sure the home base was covered.

DINAH WAS GRIM as she guided the jeep through the side streets of the Montford Avenue neighborhood, but as she accelerated up the entrance ramp and onto the highway that would take her north out of Asheville her breathing became slower and deeper. Doing something, being in action, moving fast, focused her mind, just as it did in sports: just as it had done in the Army when she went on patrol.

She stepped on the gas and got the jeep up to speed, fast but controlled. She glanced at the map function displayed on her phone when the mechanical navigation voice instructed her to proceed for fourteen miles and take the exit for the Forks of Ivy. *Must be really out in the country,* she thought. As far as she knew there was very little in the way of commercial enterprise in that area. She hoped Lieutenant Segal would call before she got there, but as of the time she rolled off the exit no call had come.

She proceeded on the curving roads. When the voice of her phone navigator told her she had reached her destination she hesitated for a moment at the end of the driveway. If Jody had been kidnapped this could be a dangerous area, for Jody and for herself. It might not be a great idea to roll in and announce her presence. She let the jeep glide past the driveway and found a place around a turn in the road where she could pull off under a couple of maple trees, out of sight.

It turned out to be a good place as she found she could slip into a patch of dense woods and approach fairly close without being seen from the house. She clipped her gun in its holster to her belt and slipped her badge into a pocket of her jeans. She exhaled slowly through pursed lips, her preparation for action.

She followed along, parallel with the driveway until she was even with the front porch. From there she could also see how the driveway bent around the back of the house, as well as the outbuildings and silo behind. She could tell from tire tracks in the dirt that some kind of vehicle had been there recently. Looking carefully, she could just make out the back of a blue van in one of the outbuildings.

Dinah held her position in the shadows of the trees for several minutes looking and listening for any sign of movement or activity. After a while she saw and heard a window sash go up in the house. *Must be getting stuffy in there by this time in the afternoon*, she thought. She saw no sign of air conditioners. In a moment she heard the faint sound of music coming from the open window. She held her breath to concentrate. It was music all right, Reggae: Peter Tosh singing *Bush Doctor.*

"Yeah, you're a bush doctor all right," she said under her breath.

She watched the windows carefully for a few more moments. Seeing no movement, she decided to risk an approach to the house. It required crossing a narrow strip of lawn, the driveway, then another strip of lawn, completely in the open. She removed her gun from the belt holster and sprinted in a partial crouch. When she reached the front of the house she pressed her back to the wall so she could not be seen from the windows. She waited, silently taking a couple of deep breaths.

Nothing happened and all she heard was Peter Tosh playing softly. She desperately wanted to see what was going on inside but couldn't tell what move would be safest.

To her right was the front porch with a door and two windows. She guessed the door was rarely used by anyone living there since all the other buildings and parking places were to the rear. At that moment she heard the back door open and shut. She heard the sound of someone crunching across the gravel, she guessed toward one of the out buildings. She figured this would be as good a chance as she was likely to get.

Dinah stepped on the end of the porch and pulled herself up by the railing. She stepped over and transferred her weight gently onto that foot and pulled the other foot behind. The boards of the porch looked old and creaky so she took her next step carefully and got into a position where she could peek in the front window.

She saw what looked like a medical exam room: chair, padded table, cabinets and counter with various bottles and boxes, a blood pressure cuff and meter hanging from a hook on the wall. She was surprised at first, but then she remembered that Mark Engel's father had been an old-fashioned family doctor before he himself fell ill.

She pressed her face against the window now so that she could see the right corner of the room, and there was Jody, collapsed in a reclining chair. She was asleep, passed out or drugged, Dinah couldn't tell which, but it didn't matter. She was dressed in her Joan of Arc armor just like in the painting. Dinah had to get her out.

She stepped sideways to the door, but found it locked when she got there. She moved back to the window. Dinah could see the latch inside and it was not engaged. Slipping the gun back in its holster, she pushed up against the lower sash with both hands. Just like every window in every old house it was stuck. She repositioned for a better lifting stance and this time it moved up, making more noise than she would have preferred. She ducked and stepped inside.

The room still smelled like a doctor's office with the slight odor of disinfectant. She went over to Jody and checked her pulse. She was out cold, breathing slowly. Dinah took her hand and patted it trying to rouse her without making noise but it was of no use.

Dinah tiptoed to the office door and peered around the edge. She saw no one and heard only the Reggae music playing softly from some other room in the house.

She thought only for an instant about what to do. She would call for backup and then try to get Jody out of there and to her jeep. It wouldn't be the first time she used a fireman's carry. She reached for her phone and punched the screen. No service. There was often spotty service out in the mountains away from town. She knew there was service out by the road because the navigator had worked. She would have to go out there.

Dinah bent over and stuck her head out the window to

begin the awkward process of stepping through it and out onto the porch. In this terrible off-balance position she felt someone grab the back of her collar and pull her forward. At the same time she felt a cloth held tight against her mouth and nose and the sweet vaporous smell of ether. She realized she would pass out if she did not free herself, and quickly.

Her first instinct was to pull away and back inside, but her weight was too far forward and the attacker was too strong. She heard her jujitsu coach speaking to her from the past: "Go with the opponent's force, not against it." She grabbed the attacker's wrist, pushed forward, and dove out the window, rolling into a summersault when she hit the porch floor. This got her out and freed her from the assailant's grip.

It was a good move and well executed. She sprung up to her feet by the porch railing. But when she spun around to face the attacker the world would not stop spinning. The ether had done its job. Her vision blurred and she felt her stomach drop in nausea. The last thing she saw was the blurry outline of a man as he advanced and put the soaked cloth back over her face.

HAVE YOU HEARD anything from Dinah?" Segal asked when he got back to the station.

"I just tried calling, but she didn't pick up, it goes right to messages," Gina said.

As he breezed by she handed him a handful of messages and mail. Segal tossed them on his desk without looking at them. No time for the routine stuff just now.

"One of those messages is from Tommy. He wants you to call him," Gina said.

"OK," Segal said. "I'll call him as soon as I can."

Walter, who had been busy at the computer screen

looked up and grinned. "I think we have something significant here."

"Well, I have something significant, too," Segal said. Gina joined them.

"First of all, do we have anything on Jody Mare yet?" Segal asked.

Walter and Gina both shook their heads no.

"Like I said, I tried to get Dinah on the phone but no luck," Gina said.

"Well keep trying and if you don't hear from her in thirty minutes or so, send someone over to the house on Montford to see what's going on."

He sat down at his desk and turned to Walter. "OK, what did you guys dig up?"

"Connections," Walter said. "Interesting connections. You already know about some of them. Koll, Hargrove, and Belincort all connected through the questionable business and investment deals."

"And you can probably throw the governor in with that group as well, or at least the governor's office," Segal added.

"And maybe the governor's family," Gina threw in. Segal winced. He knew she was getting a bad vibe from Alexa, and she hadn't even met her in person.

"Anyway," Walter continued, "Joe has access to this program that looks for business connections in public records. You put in a bunch of names of people and companies and it looks in filings and court records and deeds and so forth for connections between the entities. We got the ones we were expecting but what we didn't expect were these."

Walter spread out three pages of paper. Segal and Gina leaned over to look. There were a number of listings that included the name Dr. Stephen Engel. Also, the estate of Dr. Stephen Engel and Mark Engel.

"So Dr. Stephen Engel was Mark Engel's father, and all these legal actions were filed on his behalf," Segal said.

"Yes, Mark must have filed some on behalf of his father when he was still alive, and then for the estate after he died," Walter explained.

They examined the list closer. The targets of the lawsuits included many of the shell companies owned by Tectonic Plate investors and ultimately by Koll and the group of wealthy insiders.

"And look at this one," Walter said, "A filing with the State Insurance Commission against Bell Tower Insurance."

"Looks like it was dismissed," Gina said.

"Right," Segal said, "By a board no doubt appointed by our governor."

They took a moment to absorb the information.

"So when we heard about the rabbit skin glue we were thinking Morrison because he asked for it that day in the studio. We should have been thinking Engel, the guy tasked with making it," Segal said.

Segal filled them in on what he had found at Engel's house. He showed them the pictures from the notebook.

"They're all into making the artwork using the old authentic techniques and materials. But which one among them was the most likely to take that to the extreme? Who actually made the glue? Who had a forge to make the arrow tips?"

"That farm at the Forks of Ivy. Engel's farm," Walter said. "Remember the workshop with all the tools for repairing farm equipment, including a forge?"

They flipped to the drawing of the catapult.

"He told us he was taking history and engineering. He must have worked on the catapult too," Walter said.

"Yes, and Engel told us his father was a country doctor.

He could have left some ether and other drugs and Mark would probably understand how to use them."

They looked back over the photos from Engel's apartment. It all made sense.

"What do you think this date at the bottom means? May 30, 1491," Walter asked.

"It's the day Joan of Arc was killed," Gina said.

Segal and Walter looked at her surprised that she would have such an arcane fact in her head.

"Remember, you had me do some research on Joan?" she said.

"And today is May thirtieth," Segal said.

After a brief silence while they all took this in Walter said, "Remind me how she died."

"She was burned at the stake." Gina's voice was little more than a whisper.

"I know exactly where he's taking her," Segal said.

"That farm at the Forks of Ivy?" Gina asked.

"That's too private. He wants this to be a public spectacle. He's taking her to the festival at Lake Eden."

DINAH REGAINED CONSCIOUSNESS piece by piece. Along with her awareness came a sharp pain in her head and a sickly unstable feeling in her stomach. As her mind cleared enough to look around she only became more confused. She was in a round room with smooth walls made of glazed tile. The ambient light was dim but far above her was a random pattern of pie shaped slices of bright sunlight. The surface she was resting upon was spongy. There was a sweet organic odor in the air, sort of malty, which did not help with the nausea.

She sat up slowly and paused for a moment to let the spinning in her head stop. The surface she sat on was composed of loose material. She picked up a handful and let it pour out through her fingers. It was ground up corn stalks and pieces of corn and cob, slightly damp.

"Silage," she said under her breath. She realized with a jolt that she was in the silo she had noticed when she first observed the farmyard from the woods.

She got slowly to her feet and tried to stand up straight. With the unsteady floor, her general unease, and the smell of silage she was struck by a violent wave of nausea that sent her staggering to the wall. She bent over and retched harshly, placing one hand against the wall to hold herself up. She coughed and spat and after some moments wiped her mouth with the back of her hand. She side-stepped her way a few feet to her left, still leaning on the wall to keep her balance. When she was some distance from the mess she started taking slow deep breaths, in through her nose and out through her mouth.

With each breath Dinah felt a little stronger, a little clearer, and a little more stable. She took a step back from the wall and found she could maintain her balance. After a couple more breaths she began to assess her situation.

The walls of the silo were made of brown ceramic blocks with a shiny glaze on their surface: very old-fashioned construction. They were uniform all the way around the cylinder except for a vertical column of square doors. The doors were a little under three feet square and made of wood. The bottom one was larger. Light shone through the cracks around the door, but when she pushed on it she found it locked. A stronger push told her it was not going to budge. The hinges and bolts felt very firm.

No light shone around the other, smaller doors and she realized they must be mounted inside the enclosed shoot she had always noticed running up the side of silos. She

was no farm girl, but she assumed it had something to with
loading or unloading the contents. Apparently as the contents were used up the farmer could remove a succession
of doors one after the other, beginning at the top and working his or her way down. The good news, she realized, was
that there must be a ladder on the outside allowing a person
to climb up and remove those doors. She reached up to the
first of the smaller doors, but it was secured.

She stepped back to get a better look. All the openings
were closed with the wooden doors except for the one at
the very top. It was open. If she could manage to climb up
there she should be able to get through and onto the ladder.

That was a big if. The open door was a good three stories
up there, maybe more. Each of the wooden doors was not
quite flush with the walls but there were a couple of inches
or less of ledge to grip with finger tips or to stand on with
the toe of a shoe. She had done a little rock climbing since
she had come to the mountains. It would have been a fun
challenge if she were belayed with a rope, but of course,
there was no possibility of that here and now. Dinah's only
other option was to wait for help. That might never come
or if it did it might be too late to help Jody. Dinah would
have to go for it.

She stretched but found she could not quite reach the
ledge of the first square door. It took a little bit of a jump
for her to reach it with the fingers of one hand, then pull
herself up enough to get the second hand to the ledge as
well. Meanwhile her feet searched for something to push
against. They found a thin purchase on a ledge above the
main door. From there she began to push her body up.

Now it was her fingers that were looking for something
to grasp. The only thing they found was the vertical ledge
on each side of the door. By pushing out on these she could

just maintain enough pressure to stay erect and keep most of her weight on her toes with her body plastered against the wall of the silo.

She made it up to the second door and was pushing for the third when her foot slipped and she went down. She managed to land feet first and roll out of the landing and not get hurt. Dinah brushed herself off and took a couple of breaths. She was already breathing hard and starting to sweat. This, she knew, could be a problem if her hands got wet and slick.

She took her shirt off and tied the arms around her waist. This would help her keep cool and give her something to wipe her hands on if she needed to dry them off. She looked up at the challenge again. If she could make it past the third door things should get a little easier because the ledges looked wider.

Dinah stood back for a moment to center her concentration. She knew that once the climb began the endurance clock would be ticking. There was nowhere to pause partway up and no way to recharge the batteries. What she needed was a deliberate series of moves, not hurried or careless, but no hesitation either. She closed her eyes and visualized the first movements.

One more breath and she launched herself at the wall. After the initial scramble over the large bottom door she soon developed a rhythm of moves, hands and feet, shifting of weight, up and over one door after another. She dared not let her mind wander, no thinking about how high she was or how much she had left to go. She was so concentrated on the moment and the particular move she was executing at the time, that it was actually a surprise when her fingers reached the ledge of the top opening. Since the door was removed from this one her fingers could grip the ledge solidly and she could pause and take a deep breath.

Now the challenge was how to get her body through the opening. One more good heave should do it.

Dinah moved her right hand over for a wider grip and gave a strong pull. The block she pulled on shifted and came loose. It fell away and seemed to take forever before Dinah heard the sound of it thudding into the loose material of the floor below. Her feet had already left the thin ledge when she started the move so she was now left dangling by her left arm. Her body had rotated out a little away from the wall.

She closed her eyes and concentrated. Her body rotated back around and her right hand found a new grip. Her toes found the thin ledge once again. She pulled up, more cautiously this time, and lunged through the opening head first. There was a pause with the weight of her body at hip level, center of gravity on other side of the wall. Her hand found the rung of the ladder just where she expected it to be. She scooted on through and righted herself in the close confines of the access tube. For once her small stature was an advantage. She gave one more look over the ledge and back down into the silo before descending the ladder to the ground.

As soon as Dinah reached the ground she dropped into a crouch and ran behind the silo where she would be out of sight of the house. She took stock of the situation. The sun was getting low in the sky, telling her she had been out for some time. Her gun was gone, holster and all. No phone and no badge either. She listened closely but heard only the wind in the trees. No Reggae music either. She moved to where she could see the house, this time the back porch. No movement there either.

To her left was an outbuilding. The big front doors were rolled open and when she ventured a peek inside she saw that the blue van was gone. There were no other vehicles in sight.

She suspected that whoever had been here was decamped, but she used caution in approaching the house anyway. A few peeks inside and careful listening convinced her it was empty.

Dinah went through the back door which led through a mud room and then into a kitchen. Moving quickly to the front of the house she found the examination room where Jody had been, but Jody was gone too.

In the center of the house was a space that must have served as an entry way from the front door and a waiting room in the days the doctor had his practice there. The examination room was off to one side of this entry way. On the other side was a room which must have served as the doctor's study. Dinah felt drawn to it.

Inside she saw a desk with a comfortable looking chair and a bookcase with some medical reference books. There was an old black landline phone that excited her for a moment until she picked up the receiver and found the line dead. The only other objects on the desk were a sketch book and a folded brochure. The brochure was for the music festival at Lake Eden. She had heard a little about it before. The date was today, May thirtieth, she realized.

She flipped open the sketch book, presumably Mark Engel's. The last drawing was done in sanguine conté. It was of Jody, lying on the examination table, eyes closed, just as Dinah had seen her earlier that day, armor in place. Dinah felt a chill run through her body.

She turned away from the desk and noticed a gun case against the other wall. There was nothing remarkable about the gun case. It would have seemed out of place in a doctor's office except that this was a farmhouse too. The case contained two shotguns, a large caliber rifle with a scope, which she assumed was for deer hunting, and a smaller twenty-two caliber rifle. It was the object leaning against the gun case that really got her attention: a crossbow, complete with a quiver of wooden bolts.

It was enough to set her in motion. She ran to the examination room and found a pair of gloves. She also tore the sheet of paper off the examination table. Back in the study she spread the sheet out on the desk and placed the crossbow on it and wrapped it up. As an afterthought she grabbed the sketchbook and threw it in too.

She broke into a run when she got out the front door with her package and breathed a sigh of relief when she saw her jeep where she left it, underneath the maple tree.

TWENTY-FIVE

Grape Popsicle

SEGAL AND WALTER were in the old Volvo headed toward Black Mountain. Walter opened the glove box and pulled out the emergency flasher which could be put on top of the car anchored by magnets.

Segal nodded approval but said, "Let's turn that off when we get to the festival. No need to announce our arrival."

"I hope you're wrong about this thing at the festival," Walter said.

"I hope I am too," Segal said, but he knew he wasn't. "Why don't you call that professor at UNCA and see if they actually took the catapult to the festival."

Walter nodded and punched in the number. The call was answered on the first ring and Walter posed the question. Segal could tell from the monosyllables Walter made on his end of the call that the answer was yes.

"Four members took it over. They're meeting a fifth one there," Walter said. "The fifth man is going to operate the catapult while the other four head to higher ground to watch and record it on video."

By the time Segal and Walter arrived at the fairgrounds the sun was sinking toward the western ridgeline. Segal knew full well that once it dipped below that ridgeline the problem of finding Jody and Mark Engel would become exponentially more difficult and the danger exponentially higher, approaching what some called the Vantasner Danger Meridian. They had no time to lose.

Segal had enjoyed the Lake Eden Arts Festival, or LEAF, several times in the past as a regular music fan. It was held twice a year at the beautiful Lake Eden venue east of Asheville. This year the theme of the festival was Renaissance Fair. In Segal's opinion this was redundant as the attendees of the festival, especially the women, often chose to dress in clothes reminiscent of that period anyway.

They pulled slowly past the entrance gate, taking in the scene. The fair was big, chaotic, and decentralized. There were several stages, food booths and trucks, tents for various crafts and activities. There were a number of areas set aside for camping. Everywhere people walked around, people in all sorts of dress. There was everything from modern day casual clothes to people dressed true to the renaissance theme. Children ran around, chased each other and played, also in various kinds of dress, shoes definitely optional. It would have been a lot of fun under different circumstances.

They got out and proceeded on foot.

"How the hell are we going to find Engel or Jody Mare in this mess," Walter asked. Segal spotted an information booth at the edge of one of the craft tents. He nudged Walter's shoulder and pointed to it and they both headed that way.

Segal's phone rang. He saw that it was Tommy calling. "Not now, Tommy," he said under his breath, and he slid the phone back into his pocket without answering.

In the booth a girl in an official LEAF T-shirt was talking to a woman who seemed distraught about missing some kind of performance. Segal looked around at the dimming light, waiting for them to finish. Walter picked up a pamphlet from a stack on the counter and found a schedule inside. He quickly ran his finger down the list to the current time. He nudged Segal and pointed to the line. It read, "Lighting of the Bonfire."

Segal pulled out his badge and interrupted the conversation. "Excuse me, Miss. Where is the bonfire?" he asked. The girl in the booth started to look a little irritated, but she apparently sensed the urgency of the situation from Segal's demeanor. She leaned over the counter and craned her neck and pointed.

"You can see the stack of wood over there, across the water."

Segal looked in that direction and he could just make it out across the north end of the little lake.

"All right Walter let's go!"

They took off and the girl called after them, "Wait, no one is allowed in that area until the fire is lit. It's dangerous!"

Segal took no notice and sprinted toward the stack of wood just visible in the dusk across the face of the water which now reflected the red ball of the sun. Walter was right with him. At first they thought they would have to run all the way around the south end of the lake, but then noticed a thin strip of land that went all the way over, actually dividing the water into two lakes. They headed for that.

They spotted a rope with a handmade sign that said "Do Not Enter" hanging from it stretched across their path. They both cleared it like track stars.

There was a man in a reflective vest like the ones worn by the guys directing traffic. They flew by him in a flash and he yelled after them to stop. Segal held up his badge and yelled back at the guy, "Call for backup, police and medical." The guy fumbled in his vest pocket for a radio and raised it to his ear.

Dɪɴᴀʜ ʀᴀᴄᴇᴅ ᴅᴏᴡɴ the highway toward Asheville while her mind worked ahead, trying to anticipate what she might find. She forced herself to slow her breathing and concentrate on the present moment. She knew from experience and training how dangerous the unfocused mind was in a situation that called for extreme action.

First, she had to think about how to navigate to this place. She was pretty sure she knew approximately where it was. She knew a way to get there, but had a feeling there were short cuts. She decided to stick with the known entity for now. There was already too much unknown. She had lost her phone, along with her gun, her badge, and her keys. Thank God for the old trick her father had showed her of hiding a spare key in a magnetic box under the rear fender, or she would have been without wheels too.

She had considered stopping someplace to call the station, but instinct told her she could not spare the time.

Dinah flew south down the highway, looped around the center of town on the bypass, and headed east on the interstate. It seemed an eternity before the exit for Black Mountain came up.

She slowed as she pulled into town, not knowing exactly where to go and got quick directions from a man crossing the street. It wasn't too long before she found herself entering the camp grounds at the north entrance at which point she stopped, not sure of where to go next. A couple of teenaged girls wearing cutoff jeans walked side by side, crossing the road in front of the jeep, each working on a grape popsicle and speaking in low voices and laughing.

Dinah leaned out the window and waved them toward her.

"Hey girls, can I borrow a phone, I lost mine," she said.

The girls both looked at her skeptically. *Jeez, am I old enough to be getting that look?* Dinah thought.

"It's an emergency," Dinah said. She said it with enough genuine authority that one of the girls pulled a cell phone out of her back pocket and handed it to her without taking the popsicle out of her mouth.

Dinah wanted to call Segal but she realized she didn't have his number. She pressed the screen for 911 but got only static.

The teen who had given her the phone took the popsicle out of her mouth long enough to ask for the phone back.

"Is there no reception here?" Dinah asked.

The girl rolled her eyes and took the popsicle out of her mouth again. "It's the LEAF festival. Too many people using up all the bandwidth. Happens every year." She held her hand out for the phone. "They're supposed to launch a comet or rocket or something to light the bonfire. I want to get a picture of it."

It took Dinah a second to adsorb what the girl said and to recognize the danger it represented.

She tossed the phone back to the girl and rolled the jeep forward. She moved on carefully, surveying all around for any sign of Mark Engel or Jody or Segal or Walter. There were a lot of people now walking in the rapidly fading light. They were heading down the hill and to the right where a crowd was gathering on the shore of the lake. Maybe waiting for the comet to launch, she thought.

She moved forward slowly. There was an empty parking lot to her left. Odd, she thought. This should be prime parking. She rolled up to the entrance and saw a sign the read Handicapped Parking, but there was a rope across the entrance and a handmade sign reading "Temporarily closed." She studied the lot for a moment and on the far side by a clearing in the trees she glimpsed the top of a blue van. She got out and undid the rope and then cruised the jeep slowly into the lot.

It was Engel's van all right. Dinah remembered its unique pattern of scrapes and dents. She parked and approached it with caution. She peeked in the window and saw no one. She could see her badge and phone laying on the center console. Her holster was there too, minus the pistol. If he had not been armed before, he was now.

Dinah went back to the jeep and pulled out the wrapped package she had thrown in the back, then moved down the row of trees with stealth and caution.

When she got to the end of the row she paused for a moment to look around. To her right the hill curved down to the north end of the lake. Further on in that direction the crowd was building, and she could hear the low varied sound of the people in the distance. Across the small lake she could make out the outline of a stack of wood that would be a bonfire. She caught some movement by it in the soft glow from the lights near the crowd at the center of the festival.

To the left, behind the parking lot there was much less light. She heard movement before she saw it. A small white light came on and a mechanical ratcheting sound came from the same spot.

She moved toward it in a low crouch, trying not to make a sound. At a distance of thirty yards she could tell it was a Petzel light, like one used by campers, strapped to the forehead, leaving two hands free to work. The light illuminated a strange looking machine, but not the face of the wearer. It was the catapult she had recovered from those three knuckle heads. The wearer of the Petzel turned a crank which gave off the sound of a ticking ratchet as well as the squeaking sound like the tightening of a large spring. He stopped doing that, bent over, and picked up something a little larger than a basketball and placed it in a holder at the end of the catapult arm. She heard the click of a switch and a tiny beam of red light projected from the front of the machine, visible in the slight fog beginning to form in the mountain air. The beam bounced back and forth a little until it settled on the pile of wood across the water, a couple hundred yards away. *He's using laser targeting*, she realized.

A scream was heard from the direction of the woodpile. Dinah and the operator of the catapult both jerked their heads in that direction. Dinah looked back at the catapult as the man there struck a kitchen match and touched it to the ball in the holder. It lit with a whoosh and in the light of the flame Dinah could confirm what she feared. It was Mark Engel. He had lit a flaming ball which he intended to fling like an artificial comet across the lake to light the fire.

"Mark Engel, this is the police. Step away from that machine and hold your hands up," Dinah said in her best command voice.

He did take a step back but his hands did not go up. With his left hand he grasped a rope coiled loosely beside the catapult. With his right he reached behind his back and came back with an automatic pistol, Dinah's own gun, she realized.

"Officer Rudisill, you're going to ruin everything," he said in a plaintive voice.

It surprised her that he remembered her name.

"Mark, put the gun down and drop that rope," Dinah said in a somewhat calmer tone. She began to move forward. She figured the rope must be attached to the release mechanism, and she was getting a very bad feeling about what might happen if that fireball found its intended target.

A second lapsed but it felt much longer. Dinah registered the sound of the excited crowd and in the distance she could hear the first faint sound of sirens.

Mark Engel took a side step toward the back of the catapult and wrapped the rope around his hand. A burning drop of kerosene dripped onto the deck of the machine.

"Drop the gun and the rope, Mark," Dinah said as she took another step forward.

"This was going to be perfect and you're ruining it," he yelled again, this time more as an accusation than a complaint. The hand with the gun was by his side and shaking now.

Dinah took another step forward. Engel raised the gun and pointed it at her. His hand was not shaking now and a look of determination froze on his face.

Dinah kneeled swift and smooth, raising the crossbow to her shoulder in the same moment. She aimed as she had been taught, center of the body. She touched the trigger and the bow sprang to life.

For an instant Mark Engel stood frozen and Dinah wondered if she had hit him. The first thing to move was his hand falling and dropping the gun. Dinah immediately sprang forward toward the catapult. As Engel's body slumped away from the machine he had enough energy and focus left to jerk the cord wrapped around the other hand. At the same instant Dinah slid into the back of it kicking with all her might.

She saw the arm of the catapult fling itself up and forward with a speed and power she was not prepared for. She saw the flaming ball release into the air. She saw the spot from the laser jump to one side. But whether she had moved the machine before or after the projectile left she could not tell.

For a few seconds the world seemed to stand still, all except for the flaming ball rising in its high and majestic arc. It trailed a long streak of flaming liquid: a perfect tail for a man-made comet.

TWENTY-SIX

Arc of the Comet

AS SEGAL APPROACHED the pile of wood that would soon become a bonfire there was a slight breeze in his face. It carried with it the choking vapors of kerosene and oil. When he and Walter got closer they could see it was to be a serious fire. Segal saw movement on top and he could make out a figure standing upright but leaning at an odd angle.

The stack was composed of pieces of wood of various kinds. There was old lumber from demolition sites, broken up shipping pallets, branches and sticks from landscaping projects, rough trimmings from a saw mill, and even some old wooden furniture.

As random as this selection was, there was nothing random in the way it was stacked. The builders had formed a cylinder about fifteen feet in diameter and over eight feet high. The manner of stacking had been well considered. It was dense enough to provide a lot of fuel in a concentrated space but loose enough to allow air to penetrate and provide plenty of oxygen for the conflagration. *With the kerosene and the breeze,* Segal thought, *this thing is going to go up like a blow torch.*

Segal was first to touch the pile and he immediately began to climb up the side. Walter was right behind him.

He must have seen the figure on top too because he started to climb up the side of the stack same as Segal.

The climbing was difficult. The side of the stack went straight up. Some of the pieces of wood were large and well secured, but a lot of them were loose and they moved when he tried to grip them or step on them. Soon, one of the branches he grasped pulled out completely sending him tumbling backward to the ground.

The same thing happened to Walter.

"Boost me up," Segal said.

Walter began to protest him going up alone but realized at once it was their best chance. They circled the stack looking for a better place to climb.

"Try here," Walter said. Segal could see why he chose the spot. There were some substantial pieces of two by six that looked almost like a ladder. The stack sloped back a little near the top which would make climbing easier.

Walter stooped and made a stirrup of his hands. Segal put his foot in and Walter stood and lifted and practically threw him up the side of the stack. Segal grabbed high and found secure holds for hands and feet and felt a flash of gratitude that his partner was not only smart and generous but also strong as a bear, too.

He pulled himself up, slowly at first, but as he approached the crest he was able to do a quicker scramble and stand up on the top of the stack.

As soon as he did so he saw Jody Mare. It was exactly as he feared. She was tied to a vertical pole in the center of the wood pile.

"She's up here," Segal yelled.

"Should I come up?" Walter shouted back.

"No. Stay there so you can help her down," Segal called out.

Segal approached Jody at the center of the pile. When

he got closer he could see that she was dressed in her armor. It was strapped on over a pair of running shorts and a T-shirt and sneakers. *Mark Engel must think she was an incarnation of Joan of Arc, not just a model striking a pose* he thought. And today, on the thirtieth of May, just like in 1431, he was going to make sure Joan of Arc was burned at the stake in the most spectacular way.

Segal ran to her now as best he could over the rough surface, and her eyes widened when she saw him. A wide piece of tape covered her mouth, perhaps the most inauthentic detail of the whole setup.

He ripped off the tape in one quick motion.

At first Jody just took in a few deep breaths. The first words she said were, "He's crazy."

"I know," Segal said. He was looking at her hands now to see how they were tied, trying to move as quickly and efficiently as he could.

In the dimming light he could feel better than he could see. He touched her arm and followed it with his hand back around the pole to where it crossed her other arm at the wrist.

"Damn," he said. Engel had secured her there with one of those hard plastic zip ties. "No way that thing is going to break or slip off. Where's your devotion to authentic technology now?" he muttered.

He stood up and looked her in the eye. He could see that she was not quite with it, either from drugs or panic or a combination of the two. Her head lulled to one side. He took her face between his hands and lifted it so her eyes were looking right at him.

"I'll be right back," he said. She started to panic as soon as he turned away, and he said, "I promise."

He scrambled over to the edge and called to Walter. Walter backed up so he could see him better.

"Walter, do you have your pocket knife with you?" Segal asked. He knew Walter would. He never left home without it.

Walter reached in his pocket and pulled out a folding knife with two blades in a brown bone handle. He held it up and walked back to the pile and started to climb. At the same time Segal crawled forward and down until their hands met and they could exchange the knife. Segal carefully slipped it into his pocket before backing up. He realized that if he dropped that knife into the loosely packed wood pile it would never be seen again.

He scrambled back to Jody. She was watching him but then her eyes shifted to look at something over his shoulder and she let out a scream. He turned to follow her gaze and saw what had struck terror into the girl. In the distance, across the water he could see a blazing point of light, and he could guess what it was as well as Jody could.

Segal went behind Jody and opened the knife. He knew Walter's strategy when it came to pocket knives. It was one Walter had learned from his father. For most things he used the large blade of the knife and kept it reasonably sharp. The small blade was reserved for special jobs and it was kept razor sharp and not dulled by everyday use. That's the one Segal would need to cut through the tough plastic band.

"Hold your hands steady for a minute," he said to Jody softly.

Walter called up, "Are you all right?"

"Yeah, I'm cutting the restraints," Segal called back in a calm voice. He kept sawing away at the restraint as he said this, and then leaned in close to Jody and talked in a lower voice into her ear, "You're doing great. Almost done."

But as soon as he said that the knife slipped from his hand. He held his breath as he watched it turn one time in the air. Time stood still for a second except for the falling and rotating of the knife. And then, the falling knife suddenly stopped with a small dull sound. The point of the blade stuck into a piece of a poplar branch lying at his feet. He let out a sigh of relief and snatched the knife up again

It took only a few seconds more to cut the restraint. As soon as her hands were free Jody began to fall forward until Segal caught her. She leaned on his shoulder while Segal kneeled to free her feet. This looked like it would be quicker because Engel had used a hemp rope around her ankles.

She breathed heavily, draped over him as he worked, but just as he finished she inhaled a sharp breath and her body went rigid. He stood and turned in time to see the flaming ball launch high into the air from the other side of the water.

The fascination with watching it arc across the sky toward them was almost irresistible. But his sense of self-preservation kicked in. Jody immediately lunged for the edge of the stack.

"Jump, I've got you," Walter cried out and Jody did it without hesitation, just as the flaming ball of the man-made comet hit.

It struck the ground an arms-length to the other side of the stack, but it wasn't a total miss. It exploded on impact splashing flaming liquid and fragments of rent cloth in all directions. Enough of them landed on the stack to ignite it.

Segal made it to the edge, scrambled partway down and then jumped the last few feet. As soon as his feet hit the ground he heard a whoosh as the fumes from the kerosene ignited and the flame front ran around the stack. He felt the intense heat on his face as he backed away, trying not to think of what would have happened to him and Jody had they been a few seconds late, or if the comet had made a direct hit.

Segal glanced over his shoulder as he continued to back up in the red light of the fire. He saw Walter with his arm protectively around Jody's shoulder. Behind them he saw a crowd of people across the lake. They were cheering and laughing with no idea of the horror that had been averted. As far as they were concerned their bonfire had just been lit by a wonderful pyrotechnical simulation of a comet. A few of them started running across the strip of land between the lakes to get closer to the fire.

When the people began to arrive none seemed too surprised to see a girl wearing armor standing with two men. Nor did it draw much attention when Dinah broke into the circle of light carrying a crossbow.

SHE HAD RUN around the north end of the lake to see if they survived. The moment Dinah saw Jody standing there with Segal and Walter her body drooped as if the nervous energy she had been running on blinked out. She barely kept her balance as she walked toward them. All the other people were focused on the fire while she focused only on the trio who had narrowly escaped death by catapult.

When she got up to them she stood there with her mouth open for a second, then she looked down at the crossbow in her hands.

"I got this from Mark Engel's place," she said, and handed the bow to Walter.

Jody flinched at the mention of his name, and asked, "Where is he?"

"You don't have to worry about him anymore," Dinah said. Segal and Walter turned toward her. Segal could read from the expression on her face exactly what she meant by this.

She hugged Jody. She started to tell them what had happened, but Segal raised his hand, signaling to wait.

"Let's let the medics take a look at Jody."

They turned and began walking back around the north end of the lake toward the parking lot where Segal saw the backup that the guard had called for. Two squad cars and a medical unit, lights flashing, had arrived moments earlier.

The medics decided to transport Jody to the hospital as she still seemed under the influence of whatever Engel had drugged her with.

"What about Engel?" Segal asked as the medics pulled away.

Dinah nodded her head toward the clearing at the back of the parking lot. The three of them walked in that direction, feeling the warmth of the blacktop now in the cooling mountain air. As they walked Dinah quickly recounted the events which had led her to the farm at the Forks of Ivy and eventually here to the festival.

Two police officers were already stringing up crime scene tape around the area. Dinah and Segal and Walter ducked under the tape and approached the catapult.

"So, you were able to kick the machine?" Walter was asking.

"It moved a little, but I wasn't sure if it was enough or if it was even in time."

"I'd say it was just barely enough and just barely in time," Segal said. He blinked his eyes and thought of the scene on top of that woodpile and the terrific heat of the flames and what it would have been like if the comet had made a direct hit.

"I don't know, he might have missed anyway," she said.

"I don't think so," Walter said. He was checking out the laser beam trailing off into the night mist. It led to the exact spot the comet had hit.

WHEN CRAWFORD, the medical examiner, arrived along with the crime scene technicians they got their first thorough look at the body of Mark Engel where it lay sprawled on the other side of the catapult. Dinah had executed a perfect shot, mid chest.

"Where's the arrow?" Walter asked.

"Bolt," Crawford said.

"Right, bolt then," Walter corrected himself.

"We think it passed through the body," Crawford said, and he motioned back into the stand of trees where they could see a couple flashlights bobbing around. The others watched as the lights converged on one point while Crawford continued to examine the body. Presently the two officers with flashlights came up, one waving the short arrow, or bolt, in a gloved hand.

"Found it stuck in the trunk of a beech tree," the officer said. It was clearly one of the wooden handmade bolts, a match for the one which had killed Julius Hargrove.

"Damn," Walter said, and he looked at the crossbow he carried with greater respect. He looked at Segal and then at Dinah.

Dinah was standing there with a face empty of emotion and a blank stare in her eyes. Walter had seen that look before on the faces of people who had witnessed bad things and been forced to take drastic action themselves. He had worn that look on his own face a time or two as well.

"You OK?" he asked her. This drew Segal over too.

"Why did he do all this?" Dinah asked. "Why did this happen?"

"I think it was a combination of things. He lost his mother a few years ago, and then his father more recently. Then he found out his father was swindled out of his savings by a private investment company. Then the insurance company found an excuse to deny claims for his father's hospital care at the end of his life. He decided he would create his own justice. Not just revenge, but a statement of justice done in a dramatic and artful and public statement. After all, his master at the art studio taught him how to make his own glue and his own ink, and almost everything else they use. Why not make his own justice too? He considered himself a victim, but not a helpless one," Segal reasoned.

Walter looked at her face and must have read there the physical and emotional exhaustion. Segal saw it too. He put a hand on her shoulder and turned her, walking her away from the scene. Walter walked on her other side.

"So, he kills the crooked investment guy, who was also involved with the militia, using an assault rifle," Walter said. "Actually, he doesn't just kill him he goes to the excess of using a full magazine of ammunition to embellish the point. The manner of death matches what the man did in life. Guns and greed. I think the straw that broke that camel's back was when he found out Koll was buying the painting of Joan to hang in the meeting room of the White Hog Militia. Given how he felt about Jody it must have been intolerable to think of Hogs gawking at her."

By this time they were approaching the end of the lot where Dinah's jeep was parked. They could hear the babble and laughter of the crowd over in the main part of the festival grounds.

Segal nodded. "And Hargrove was working on a painting from the fifteenth century using techniques from the fifteenth century, so he gets killed by a weapon from the fifteenth century. Makes sense, and makes justice, at least in a twisted sort of way. Besides that, Engel himself sort of lived in that time period."

They all jumped when they heard some fireworks go off near the bonfire.

"What about John Belincort, why death by wrecking ball?"

"I'm pretty sure when we check the fine print of the life insurance policies his company sells we will find a clause excluding payment for deaths in exceptionally dangerous places like a building scheduled for demolition," Segal said. "So, had Belincort died in that building as planned, his estate would have been denied coverage, same as Engel's father."

"So, it's clear what he had against Belincort and Adrien Koll, but what turned him against Hargrove and Jody Mare?" Walter asked.

They walked in silence for a moment, then Dinah spoke up.

"I think I know the answer to that. He saw Jody and Hargrove in the studio that night, looking in through the skylight. He thought they were together. I mean sexually together. The way he felt about each of them, it would be like a guy finding his girlfriend with his father. He probably hated both of them for it. It got in the way of his fantasy about Jody."

"That makes sense," Segal said. "Everything about this beautiful painting and the story he made up in his own head turned sour. His hero, Hargrove betrays him. The girl he idolizes is not the saint he made her out to be, and the painting itself is going to be owned and used by a bunch of hateful militants. His whole belief system collapsed. He was probably planning something like this for a while, but that was the spark that touched off the powder keg."

By now they were at Dinah's jeep.

"You OK to drive?" Segal asked.

Dinah nodded, but asked, "Don't you need me here? Or should I go into the station and give an official statement?"

Segal could understand how it would feel wrong to her to just drive off and leave this mess to her fellow officers.

"You can do that tomorrow. Maybe in the morning you could go over to the hospital and see how Jody's doing," Walter said.

"Yeah, that's a good idea," Segal said, "And send us a text and let us know if she's OK." She still held her phone and badge in her hand.

She nodded in agreement and Walter and Segal watched her drive away.

TWENTY-SEVEN

All Men Depart

SEGAL AND WALTER stayed until the forensic techs and the medical examiner were finished with their work and the body was taken away. They arranged to meet with the festival organizers the next day and made sure the site would be covered by uniformed officers through the night to keep the curious away. It was past midnight by the time they felt they could leave.

Segal got behind the wheel and they pulled out in silence.

"So that was it," Walter mused. "People telling crazy stories, making up crazy stories, believing crazy stories."

"It's what makes the world go around, Walter. The power of the story. It controls how people see the world more than what they see with their eyes or hear with their ears."

Walter nodded and smiled.

"You think that's just me being philosophical, but it's the truth," Segal said.

"I believe you, professor," Walter said, then, after a moment of silence he asked, "So Segal, if someone were going to knock you off in a way that matched how you live your life, what would they do?"

They were nearing downtown Asheville by then. Segal made a face as he thought about the question.

"Maybe I get killed by a giant avalanche of paperback books."

Walter grinned and nodded.

"What about you," Segal asked.

Walter seemed to think about it, but before he got far, Segal's phone sounded. Segal pulled it out of his jacket pocket and answered. He made a few sounds of acknowledgment finally said OK and hung up.

"There's a crazy guy scaring people over on Church Street," he said.

"You think it's Tommy?" Walter asked.

"Sure sounds like him," Segal said. "I better get over there and check it out. You want me to drop you at the station first?"

"Nah, it's OK, Segal. Let's go see what your boy's into this time. At this time of night what's another twenty or thirty minutes?"

When they turned into the north end of Church Street the scene was dominated by the flashing blue lights of two squad cars pulled up, blocking the road. They coasted to a stop behind the squad cars and got out. One of the uniformed police officers recognized them right away and seemed relieved to have some help in dealing with the strange situation.

"We got the call about twenty minutes ago, Lieutenant," one of them said. "One of the church wardens noticed a guy hanging around the entrance and he couldn't get him to say anything sensible. He thought the guy might be in trouble. He gets very agitated and just yells the same thing over and over again when we try to approach."

"Really?" Segal asked. "What does he yell?"

"Something like, 'On pain of death, all men depart.'"

"Yeah, that's Tommy all right. I guess it's the death part that has everyone worried."

"What's he talking about?" the officer asked.

"It's a line from *Romeo and Juliet*. It's what the prince says when he and his men break up a fight between the Montagues and the Capulets. He's pissed and he reads them the riot act and he ends it like that, *On pain of death, all men depart.*"

"Why is he reciting Shakespeare?" the officer asked.

"It's a long story," Segal said. "Where the hell is he anyway? I can't see him."

"He's up there, at the top of the stairs leading to the church entrance," the other officer said.

Segal looked again and saw movement in the shadows behind one of the stone pillars.

"Tommy, is that you?" Segal called.

There was a short pause, then they heard his voice. "On pain of death all men depart."

That's a strange line for him to get hung up on. Now he's pretending to be the prince, Segal thought.

"Everyone is going to depart, Tommy, but first I'm coming up where I can talk to you without yelling." Segal started walking forward.

"On pain of death all men depart!" they heard again. This time Tommy's voice sounded more frightened and upset.

Segal held his hands up and said, "It's all right, Tommy, it's just me." He continued to advance with slow even steps. "I'm sorry I couldn't take your call earlier tonight."

"Throw your mistempered weapons to the ground."

"Nobody has any mistempered weapons, Tommy." He took another step forward, thinking, *at least he's moving on to a different line in the scene. I'll take that as progress.*

"I mean it, Segal! On pain of death all men depart!"

Now the voice seemed pleading and desperate. As he said it he stepped out from behind the pillar and Segal could see him. His figure looked crumpled and ghostly in the dim blue illumination of a street light. His left hand lay high on the pillar as if for stability. His right hand was straight down by his side. Even though he was little more than a dim outline Segal could tell just from his posture that he was not all right.

Segal took another step forward, more cautiously this time.

Tommy raised his right arm.

Walter yelled from behind the squad cars, "Gun! Segal! He's got a gun."

Segal looked back at Walter. He could not process what he had heard. Tommy couldn't have a gun. No one would give Tommy a gun. He was about to tell Walter he was wrong when he saw the four uniformed cops pull out their side arms in unison, focused on Tommy.

Segal swiveled back toward Tommy. Tommy stepped forward into the light where Segal could see that he did have a gun in his raised hand. His instant thought was, *This can't be. It's a toy, a stage prop.*

"On pain of death all men depart," Tommy said once more. His right hand shook so he steadied it with his left.

Segal thought his voice sounded a little calmer now. He slowly took half a step forward, this time with hands raised.

Tommy's gun fired without further warning. Segal was thrown backward as he shouted, "No! Tommy!"

Segal closed his eyes. He heard the horrible blast of shots from the direction of the squad cars and he knew that the officers had done what they had to do, what any law enforcement officer would do when they saw an out-of-control man shoot at a fellow police officer.

He managed to sit up. He registered the hot burnt smell of the gun shots in the air and the crumpled body on the steps of the church. He felt light-headed and only then did he realize that he had been hit by Tommy's shot.

And then he felt weak, sick. Followed by darkness.

SEGAL WOKE TO fluorescent lights and stainless steel and the sound of squeaking wheels. He realized he was moving, then he realized he was in a hospital on a fast moving gurney. An IV was taped to his left arm and the plastic tubing leading to it was red with a blood transfusion. He moved his head and tried to speak, but his voice sounded muffled. There was an oxygen mask covering his nose and mouth. He felt the mask with his right hand and began to pull it away, but another hand landed gently on his own before he could do so.

"It's OK, Segal, let's leave that in place for a while." The voice came from a figure in blue scrubs and a surgical mask. The eyes above the mask were kind and smiling and vaguely familiar to him. He dropped his hand to his side.

"You're going to be all right," the woman in the mask told him. "You've been shot in the leg and you lost a lot of blood. We're taking you into surgery now. We've got some bone fragments to deal with but you are going to be OK."

"Tina May?" Segal said. He just realized it was the woman his friends had introduced him to at the roller derby bout, then he remembered she was an ER doctor.

"What about Tommy? What about the other man injured at the scene?"

The eyes above the mask changed.

"I'll see you in the recovery room." Dr. May said. She stepped aside and Segal felt the foot of the gurney hit a pair of swinging doors. He went to sleep again.

TWENTY-EIGHT

Twelve Bones

SEGAL SAT QUIETLY in a wheelchair at the end of the hall in the hospital ward. He was in front of a window which looked northwest out across the city and to the mountains beyond. If he leaned forward he could see Mount Pisgah etched against the sky.

He was thinking about hiking. Actually, it was more remembering than thinking, remembering some of the hikes he had been on and the people he had been with. The physical therapist said it was good to visualize a goal, to see yourself in your mind's eye doing something that you want to do, something that you are not able to do just now. See it like it was a reality. At that moment it was hard to imagine himself walking along those ridgetops.

He closed his eyes and tried to evoke an image of a place on the Coon Tree Loop, one of his favorite places. On that trail was a spot where two streams converged to form one. He could see it clearly, but as soon as he imagined lifting his right leg to step up onto the log bridge that crossed the steam below the confluence he felt a sharp pain. *You at least have to do it in your head before you expect your body to follow*, he could hear the therapist say.

His mind next drifted back to the case. *Make sure ev-*

eryone gets exactly what they deserve. That was what his boxing coach had told him. He blew out a breath. They had solved this case, but did anyone get what they deserved?

It added to his feeling of melancholy and he spun the wheelchair around to return to his room. As he neared his door a figure darted around the corner of the hall and pulled up face to face with him.

"Shirley Dawn!" he said. The melancholy disappeared.

"Segal!" she said, matching his tone. She had a heavy bag slung over her shoulder but she managed to give him a hug anyway without dropping it or dumping its contents on the floor.

They proceeded into the room and Segal decided to remain in the wheelchair for her visit rather than hauling himself into bed.

"I brought us some lunch," she said in a conspiratorial whisper. She started removing items from the bag and placing them on the wheeled table that could swing over the bed.

"Pulled pork sandwiches from Twelve Bones," she said.

Segal smiled and nodded.

"Some fries and coleslaw," she continued, "sweet tea, and for desert, double fudge cookies."

Segal beamed. She had remembered his favorites.

"Thanks, Shirley. You didn't need to do this."

"Hey, Segal, you've only bought me about a thousand lunches."

"Well, thanks," he said.

They both reached for the sandwiches and dug in. With the first taste a hunger came to him he didn't know he had.

"So, fill me in on the latest news, news lady. All I get here is what I read in the paper," Segal said after the first bite followed by a sip of sweet tea.

"You're the one with the inside track," she said when her mouth was empty enough to answer.

"What do you hear about the governor and Mrs. Price?" Segal asked.

"Looks like they're going to skate out of this. People like them always skate," Shirley said.

"Not always," Segal said. "There are a few rare cases of determined media coverage getting in the way of some pretty big plans."

Shirley grinned. "There are rumors that the governor is being groomed by the party for a presidential run. You haven't heard from them?"

By "them" Segal knew she meant Alexa.

"They sent those flowers," he said, nodding toward a large bouquet of lilies on the side table.

"You probably heard that John Belincort has been indicted."

"Yeah, I did hear that," Segal said. "I suppose Adrien Koll would have been, too, had he not been killed with his own assault rifle."

"It was his own gun?" Shirley Dawn asked. "See, I knew you would have the inside scoop."

"Got me," Segal said, though he didn't really feel it was much of a disclosure. "Anything happen with the White Hog Militia, losing their leadership and funding and all?"

"Oh, the Hogs will land on their cloven hooves. But from what I hear several agencies of local, state, and federal government have their eyes on them. The governor is doing a great Schrodinger's Cat thing of being inside and outside that particular box at the same time. I interviewed my contact inside the Hog organization and none of this seems to bother them in the least. In fact, he told me attendance at their latest rally was higher than ever."

"They say there's no such thing as bad publicity." He said it lightly but he looked thoughtful as he took another bite of the sandwich and followed it with a french fry. He strongly suspected they were the ones who hooked Tommy up with a gun. One day he might be able to prove that.

"Did you hear Koll's estate refused to pay for the Joan of Arc painting now that it's done?" Shirley said. Segal looked surprised that she knew this.

"I heard from the other Marks brothers that it was Koll who had commissioned the painting. I guess Hargrove was pretty pissed when he found out it was for the militia, and that the governor was one of Koll's preferred clients. That's when he started messing with the background message."

"Where is it now, anyway?" Segal asked.

"Pipo finished it and the estate, meaning Margery and Alexa, donated it to that church downtown that your buddy, Isidro, runs."

Segal sat up a little taller and smiled. "Have you seen it? What did he do with the background?"

"If you look at it from one angle the figures in the background look like apostles from the Bible. If you move and look at it from another angle they look like dinosaurs. Not too surprising for Colebrook."

Segal grinned when he thought of Izzy with that painting.

"That whole White Hog Militia thing, Segal. What do you think of it? Are they a real danger?"

Segal thoughtfully swirled a french fry in a pool of ketchup and consumed it before answering. "As a friend of mine says, it's hard to resist a good metaphor or a good story. It's the power of the story. Stories move people more than any set of objective facts. The militia guys see themselves as warriors: defenders sent by God. That's a powerful story to tell yourself. Pretty much gets you off the hook in terms of truth or rational analysis. So, yes, if you have political leaders reinforce and focus that story and throw in some modern weapons into the mix, I think it's a formula for real danger."

Shirley Dawn scowled and chewed hard to empty her mouth. "Do you know how hard I have to work to verify the truth of everything I write? To make sure it's accurate? Why should I bother if these fantasies move people more?"

Segal smiled. "No, Shirley, you keep doing what you're doing. We need that."

"We need you, too, Segal. We need you back."

"They tell me that's going to take a little while. Damage to the bone and nerves."

They ate for a moment without saying any more. Segal made it through half the sandwich and put the rest back in the waxed paper wrapper. He picked up the bag of cookies and noticed several were already gone.

He looked at Shirley Dawn and made a gesture of weighing the bag in his hand.

"That re-sealable flap on the front of the bag comes in handy, doesn't it?" he said.

Shirley brushed her mouth with the back of her hand and grinned. "The guy that invented that should get a Nobel prize."

Segal took a drink of the tea and leaned back in his chair. Suddenly he felt tired. It must have shown on his face because Shirley Dawn leaned toward him and looked serious.

"How are you doing, Segal, *really*?"

"I'll be OK, it's just going to take some time and a lot of therapy to get back."

"Back to normal?" she asked.

"Back to whatever normal is."

"Have you seen Tommy's mother yet?"

"She was here a few days ago. We had a good cry over Tommy. She doesn't blame me for anything, but there's no getting around the fact that I failed to help him, and I gave him that Shakespeare play."

"Someone else gave him the gun," Shirley pointed out.

"But I think the play was the more dangerous of the two."

Shirley looked thoughtful and grabbed a couple of cookies for herself. Her sandwich was gone, as were her fries and slaw. She popped up out of her chair and announced it was time for her to bounce. She gave him a little kiss on the cheek and turned to go but pulled up short.

She picked up the half sandwich he had left on the table and asked, "Are you going to finish this?"

Segal shook his head. "Take it."

Shirley leaned over and gave Segal another kiss on the cheek, just as Tina May rounded the corner into his room.

"Oh, I'm sorry, I didn't realize you had company. I'll come back later."

Shirley and Segal both said, "No, it's OK." But it was too late. Dr. May was already gone.

Shirley snatched up the sandwich and said, "As soon as you get out of this place you and I are going back to Katmandu."

"My treat," he said, and watched her skinny butt disappear around the corner.

SEGAL WISHED TINA MAY had not run off. He pressed his call button but when the nurse answered he fumbled for what to say.

"Uh, if you see Dr. May, could you tell her my guest is gone now," was the best he could do.

He looked around and picked up a paperback copy of *A*

Farewell to Arms by Ernest Hemingway, and let his mind be carried away. Carrying his mind away was not too difficult since he was still on a low dosage of pain medication.

He dozed off, for how long he could not say. He smelled Alexa's perfume before he opened his eyes and saw her standing at the foot of his bed.

"What's the scent you're wearing?" he asked.

"It's called Cairo Parchment," she said. She held her gaze on his eyes for a moment, taking off her sunglasses like she was taking off a piece of clothing. He drew in a breath. To him it smelled like a salty beach mixed with a little lemon and some Middle Eastern herbs and spices.

She looked him up and down and smiled. "You look better than I thought you would. I mean, they were making it sound like you were at death's door."

He wanted to tell her she looked awfully good herself, but it seemed too foolish. She was wearing a simple green shirt dress with a sash and bow at the waist, but something about the way she wore it made it look like high fashion.

Instead, he asked, "How are you?"

She looked surprised that he asked.

"I mean, losing your brother, and the thing at the Grove Park and everything else."

"Well, we had the funeral for Jules. Margery and I planned it together if you can believe that. So many people came and sent flowers. We didn't do any of that, 'In lieu of flowers…' stuff. Jules always liked flowers. He used to talk about how they're a great metaphor for life. We sprout up and bloom and then we fade. Jules always said he was a sucker for a good metaphor."

"Who the hell isn't," Segal mumbled.

Alexa turned away from him and looked around the room for a few seconds, then continued.

"As far as the little incident at the Grove Park Inn, no harm, no foul, and no hard feelings. That was just Margery being dramatic. Being dramatic was one of the things that drew my brother to her in the first place." She added, "I never liked that vase anyway."

"Neither did I," Segal said.

She looked down with what Segal thought was a somewhat sad and wistful expression. He wondered, for the hundredth time, how much of her flirtation with him was genuine, and how much was an act calculated to support her husband. Or maybe the two were so mixed up it was impossible to tell anymore.

"I heard your husband might be headed for some higher level in the political world," Segal said, as much to fill in the ensuing silence as out of any real interest in the man.

"Oh, yes," she said, turning away again. She rearranged the flowers in the vase by the window. "He'll be moving up the ladder, at least if Davenport and that crowd have anything to say about it." She said Davenport's name like it was a nasty word. "At least they did well at the Grove Park Inn fundraiser. I guess being shot at brings out the patriot in people."

"I'm sure you will continue to be the perfect politician's wife," Segal said.

She came back and stood by the side of the bed and placed a hand softly on Segal's chest.

"Being the politician's wife, they wanted me to ask you a question. Did you ever find the sketches Jules made for the background of that Joan of Arc painting?"

He looked into her eyes with more than a hint of disappointment and placed his hand on top of hers. So, this was the real reason for the visit.

"You can tell your husband and Davenport that the

sketches are with a private collector and I see no reason they should ever become public so long as certain people behave themselves."

She smiled and bent her face down to his and planted a long, firm kiss on his mouth. "Get well, Lieutenant," she said.

He watched her turn and walk out and only when she got to the door did he see Tina May standing there to one side of the doorway to let her pass.

SEGAL AWOKE FROM a nap later in the timeless fluorescent afternoon of the hospital world. There was a nurse fussing around with the blood pressure cuff on his arm. When she had the reading, she bent over and told him softly, "You have a visitor."

He straightened up and saw Dinah sitting in the visitor's chair, dressed in running shorts and a light sweatshirt with the arms cut out. She looked like she belonged in the outfit which did a great job of showing off the muscles in her arms and legs. Her bundle of frizzy hair was pulled back and plaited into a single thick braid.

Segal sat up in the bed. She stood.

"Don't get up on my account," she said but Segal pressed a button to make the bed come up to a sitting position.

"Have you been out running?" he asked her when the whirring of the bed's motor stopped.

"I wanted to get a few miles in, so I thought why not run in this direction and stop in and see how you're doing."

"They tell me I'm going to be OK," he said. "It might take some time and a lot of PT, but I'll make it back."

"I'm sure you will."

"How are you doing?" Segal asked. He had heard more of the story of that day including her escape from the silo.

"I'm fine," she said.

Segal gave her a serious look and said, "Really, how are you?"

Dinah met his gaze and said, "I really am working through it. What I learned in the service is after you have a close call, focus on what really happened instead of what almost happened. What really happened is that you survived. That's the most important thing."

"How's Jody Mare?" Segal asked.

"Jody's bouncing back. She's posing as Mary Magdalene for a fresco the other Marks brothers are doing in a church."

"I didn't know anyone did frescos anymore," Segal mused.

The conversation stalled for a moment and they looked at each other.

"Walter told me he's moving on," Dinah said.

"We had a long talk about that a few days ago," Segal said. "He really impressed some people in Raleigh with how he put together the financial and business fraud part of the case. They offered him a position in the Attorney General's office in Raleigh working with the white-collar crime group. They liked the idea of having a real live detective on the team. He said he wasn't going to walk out and leave me in the hospital."

"The code of partnership." Dinah nodded. "Walter is a good man."

"Walter's the best," Segal said, "but I made him take the position. For one thing he can have more impact in a job like that. I mean what's more important in the long run, catching a few local miscreants or shutting down stuff like Continental Drift investments or even bigger scams?"

"You guys were able to do both in this case."

"Well, Walter's wife is going to like it a whole lot better this way. She was already worried about him being in this line of work, and I think me getting shot just made it more real. I had to make him take the offer."

"Where are you going to find a partner like that?" Dinah asked.

Segal smiled but did not answer. A thought was forming in his mind.

"I brought you something," Dinah said. She turned around, snatched a bag off the chair, and presented it to Segal. The bag bore the insignia of Malaprops Bookstore. He opened it and slid out a hardback book and looked at her with a smile.

"I remembered you telling me about Elmore Leonard, and I knew you didn't have this one because it was just released two days ago."

"I didn't know they even came in hardback," Segal said. He flipped the book over and glanced at the cover summary and blurb.

"I read a couple of the paperbacks you recommended," she said, "the ones set in Detroit and Miami."

"Did you like them?" Segal asked.

"If by like them you mean I couldn't put them down, then yes, I liked them a lot."

Segal lowered the book and looked at her again, standing there.

"I'd better get going," she finally said.

She hesitated a moment then bent over and gave him a hug.

"Come back soon, Lieutenant," she whispered.

"Soon as I can," he whispered back.

When she straightened and turned to go, Dr. Tina May was standing in the hall, leaning against the door jamb with her arms crossed and a wry smile on her lips. The two women nodded to one another as Dinah walked out, and the doctor sauntered into the room.

"You're a popular guy with the ladies, Lieutenant Segal."

He opened his mouth and started to say, "If by popular you mean..." Then he just smiled and said, "Never mind."

* * * * *

ACKNOWLEDGMENTS

MANY THANKS TO Steve Kirk for his generous guidance with early drafts of this book. I am ever grateful for his insights and encouragement. Also thanks to my wife, Jen, for her patience and willingness to comb through manuscripts, correcting my numerous errors.

I offer a special thanks to the team at Wild Rose Press and especially to my editor, Morena Stamm, for turning a manuscript into a book.

Finally, thanks to the readers of my earlier books who have given me such sustaining support. I hope you have fun with this one.

A WORD ABOUT THE AUTHOR...

KENNETH BUTCHER IS the author of *The Middle of the Air* (2009) which won Ben Franklin and Independent Publishers awards. He also wrote *The Dream of Saint Ursula* (2014) and *As the Crow Dies* (2020). He is a materials engineer and researcher with 16 U.S. patents and lives with his wife in the mountains of Western North Carolina.

www.kennethbutcher.com